Chronicles of Aragore

Part One: Naming

Tyler A Mann

ISBN: 979-8-990044

ISBN-13: 979-8-9900443-0-2

To the D&D group that helped me tell this story. Hoping each of your characters speaks to the soul of what you had in mind.

CHAPTER ONE

Desert Heat

If there was one thing the troll feared, it was fire. Alas, it seemed he was destined to be surrounded by desert sand and oppressive rays of sunlight that kept him from thinking of anything else. The shifting nature of the sand around him made him feel like he was going to, at any moment, be pulled under a lake of burning fire and perish in its flames.

"Hold there, Troll-Man. The sun is high in our sky and the time is nigh for rest and relaxation. Take your load and lay it down."

The troll stopped in his tracks and looked around. The rest of the caravan had stopped and were setting up shelters to provide shade from the sun's harsh rays as they waited for it to pass its zenith. The sleds that held valuable goods and supplies for the caravan's journey were being brought into the center of a roughly circular campsite, and the other guards were taking their posts along the outside of the perimeter.

The source of the command that stopped the troll stepped up next to him as he let himself fall to a sitting position in the sand, eyes turned toward the dunes on the horizon. The man was small, even smaller than most people the troll had met. Standing straight up, and with the troll sitting in his slouched position, the man still only came up to the troll's shoulder.

He was a stout man with pointed ears and a long and sharp face. His cheek bones were high and sharp, and his eyes were bright and keen. His posture was relaxed and open, and his smile always seemed to twinkle with mischief.

The troll didn't greet the small man. The troll had learned on their journey his kind were called gnomes. The small man tried to tell him a number of stories that he claimed would highlight what it meant to be a gnome, but he always seemed to want to tell these stories around a campfire, and the troll couldn't get close without his fear paralyzing him.

Instead of looking at the gnome, the troll kept his eyes locked on the horizon, watching for anyone who would want to threaten the caravaners. After a moment more of waiting, the gnome walked away toward where the water was being distributed.

The troll continued to watch the horizon. He thought about his homeland. He was from a forest that was much cooler and more seasonal than the desert he was in now. Here, there were only two seasons: hot and dry, then windy and stormy.

He was very much a product of the forest he'd come from. His complexion was a dark forest green, his eyes were the rich brown of earthy topsoil, and his nose had a crooked and pressed quality from regular breaking during his childhood. His face was as scarred as his torso with lines and blotches that gave his skin a mottled quality. He missed all the plant life that let him blend in with their shade and leaves.

He was brought back to the present by the approach of another caravan guard. He was a foreigner from somewhere across the ocean. He wore a robe made of an unfamiliar material. When he allowed the troll to feel it once, it was smooth and soft unlike anything the troll had ever felt before. He had hooded eyes with sharp green irises and a look that belied his keen understanding of the world around him.

"The loud one," he said gesturing to the gnome who'd walked away a moment ago, "he calls you 'Troll-man'. He knows your name, yes?"

"I... umm... well..." the troll didn't have a name. His parents always simply called him boy, or the child. The Ringleader from the circus never cared to ask about a name and everyone else he had ever met simply called him 'the troll'.

He stood from his seated position. The hot sand was making his backside feel uncomfortably warm, and it was easier to hide the shame on his face if he forced the warrior to look up at him. He kept his eyes locked on the horizon and let the man's question go unanswered.

"You have a name. Would you share it?" The troll was surprised at how much the man was speaking to him. Usually the man was quiet and answered direct questions with as few words as possible.

The troll shook his head. The other guard looked at him blankly, and the troll caught the end of a gesture he made as he looked down during their silence.

"I don't have a name. I hope to get one from House Morkae. That's why I'm acting as a caravan guard. They said if I could keep this caravan safe, I'd be allowed to be a part of their family."

He caressed the bow they had given him. House Morkae was powerful and wealthy enough to hold sway over many things. The troll hoped their influence would let him earn a name by serving them.

The bow itself was the first sign of their favor. They claimed it was magic and the only the strongest warrior in the desert would draw it. The troll wasn't sure about all of that, but he'd learned during his time among humans that he was stronger than any of their kind. He'd been able to draw it and shoot clean through the target they'd let him practice on.

"This thing is not what families do. They don't make you a slave." The man's words rang hollow in the troll's ears.

The troll frowned and looked at him. "What other choice do I have? At least they're willing to accept me."

The warrior's hand flicked again. "My name is Gan Jiang. I would accept you. If this family does not."

The troll was taken aback by this statement. This was the first time he had spoken to this man since he'd started guarding the caravan. "Thank you, Gan," he said.

The warrior flicked his hand again. "That is my family name. You may use it. It is amusing to hear me called this way."

"Gan is your family name? That would make your name Jiang?"

Jiang nodded.

This was very confusing to the troll. He had always heard a house name used second. Was this one of the things that differed between this man and House Morkae? Or was he mistaken and he would be

3

expected to put the name Morkae before whatever individual name they gave him?

Jiang started making a series of slow movements. The troll watched him as he took a step and shifted his weight. He moved his hands and brought his back foot up until he was balanced on one foot. The troll watched him move through steps as if practicing an intricate dance. The dance was interrupted almost immediately when a shout came from one of the other guards.

The troll turned in time to see a charging person in full leather armor slam a lance into his shoulder. The weapon shattered on impact, and the troll spun to the sand as he felt blood pour out of his wound around the metal tip.

The troll felt the wound begin to heal itself, and he dug around in the closing flesh for the metal bit. It was excruciating and his vision fogged from the pain, but he didn't want the metal to be stuck under his skin if the wound closed around it.

When he'd gotten it out, and his vision stopped swimming, he saw the other guards had taken a defensive position around the merchants and their trade goods. The troll stood and looked for his assailant.

He spotted the leather-clad warrior dismount a horse that faded from view the moment their boots touched the hot sands. If he hadn't been charged down by it, the troll would've assumed the horse itself was an illusion. Where did anyone find such a creature in the desert?

There was no time to ponder that question, however. The assailant made no move toward the caravan. Instead, they pulled out a long spear with a serrated tip and walked toward the troll, menacing it out in front of them.

"You will kidnap no more innocents. Your slave driving days are over beast." It was only when she spoke that the troll realized this person was a woman. The armor she wore covered her completely and the only markings on it where a sword pointing down behind a stylized sun-disc.

The troll looked around, somewhat confused, and spotted Jiang standing with another guard wearing a steel breastplate. They had both drawn weapons: Jiang his curved two-handed sword, and the other guard had a long pole with an axehead and a spike at the top.

"I don't know what kidnapping you're referring to," the other guard said, "but you are attacking a caravan of innocent traders. Stand down, or I will be forced to subdue you."

"Stay out of this! This is between me and that overgrown brute you're harboring." The attacker charged the three guards.

The troll crouched to string his bow and looked around for the quiver he'd dropped when he'd fallen to the sands. Before he could do either task, the other two guards stepped forward to defend him. Jiang used his sword to guide the head of the spear to the side, and the other guard used the parry as leverage to chop the haft and break the spear into splinters.

He moved expertly with the momentum of his weapon until he had the attacker against his own haft. He shoved her to the sands, but before he could pin her, she rolled out from under him and leaped away.

While everyone stopped for a brief moment, the troll heard music from the spot where the caravaners were hiding behind their guards. It was some kind of rousing battle hymn, and he recognized the music. It was coming from the lyre the gnome was playing earlier.

The woman attacking them closed her eyes and touched her breastplate. She muttered something the troll was too far away to understand, and her horse reappeared by her side.

It charged the other two warriors, who had to dive to avoid the large beast. When it got to the troll, however, it meet a wall of resistance. The troll felt the music somewhere deep inside, and it gave him a strength greater than what even he was used to. He dug in his heels and he felt something crack beneath the horses muscular frame. It whinnied in pain and backed away.

The horse retreated to its partner, who whispered something to it that soothed it and made its stumbling posture firm again. She mounted the beast and summoned a blade that was nearly twice as big as Jiang's and charged again.

The troll met her charge for charge, feeling something stir at the sound of the music and the feeling of the fight. When he came close, her horse reared and threw her off. The troll grabbed it by its front legs and forced it down on top of her. She dismissed it before it crushed her.

He began to understand that she was using magic, but the fight and music had already awoken something else inside him. Rage he knew well was driving him as he approached to prone and helpless woman.

Why had she attacked him? He touched the newly sealed wound on his shoulder. What had he done to deserve her ire?

He put his fists together and slammed them down on the woman. She cowered under a conjured shield while the troll slammed his double fist on it. The shield splintered and shattered before the troll heard the music shift from a battle hymn to a lullaby.

The notes reminded him of a mother he saw while he was on the streets. Her baby was crying from hunger. It was obvious to the troll that she was weak from hunger as well. She just sat there, singing, desperately trying to get her crying child to sleep.

When he broke out of that memory, he saw another woman. She muscular and strong, but nevertheless as she cowered below him, he saw the same vulnerability in her. He saw the shattered pieces of wood around the two of them. The troll fell to the sands and began to weep. He had lost control and his Rage had cause someone pain. Again.

When he pulled himself together, the woman was gone, and Jiang was sitting beside him. The troll looked around and saw the other guards and the bard hovering behind him. They sat there silent for a moment. The bard's voice broke the silence.

"Sorry about the song. I wasn't expecting my music to have such an effect on you. I guess my music effects trolls differently than other sentient races."

The troll wiped his eyes and shook his head. "It wasn't the song. That happens to me from time to time. Part of the reason people think of my kind as monsters, I suppose."

"I told you," the bard said, turning to the guard that fought alongside Jiang. The man gave him a withering glare, and the gnome crossed his arms and looked away.

"Anger is something we all have to deal with," the guard said as he turned back to the troll. "True strength comes from finding a way to channel powerful emotions like that to something constructive.

"I can't say the way things ended with that paladin was ideal, but she was obviously trying to kill you. You shouldn't feel bad for defending yourself. Just remember where to stop so people like that can be subdued."

The troll nodded.

The guard put his hand on the troll's shoulder. "Why don't you join us for a water break? I'd guess that the other guards are willing to fill in for you while you recuperate."

The troll nodded again and stood. He followed the other three to the water barrel, where he drank two ladles of water.

"What was your name by the way? I can't seem to remember," the guard with the strange ax asked.

"He hasn't one." Jiang said.

"No name? How is that possible?"

"I've just been calling him Troll-man," the bard volunteered.

The guard shook his head. "That will never do. Everyone needs a name."

"House Morkae promised me one once I'm done guarding this caravan."

"How long will that take?"

The troll shrugged.

"Well I'm not going to call you Troll-man until someone picks out a name for you." The guard paused for a moment to think. "How about Pax? I think it means 'peace'."

"In what language?" the bard asked.

The guard shrugged. "Not sure. The men in the monastery that raised me used the word often. That's what it always seemed to mean when they did."

"Pax works. I am Pax," the troll declared.

"It's good to meet you Pax. I am Korivare, Knight of Mt. Koyasha. The annoying one is Gerald. Your name was Gan, right?"

"Jiang is his name. Gan is his family name," Pax explained.

Jiang's left hand flicked again. Pax gave him a questioning look, but he just shook his head. Instead, Pax moved to an out-of-the-way part of where the caravan had stopped. He was surprised when he turned around and saw the three men that had just introduced themselves standing with him.

"It's usually a bad idea to stay by yourself in the wilderness," Korivare said. Pax didn't understand what he meant. Pax had been staying away from everyone else this long and no one had said anything. Still, he supposed he didn't have a reason to object to their company, so he shrugged and sat down on the sand again.

Pax started retwisting his hair while the other three told stories about their past. They were mostly simple stories. Jiang was a warrior for a noble in his home country. He was sent here to guard a shipment of silks, which was the strange material he was wearing.

Korivare was raised in a monastery in the mountains. After he reached his majority, the monks encouraged him to go out into the world to find his true purpose. He'd been moving from place to place doing his best to protect people and be a force for good in the world ever since.

Before Gerald could explain how he'd come to be a part of the caravan, the Caravan Master signaled to them it was time to move on and the four men retrieved their belongings and caught up with the tail end of the train.

CHAPTER TWO

Strange Signs

That night they stopped at one of the oases that peppered the desert wilderness. This one had several strange pillars that seemed to be made of the surrounding sand. They were scattered in a seemingly random spread, but their presence disturbed Pax as he helped fill the water stores.

The caravaners had a technique to filter out the sand from the water to make it drinkable. Afterward, Pax would normally have stayed by the sand-sleds and oiled his bow, but Korivare waved him over to the fire that he, Jiang, and Gerald were sharing. Pax came over to Gerald playing a meandering tune on a warn lyre. The other two were oiling their gear: Korivare his breastplate, and Jiang his blade.

"Troll—I mean, Pax. What is your favorite story?"

"I don't know many stories. I do remember one from… from before. It was about a heroic warrior. I can't remember his name, but he fought in a lot of wars. Or maybe it was one big war."

"Tehrul, the Mighty? Braedon, the Lancer? The Storm King?"

"None of those sound right. Sorry. I wish I could remember more."

Gerald strummed his lyre. "Perfectly alright. Perhaps we'll happen upon the story on our journey. For now, does anyone want to hear about a place with screaming winds that tear flesh, floating islands that are the only solid ground, and birds the size of mountains?"

"This place. It does not exist. It is myth."

"Oh? Jiang must be the child of a Wanderer. Perhaps you could tell us how you know for certain this place is a myth."

"Place with only sky? Makes no sense. Where would birds land when they tire?"

"I just told you there is land. Floating islands."

"What makes islands float? Is there no gravity?"

"I— you know, I don't think the story ever specifies. Surely if one couldn't land on the floating islands in some way it would be an important detail to mention."

"You're the one who claims to know the story," Korivare pointed out.

Gerald shrugged. "Maybe a different story then. Jiang, do you know any stories from your homeland? I'd love to have some Techarian stories in my memory palace."

"What's a memory palace?" Pax asked.

"Something Gerald insists helps him keep track of all his stories. Despite the fact that he can't seem to remember when his imagined places have gravity," Korivare explained.

"It does work, and I already told you the story doesn't specify how the floating islands work. They just... float. Maybe if there's not any ground to pull down on them, gravity doesn't work."

The discussion between the two men continued, but Pax's attention was drawn to the fire they were all sitting around. It was so dangerous, so primal. How could they expect to control it? He watched as a glowing ember popped out of the fire and landed on the sand in front of him. He jumped back, and that made Korivare turn to him.

"Pax? Are you alright?"

"I... can't... I don't..." He tried to put the words together in his mind, but that ember was still glowing a mere handspan from his feet. He felt his anxiety grip his chest.

It started to tighten and his breathing became too shallow for him to speak. He started to shake. He barely noticed someone move from the other side of the fire, and he heard Gerald start to sing. It was another lullaby, different from the one earlier in the day.

Pax looked up and their eyes met. The music washed over him and he felt the grip in his chest loosen a bit. It was still hard to breath, but he could, with effort, take a deep breath. The grip started to slacken more. Pax focused on the melody: low and sweet.

The ember at Pax's feet went out and he took a deep, long breath. He fell back and lay on the sand, focusing on nothing but his breathing. Soon, Korivare and Jiang were standing above him, looking at him with concerned faces.

"I... umm... don't much like fire. It's one of the few things that can hurt me permanently." Pax was suddenly very aware of the scars on his back.

Korivare nodded. "I understand. I noticed how quickly you healed when that paladin attacked us. I'm guessing that doesn't happen from burns."

Pax shook his head.

"Hold on," Gerald said. "How did you know she was a paladin?"

"All paladins wear their order's symbol as a crest on their breastplate. I didn't recognize the symbol, but it was obviously from some kind of order."

Gerald nodded. "It looked like some version of the symbol of the Soldier King, the god of war and battle tactics."

Korivare nodded. "That would explain why she was so quick with her weapons. Each order has its own philosophy on when attacking is an acceptable course of action. The monastery I grew up in taught that it should be among your last courses taken. I suppose her order doesn't teach the same."

"That, or she's crazy. Didn't she call Pax a slave driver or something?"

"And a monster," Pax added darkly. He was still lying on the ground. "That was right after she sent a lance through my shoulder."

He pressed his hand against the spot where the lance stabbed him. It stopped hurting soon after the wound closed, but it had left a slightly lighter bit of scarred skin, adding more shading to his mottled green skin.

"Did it seem to anyone else that she had been sent by someone? Pax doesn't come off as anyone who'd be driving this caravan," Korivare said. "No offense to our large green friend."

Korivare looked at Pax, who shrugged.

"I can't think of any reason she'd assume he was kidnapping anyone. She must have been told by someone that such a thing was happening."

Everyone stayed silent. Pax worried what that might imply about his situation. If people were sending paladins to kill him, he would be putting the caravan in danger by staying around.

"Well," Gerald said as he stood, "this little chat has been fun, but assuming our muscley green friend won't need my music for the rest for the night,"

Pax shook his head.

"I'm going to turn in." Gerald took a bedroll out of one of the sand-sleds, along with a blanket.

"We should all get some rest. Tomorrow will bring another long day of moving forward," Korivare said. He set aside his freshly oiled breastplate and laid back on the bare sand, using only his gambeson as a pillow.

Pax went to sleep next to the sand-sleds. He wouldn't be able to sleep so close to the fire, and the cold desert nights hadn't bothered him since his first years here. He moved and shifted in the sand until he had a small nest-like indent. After that it was still several moments before he fell asleep.

Pax normally didn't dream as far as he could remember, but that night was very different. He dreamed of the forests he grew up exploring. The trees were covered in leaves of so many shades of green, his mottled skin seemed to disappear against the canopy.

He rushed through the underbrush without fear of stumbling. Before he could get back to the cave he called home, the scene shifted and he was on the bank of a river. The river seemed to flow strangely, but Pax couldn't put a finger on why. Without reason, Pax could tell the river was flowing the wrong way.

Pax spotted an old woman on the bank of the river washing blood off a breastplate that seemed familiar, though Pax couldn't quite place it. The woman started cackling when Pax got closer, and the sound of it sent a chill to his core. Something about this woman told all the wild instinct in Pax that she was dangerous and to be feared. That's when Pax woke with a start to a rising sun and a rousing caravan.

CHAPTER THREE

Storm's Rage

Breakfast was a handful of dried fruits and spiced meal made from an unfamiliar grain and the water from the oasis. For Pax, cooked meals of any kind were a luxury he only recently had been exposed to. He enjoyed the flavors that cooking seemed to bring out in foods. He did occasionally miss the warm squirt of blood that came from raw meat, but it was a small price to pay to prove he could be civilized.

After they ate, Pax and the other guards helped the caravaners pack up the sand-sleds. Then, Pax noticed the sand shifting in the distance. He looked at it, and Korivare spotted him.

"What is it?" Korivare asked.

"Does the sand look… like it's moving toward us?"

Korivare looked toward where Pax was pointing. He had to shade his eyes against the sun, but he still didn't seem to see what Pax was seeing. He shook his head. "It might just be—"

Pax didn't hear the end of his sentence. A giant form rose up out of the sand, snatched him by the neck with talons like spear heads, and flew high into the air.

The creature's scales were a speckled tan on top, but its under belly blended in with the sky behind it. Its massive wings beat and lifted a mass of rippling muscle. It had a long neck that reminded Pax of a constrictor, and it ended in a massive head with sharp, discerning eyes.

Pax was able to take in the full form of the huge dragon as they flew up and up. The creature's grip on Pax's neck was beginning to draw blood. Just when Pax thought he was going to suffocate, the beast dropped him.

Pax felt weightless for the space of a few pounding heartbeats as he fell like a rock toward the sand. When he landed, he heard a crunch and felt several bones shatter.

He gasped, but between the pain and the fall, he couldn't suck in a breath. Pax felt his bones start to reknit. He clenched his fist. Broken bones were always the most painful thing to feel putting themselves back together.

When the pain subsided enough for him to move again, he got up to see the dragon flying down toward the caravan. It opened its maw and a bolt of lightning shot down toward them.

Pax's muscles clenched, but before he could do anything, the bolt was split in midair and sent to the sand, making two new strange pillars. Jiang was standing between the dragon and the caravan. He saw Pax looking at him and his left hand flicked.

The dragon roared, flipped around in midair and flew toward the horizon. Pax let out a sigh of relief. He jogged up to Jiang to ask about how he diverted that lightning, but Jiang was still looking toward the horizon.

Pax looked as well, and his heart sank. The dragon was flying back toward them. Pax scrambled toward his bow where he'd set it down.

The dragon shot another bolt down toward Jiang, who had been chanting a bunch of unfamiliar words. When the bolt reached toward him, it was pulled into his sword, which he pointed toward the dragon.

Lightning shot back out of the blade and hit the dragon in the chest. The dragon gave a serpentine grin as the electricity was absorbed by his scales, making them glow.

The glow faded as the wind began to pick up and swirl around the oasis. By the time Pax had strung his bow, the wind had kicked up enough sand that Pax couldn't see further than a few feet in front of him. He stumbled around for an unknown amount of time, trying to keep the sand out of his eyes. His head was down when he ran into something and heard Jiang grunt as he hit the sand. Pax bent down to help the fallen warrior stand.

"What happened? This storm came out of nowhere,"Pax said. He had to shout to be heard over the blowing wind.

"The dragon. It's magic." Jiang's eyes were watering as he tried in vain to blink out the sand.

"Is there anything we can do?"

Just then, Pax heard a strange melody coming from a direction he couldn't place. It was so quiet he was sure he was imagining it, but it was simultaneously eerie and entrancing. Soon, the wind began to die down, but the melody continued its quiet dance in Pax's ears.

When the sand finally settled, Pax saw Gerald strumming his lyre. His eyes were red and watery, but his face was a determined mask as he played relentlessly. When he saw the other two standing before him, he let out a breath and collapsed into the sand. The music in Pax's ears slowly faded. Pax looked around and realized they weren't near the oasis anymore.

"Where are we?" he asked. He looked around, but there was nothing but dunes on the horizons all around them. He spotted Korivare a bit off in the distance, and waved toward him. Korivare jogged toward them, huffing and puffing. He had on his chain shirt and was wearing his side sword, but his shield, bow, and big pole-thing were nowhere to be seen.

"I see you got caught in the storm as well," Gerald said. He gave a weak grin. Pax started to worry about him.

"The dragon caught me completely off guard. Thank the Light Jiang was in a position to protect the caravan. Where did that storm come from anyway? Surely we should've been able to see it on the horizon."

"Not storm. It was magic. From the dragon."

Korivare nodded. "That makes sense. It's a common battlefield tactic: divide and conquer. I guess that means the dragon is attacking the caravan as we speak."

"Which means we have to get back. We have to protect them." Pax couldn't let this opportunity slip through his fingers.

Korivare took in a deep breath and nodded. "To do that we have to find out which way the—"

SMACK. A giant scaled tail burst out of the sand and flung the knight away.

He landed and rolled in the sand, making a strained moaning sound. The last time Pax heard a sound like that was when he saw someone land wrong during an acrobatic stun. He brought up his bow, and he realized what he was missing. His quiver of arrow was still in the sand-sleds at the oasis.

"Draw it back!" Gerald shouted. He had sat up and was strumming his lyre. Pax had been warned about dry firing it, but there wasn't anything else he could do. He pulled the string back with noticeable effort.

Pax watched as the air coalesced into an arrow of swirling wind. There was a moment of amazement before Pax forced himself to focus. He leveled it at the dragon as it emerged from the sand, let out a breath, and loosed the arrow. It sailed through the air and hit the scales of the dragon with a sound like clapping thunder.

The dragon let out a loud roar. It seemed whatever protection saved it from lightning didn't extend to arrows made of magical wind. The dragon brought its wings up, no doubt planning to take to the air.

Pax drew his bow again, and, again, Gerald summoned an arrow made of wind. Pax glanced at him, and he was concentrating hard on his lyre. Pax aimed for the membrane that made up the wing and fired. The arrow flew far above the dragon, but it distracted the dragon long enough for Jiang to land a hit with his sword.

The dragon roared in anger, snapped at Jiang, forced its wings down, sending sand spinning around it and Jiang. The heroes had to turn their faces down and shield their mouths.

When the sand settled, Pax still hand to blink a lot of it out of his eyes. Once it was out of his eyes, he looked up, shading his eyes from the sun. He saw the small dark shadow that was the dragon circling them far above. Pax realized what it was doing. It was looking for an opening.

Pax looked at Gerald. He was looking up, watching the dragon as well. Pax saw the fear in his eyes, but his fingers were hovering over his strings.

"Do you have healing magic?" he asked the bard.

Gerald nodded.

"Can you help Korivare?"

Gerald nodded and headed over to the knight. Pax walked over to Jiang, keeping an eye on the dragon above. He was clutching his sword arm, which was bleeding. "Do you have any magic that can kill a dragon?"

"Dragons. Masters of Magic. I know a little."

Pax grimaced at that. "We can't let that creature get back to the caravan."

Jiang nodded.

"So, we have to find a way to slay it. Here and now."

Jiang nodded again.

Gerald and Korivare appeared next to the pair. "Turns out," Gerald said, returning with Korivare right behind, "I'm not the only one with healing magic. Good thing too. I wouldn't want to be the sole responsible party for your survival." He grinned, but his face was pale.

The dragon began to descend on the group of four. Gerald started a new song; Pax put his fingers on the string of his bow and pulled back; Jiang began chanting as he lifted the point of his sword toward the dragon; Korivare hefted his shield, moving gingerly. Did he break a rib?

Before the dragon landed, it let out another bolt from its mouth. It shot toward Pax as he loosed another wind arrow. Jiang's spell came just a moment too late, and the bolt only bent, hitting the ground next to Pax. A sand pillar shot up from the ground and cut his arm. The pillar was sharp like glass.

Pax clutched his shoulder, trying to stop the bleeding. The dragon landed and Pax heard it roar. The dragon lifted its wings. Pax closed his eyes as a wave of pain hit him, and the Rage in him swelled.

He heard the sound of a sword slicing against stone. He didn't know if it was Korivare's or Jiang's sword, but the dragon let out an angry hiss. When Pax opened his eyes, he had to immediately close them again as the dragon beat its wings and created another downdraft of swirling sand.

When Pax finally blinked out the sand, the Rage in him was subsiding. He saw the dragon in a heap in the sand. It seemed, when it attempted to fly away, it fell out of the sky. Jiang fell to one knee, still clutching his sword arm. Korivare put his hands on the wound and whispered something. Jiang's skin closed around the wound, and the two warriors shared a moment of camaraderie.

As Pax approached the dragon, he realized it was unconscious. It was breathing heavy. Pax looked at the wounds they had inflicted on it. There weren't enough for it to have lost that much blood.

"Well," Gerald said as he appeared next to Pax, "I guess that's the end of that epic struggle. Who's going to finish the job?" Pax's three friends had followed him to where the dragon lay.

"What?" Pax said. "It's helpless. We set out to keep it from attacking the caravan. If we find them soon, we can get them away from where this dragon can find them."

"Sounds like a couple pretty big ifs: IF we'll be able to find them at all and IF we can get them to safety. Still, I'm not saying we should kill it out of malice.

"It's clearly already overheated. If we leave it, it'll die of exposure before it wakes up. So, unless you have a way to drag it an unknown number of miles to some kind of shelter, it'd be more merciful to just end it here."

"Bard is correct. Kill dragon."

Pax looked at the helpless creature. He thought of all the people and animals he had hurt while Rage overwhelmed him. "I... I can't."

"I'll do it. Like you said, it's a mercy," Korivare said. He moved carefully as he picked up his sword from the sand and thrust it in to the dragon's neck. The body convulsed, and the eyes opened, but soon the dragon stilled: no breathing, no stirring.

Pax just looked at the massive beast for a moment. Gerald and Korivare were right. He did believe it, and that's what hurt so much. He wanted to be a hero like Korivare, but he couldn't help feeling more kinship with the dragon lying dead in the sand. He turned and walked back up to the other three as they were discussing which way to go.

"Look," Korivare said, "there's no way we're that far from the oasis. The storm didn't last that long and I bet we were walking in circles for most of it."

"That's just what I'm saying," Gerald explained. "This doesn't look anything like where we were. I'm worried that storm somehow transported us further than we think."

"How could something like that be possible?"

"You ever face a dragon before? Those things are usually full of strange arcane secrets."

"Even if you count the storm, that monster barely did any magic." Pax winced at the word "monster." Korivare didn't notice. He was already trudging over the closest sand dune.

"If you'd just listen to what I'm saying," Gerald continued, "I'm trying to explain that there's something completely off about..." he tailed off as he caught up to Korivare and saw what he was looking at.

When Pax saw it, he didn't understand at first. What they thought was another sand dune was actually the rim of a massive pit that surrounded a large hole in the rock below. "What is it?" he asked.

"It's a sand trap," Gerald explained. "Certain small desert predators use them to catch prey, but this one is massive and there's no telling where that hole leads. We have to—" the sand shifted below him and all three men fell into the trap, sliding down into the waiting hole. Pax's last sight was of Jiang coming to their aid only to fall into the same trap. Then he fell into the hole.

CHAPTER FOUR

Into the Unknown

Pax awoke to his bones re-knitting for the second time in a day. He wished the pain of bones forcing themselves back in place could be dulled. When he remembered what had happened, he shot up, and pain shot through his back. He saw spots, and he had to lie back down while his spine finished healing. Where were the other three?

He heard a stirring and then, out of nowhere, beautiful music that made him feel invigorated. He got up and looked toward the source. Gerald was sitting on a rock, strumming on his lyre.

Some color had returned to his face, but he still looked exhausted. While the melody echoed around them, the two warriors began to stir and wake. Pax let out a sigh of relief as he watched his friends sit up and hold their heads.

"What in the Nine Hells?" Korivare said, looking up toward the small disk of light that marked the hole they had fell through.

"As far as I can tell," Gerald explained, "the sun seems to be at its zenith. We've been unconscious for at least a couple hours."

"How are we alive? That fall is at least thirty feet onto bare stone."

Gerald shrugged. "We all know our big, green friend can survive a fall like that, but the three of us should be dead at least twice over."

"Magic. I stopped the fall." Jiang looked up at the hole. "Partly."

"OK, so that explains how we're alive. So, where are we?" Gerald asked. Then, as if to answer his own question, Gerald switched the melody of his song and the chamber they were in lit up with an ethereal blue light that came from the strings of the lyre.

The light fell on a huge cavern that was shaped like a massive tunnel. It was too regular to be a natural cave, and it had strange symbols carved into the rock.

Gerald let out a long whistle. "Now this is more like it. If my understanding of runic inscription is worth half a damn, these were meant to act as traps. I think this is the dragon's lair."

He started walking around the large tunnel. "If it is, that explains a great deal. I bet the dragon made that sand trap that brought us here, and if it wasn't used to people with the magic our foreign friend wields, it's likely the dragon expected people to die from the fall."

He touched some of the runes on the walls. "Which means these are probably a defense against people who find a way to survive. Fascinating."

"To what end? Is this all merely a defense mechanism?" Korivare asked. "If dragons are so cunning and powerful, if they are such practiced arcanists as you insist, should we be concerned? It seems like this place will be dangerous if that's the case."

"No. Dragon's dead. No more magic," Jiang said.

"Correct! Any spells we would've encountered in this liar would've lost their magical endowment with the death of its caster."

"So, what's at the end of this cavern that is worthy of all this protection?" Korivare turned toward the awaiting darkness that the light spell didn't pierce.

"Only one way to find out." Gerald started walking down the cavern, bringing the light with him. Pax fell into step beside him, not wanting to be caught in the flanking darkness a dozen steps in either direction.

Normally, having grown up living in a cave, Pax didn't mind the darkness. In fact, if the decision was between a dark cave and a place lit by candles or other kind of flame, Pax felt safer in the dark. This darkness, on the other hand, felt different. Even if the magical traps had been disabled, something made this darkness feel oppressive.

The light of the spell fell on a wall that was covered in scratches: some of them runes and some of them simply gouges in the rock that reminded Pax of a number of cave-dwelling predators. The light didn't reveal any side tunnels, however, and it seemed this entire cavern was gouged out of the rock by the dragon itself.

21

"Something is bugging me," Pax said after they were flanked on each side by growing shadows deep enough that it further stirred his anxiety.

"I'm listening," Gerald said. He was still strumming the tune that made his lyre glow, but it was quiet enough to not interfere with Pax's speech.

"You said the dragon had constructed an elaborate sand trap to protect its home, right?"

"Elaborate is a strong word for a hole in the ground and a few warding runes, but that's what it seemed like to me."

"That's what I mean. Why should it dig the hole? It can clearly move through the sand with no problem." Pax rolled his unbroken shoulder for emphasis and Korivare touched his ribs. "So why not just cover the entrance, so people can't find it at all?"

"Hmm," Gerald said as he thought. "There's something to that, Pax."

"And you mentioned smaller predators use them to catch prey, right? So, wouldn't it make sense that the dragon was doing the same?"

"That is an excellent point," Gerald said.

Pax beamed at the recognition, but his face fell when Korivare objected.

"But traps are usually lain by passive predators, and the dragon attacked us rather actively. Why would it do that if it was relying on the trap for its meals?"

"Seems reasonable to me," Gerald said, "that the dragon merely got impatient. You didn't notice many corpses or bones near where we landed did you?"

Korivare shook his head.

"Exactly. And anything that size needs regular meals to sustain itself. Unfortunately, deserts aren't known for their abundance. Maybe the dragon tried it, found it wasn't working, and started hunting again."

"No. The trap. It brought us here."

"Good point Jiang. Like I said up top, I'm certain that storm the dragon summoned did more than blind us and leave us wandering around.

"It may be that the dragon decided the trap would work if it could find something to push into it. We were probably at a favorite watering hole of its, judging by the petrified lightning by the oasis."

"That seems like a lot of effort to go through for a meal."

"Spoken like a man who has never been well and truly hungry. You are right, though, to a certain extent. That dragon could've simply attacked our caravan, gobbled up half the merchants and flown away in the time it took him to bring us here.

"Dragons tend not to think that way though. A lot of them take a great deal of pride in being over the top, even when it comes to hunting. I guess it gets boring at the top of the food chain, so they have to make a game of it."

Gerald's light fell on something glittering in a chamber at the end of the cavern. When they made it to where they could see what it was, each of them was stunned silent by the treasure trove that lay before them. A bed of gold and gems twice as large as the dragon lay at the center of a vast store of spices, silk, and weapons. Pax hadn't seen such wealth, even in the Mansion of House Morkae.

"Empty your pockets boys," Gerald said. "I doubt there's a bag big enough in all the world to carry this for us."

Pax looked down at his wrappings: barely even coverings, much less any kind of clothes that would have pockets. Gerald's melody changed slightly and the light that had been causing his lyre to glow popped out of it and flew over to the top of the pile of treasure. "There, now my fingers can get to work on their second favorite job."

He and the other two men broke up and started looking around. Pax just stood there trying to think of something he could use to hold his piece of the treasure.

Korivare looked back at Pax standing at the entrance to the chamber. He looked down at the wrappings on Pax's body, and seemed to come to a realization.

"Gerald," he turned to the bard, "keep any eye out for something that Pax can have. I doubt he'll want to carry handfuls of gems back to the Shatka caravan without somewhere to put them."

"You're not my dad! You can't just order me around," Gerald said. He turned to look at Pax. "That being said, our green friend does seem to need pockets. Pax, come here."

Pax approached. Gerald pulled something out of the hoard that looked like a giant sheet of canvas. Upon closer inspection, Pax realized in was a pale tan cloak. It was large enough that, when Gerald draped it over his shoulders, it felt like it was tailor made for him.

He tried to imagine what huge adventurer this was made for. When Gerald clasped the cloak around his shoulders, however, he clutched it in his hands. This was the first piece of proper clothing he had ever worn, and it was his.

"What do you think?" Gerald asked, but there were already tears in Pax's eyes. Gerald grinned at him. "You're welcome."

Gerald turned to walk away, but Pax pulled him into a crushing hug. "Hey now." Gerald had to gasp out the words. "We can't all just reknit our bones like you can. Be gentle."

Pax released his friend and Gerald started to rub his chest. "There's probably a dozen pockets sown into that thing," Gerald said. "So you should be able to carry plenty of stuff. Go nuts. You've certainly earned it."

Pax sprinted off, but it quickly became a skip as he failed to contain his excitement at his new gift. The bow from House Morkae was the only other gift he had ever received, and Pax wasn't sure which meant more to him. Luckily, no one was going to make him choose any time soon.

He walked through the piles of treasure. A quiver of arrows with bright red fletching caught his eye and he picked them up. He had left his arrows with the caravan and there was no telling how long it would take for them to get back to them.

"Careful. Those arrows. They're dangerous." Pax turned to see Jiang looking over his shoulders at the arrows.

"What are they?"

"They are... magic... what is the word?"

"Enchanted?"

Jiang nodded. His face was placid, but his hand flicked out.

Pax looked at his hand. "What is that you just did?"

Jiang looked down at his hand. He flicked it in the same way. "It means this." He pointed to his face and gave an excited grin that gave Pax an uneasy feeling. It looked like Jiang had long ago forgotten how to smile and was trying to imitate one after hearing it described.

"And doing that with your face is bad?"

Jiang shook his head. "It's bad. Only for me."

"I don't understand."

"For you, it's good. For me, it's bad."

"Why is it bad for you?"

"I am a warrior. Emotions are not good. Leads to men who are wrong in their thinking. When a warrior does this, it is bad."

"So, you use your hands to convey emotion instead of your face? What's the difference?"

"Yes! If I do it with hands it goes further. More time to think."

Pax gave him a questioning look.

His hand flicked in a way that seemed… exasperated? "Your face is right next your mind." He held up his hand. "This is further. Emotions travel further. More time to think about them."

Pax was trying to wrap his head around this idea when Jiang gestured toward the arrows. "Those arrows. They're magic. Enchanted with fire. Be careful."

"I will."

Jiang nodded and walked away.

Pax went back to scanning over the hoard. Something caught his eye, glimmering behind bags of spices. He walked up and moved the bags over.

It was a small, blue, glowing gemstone set on a gold chain. When Pax picked it up, he could see a faint outline of what looked like a miniature lightning storm inside. He put the necklace on. After that, he decided that gold pieces were the easiest thing to hold in pockets and filled his pockets.

"Guys," Gerald said from the other side of the gold pile, "we have to leave. Now."

"What?" Korivare asked. "Why?"

"I just found a nest."

Pax climbed over the treasure pile to get a look. Korivare was already there inspecting it. "These shells are all broken. If the babies aren't here, then they're most likely long gone by now."

"You don't understand. Blue-bellied dragons, they mate for life. If this one had kids, that means its mate could come back at any moment. Killing one was hard enough, and I don't want to stick around to see if we could take another one."

Just then a deep, rolling voice came from outside the chamber, "Kra etre hs lesha!"

Gerald mouthed "hide!"

Pax dove behind the spice bags where he found the amulet. Gerald and Korivare moved to crouch behind a rack of weapons as a creature much larger than the one they had faced lumbered into the chamber.

Its eyes were seething with anger and it searched the chamber, carefully scanning each nook and cranny. Pax hadn't seen where Jiang had hid, and he prayed to any gods that may be listening that the dragon couldn't either.

After several racing heartbeats, the creature turned and trotted out of the chamber. Pax caught Gerald's eye and he gestured above Pax's head. Pax looked up to see an opening in the stone.

He gestured toward Gerald, who moved silently next to him. He lifted the bard toward the opening. When Gerald scrambled into the tunnel, Pax looked around to see if he could spot either of his other two friends. He spotted both of them crouching nearby just as the beast at the other end of the tunnel let out a loud, angry roar. He gestured to the two warriors and they scurried over to him.

He lifted them into the opening. That's when he realized it was too high up for him to be able to reach it on his own. He was going over his options for how he could survive an encounter with that great beast when a rope fell in front of his face.

It dangled for a moment before he was able to focus on it. When he tugged on it, he found that it was secure and he used it to shimmy up to the tunnel above. Pax's height meant that he had to stoop to fit inside the tunnel. It was so small, in fact he wondered how the dragons could've carved it out of the stone.

He was pulled out of this thought when Gerald waved him deeper into the tunnel, and the four walked slowly down the tunnel until they were able to whisper without being heard.

"Where are we? I didn't see this tunnel when we first got in the chamber."

"It's probably an air vent they scratched out in case of cave-ins. If that's the case, it should lead outside somewhere."

Gerald started to walk carefully down the new tunnel. He didn't recast his light spell, and Pax realized why. He looked back to the glowing light emanating from the treasure chamber. The longer the orb stayed put, the longer the dragon believed they were still somewhere in the chamber. As long as they didn't draw its attention, they'd escape out the other end into the desert.

Pax didn't know how long they were walking through the tunnel when Jiang stumbled and grunted, breaking the silence in the tunnel. Pax heard his heart beat in his ears when he turned to see how far along in the tunnel they were.

He saw the pinprick of light from the chamber they left just before it was blocked by a shadow. He pushed Gerald and Korivare through the tunnel and all four men fell to a slightly lower floor. Just as they ducked down, a bolt of lightning arced overhead.

The dragon roared its rage and scratched at the stone, sending an awful screeching noise through the tunnel. Gerald decided that the jig was up, and summoned his orb of light, allowing them to see that they had stumbled in to a tunnel running perpendicular to the air vent.

CHAPTER FIVE

Tomb of Mysteries

The dragon's scratching lasted long enough for Pax's heart to slow to a steady, if fast, beat. After it stopped, he looked up to see a mural painted on the wall opposite him. It was cracked from age, but it seemed to depict a large company of people: some with weapons, some with what looked like grain stalks, and some that had their hands up toward a towering figure that was facing the mass of people.

Pax stood and walked over to get a better look, but the dragon let out another roar. He decided he'd rather keep up with the others, and he jogged a couple steps to catch up to the other three who had started walking down the new tunnel.

Where the mural ended, the wall was covered with strange symbols that Pax didn't recognize. Pax didn't know how to read, but he'd seen books and scrolls before. He knew what words looked like when they were written down, and this was not it. The symbols in books repeated a lot, but these symbols seemed to repeat a few times if at all.

The scrapping stopped and the dragon let out one final, anguished cry. It seemed they were safe from its wrath, but Pax felt they weren't safe yet. Wasn't that tunnel supposed to lead to the surface? Where were they instead?

"Now this is a whole new kind of interesting," Gerald said. He was looking closely at the symbols carved into the wall. He had stopped strumming his lyre, so Pax went to go see what had him more intrigued than his music.

When he got closer to the wall, he felt something shift inside him. Suddenly the meaning of the symbols on the wall opened up to him. It was a warning that this was the tomb of a king called Lethehotep. According to the inscription, trespassers faced all kinds of deadly traps and challenges and only the worthy could approach the dead king.

The symbols themselves hadn't changed, but Pax understood what they meant. That was impossible. He had seen words before. House Morkae had given him a writ of some kind, but he couldn't read. These symbols were something completely different, something he'd never seen before. Why, then, could he read them? He looked at Gerald. "Did you do something?"

"Something like what?"

"Why can I read this inscription? I've never been taught how to read and I've never seen these symbols before."

"You got me. I certainly didn't do this. Maybe our dear warmage has a spell we don't know about."

"No. I can read it, but it wasn't not me."

Pax jumped. He hadn't seen Jiang approach.

"So, three people suddenly can read a language they've never seen before, and no one cast a spell?"

"Four." Korivare said. "And no, before you ask, I didn't do this either."

"Four people finding themselves fluent in a new language. No apparent magical cause. This is quite the mystery," Gerald said.

"This inscription appears to be a warning of some kind. Is it possibly enchanted to be readable by everyone regardless of language barrier?" Korivare asked.

Gerald thought about this for a moment. "For a spell to be sustained after the caster's death, the spell would need to somehow be tied to an energy source that would keep it going. That usually requires a leyline of some kind.

"Not to mention it would take a lot of coordinated effort to give the spell the proper permanency so the focus doesn't degrade. It's possible, but highly unlikely considering how old this place has to be."

"Why do you think it's old?" Pax asked.

Gerald pointed toward a section of the wall. "That part talks about Lethehotep being a 'great unifier of Maskohma.' The last people to unify the upper and lower regions of Maskohma were the Araka Empire, and that collapsed over four centuries ago.

"Only Shatkas, clans of nomadic traders like the one we were with, are allowed across the River-Line. That's one of the things that makes them so valuable to the noble houses."

Pax nodded. House Morkae had mentioned some of this, but he didn't really understand the scope of it all. As far as he was concerned, if they asked him to protect something, he'd do it. Except if he didn't get back to the caravan, he will have failed at that task and lost all hope for a family and a true name.

"Well," Korivare said as he started walking down the tunnel, "we aren't going to be freed of this place by standing around talking about history. Which way do we go?"

He pointed down the deep cavern. "Toward the dark unknown, or," he pointed back the way they came "toward the death beast?"

Just then another roar came from that direction. The whole chamber shook and sent dust into the air. Pax wondered if the creature was slamming against the wall, and, if so, why?

"That sounds like an answer to me. Into the unknown brave adventurers!" Gerald declared. He marched down the tunnel, taking his glowing orb with him. Pax followed, not wanting to be left alone in the dark tomb of a dead king. The other two men followed soon after.

The inscription gave way to additional murals, and soon after Gerald stopped suddenly in his tracks, causing Pax to run into his back. That almost sent him tumbling, but he was able to catch himself against the wall. "What's wrong?" Pax asked.

Gerald bent down and drew a knife from his belt. Using it as a lever, he pulled up one of the tiles that made up the floor. Under it was some kind of lever. "It's a pressure plate. Now that there's no plate, we're under no pressure. This must be one of the traps the inscription warned about. I wonder what it was meant to do."

"Honestly," Korivare said from behind Pax, "I'm not keen on finding out."

"I suppose I can put off my study of ancient traps for a time where we aren't being pursued by a giant lightning breathing, desert lizard," Gerald mused.

Gerald hopped over the newly revealed lever, and continued down the tunnel. The other three followed him down the tunnel further. Pax continued to watch the murals change from people clutching various objects to a strangely angular pyramid structure with a robed woman carrying a glowing circle.

A few more feet down the tunnel the party heard a *click*. Gerald's eyes went wide and turned around as a dart shot out from the side of the wall and hit him in the side. "Oh dear," he said as he clutched his side.

Pax caught him as he fell to his knees and tipped forward. "Are you OK?" Pax asked. The bard's skin was clammy and hot.

"I'm fine. I guess I pushed myself a little hard with all the magic I've been doing. I'll pull through I'm s—Ahh!" He let out a yell of pain as Korivare pulled the dart out of his side.

"Don't be so sure," Korivare said. "There's poison on this dart. I can't tell what kind; it may be some kind of venom."

"A venom that's centuries old?" Gerald asked. His breathing was getting heavy, and he was starting to shiver. "Does venom expire? I honestly have no idea."

"Whatever it is, it's acting fast. We need to find a safe place. I may be able to help, but not if I'm constantly worried about traps or a dragon."

Gerald lifted a shaking finger down the tunnel. The light of his floating orb had revealed a chamber. Korivare shook his head. "No. We don't know what kind of traps are in that place."

"Do you want to head back toward the dragon?" Gerald asked.

Korivare rolled his eyes and gestured for Pax to pick up the shivering bard. They walked swiftly but carefully toward the chamber. The orb rested above a strange pool of clear water. Pax wondered how water could stay so clean underground like this. Korivare helped him set Gerald down gently against the wall that made-up the rim of the pool.

Korivare began whispering and his hands glowed with magic. Pax watched Gerald's wound close. It was slow on the visible scale, but much faster than the natural healing Pax knew other creatures were capable of.

Some color returned to Gerald's face, and he began to breathe a little easier. Korivare, however, was hunched over him with his brow knit

31

in concentration. Pax started to worry that they were merely trading one incapacitated person for another.

A thought occurred to Pax, and he started looking around. If only one of them had a... there! He didn't know whose it was, but he picked up the waterskin and went over to the rim of the pool.

When he looked into it, however, he didn't see the water he originally thought was in the pool. Instead, it was merely a swirling mass of colors that were shifting and mixing around. It was so hypnotic that Pax almost forgot what was going on around him.

Until, that is, he heard Korivare calling his name. It sounded like it was coming from the other end of a long tunnel, and, when Pax looked up, he was expecting them to be back toward the chamber's entrance. Korivare was sitting right next to him, however.

"Don't you go catatonic on me. We don't need you helpless as well." Korivare's face was glistening with a sheen of sweat. "Mind if I have some of that?" He nodded toward the waterskin Pax was holding.

When Pax hefted it, he realized it was full. It was definitely empty before... right? He dumbly held out the waterskin to Korivare who took it and drank greedily. When he was done, he poured the remaining water into Gerald's mouth. Gerald coughed, but then drank in what he could. Korivare went back to his whispered prayer.

Pax realized Jiang was looking at him. His face was blank as ever, but he made a gesture. Pax guessed it was meant to express concern so he just shook his head. "I'm fine," Pax said. He made a point of not looking into the pool again.

Korivare's whispering started to get strained and Pax was about to ask him if there was anything he could do to help. Before he could, Korivare sat back, breathing heavy. "We both need to rest. I've done everything I can do." His voice was weak, and after he finished talking, he closed his eyes. His breathing was still heavy, but it was steady.

Gerald, for his part, had stopped shivering. He was covered in sweat, but he seemed to be stable. His eyes were closed as well. Pax and Jiang looked at each other, and Pax shrugged. He sat on the tiled floor and put his back against the rim of the pool. He faced the tunnel from whence they came and looked into the wall of darkness where the light didn't reach. Pax didn't even notice when he fell asleep.

CHAPTER SIX
Chaos Reigns

Pax awoke in the middle of swirling pink petals falling from trees he hadn't seen before. Their trunks had a dark brown bark and any existing leaves where invisible behind the pink petals that the trees seemed to shed.

It took him a moment to remember where he was supposed to be, and he stood up and looked around, confused. The walled off pool he had been sitting against was still there, but the tunnel they were in was nowhere to be found. Neither was the dessert that it had been in.

Everyone else was still asleep. As Pax looked around, the swirling leaves never seemed to collect on the forest floor. They just seemed to swirl downward forever, never touching the ground. He paused for a moment. He felt like he was thinking through syrup, but something wasn't right about his surroundings.

He looked up through the branches. The sky was covered in a massive cloud that made it appear like the sunlight was shinning down from the whole sky. The clouds themselves were white and puffy. Clouds he knew well from the forests he'd grown up in, but unlike any he'd seen in the desert.

There was something about this place that felt off. Pax remembered few of his dreams from throughout his life, but he remembered waking up realizing that a great deal of what had happened didn't make any sense. In the moment, however, it never seemed confusing. He was familiar with the feeling of confusion, and he always felt it upon waking, but never in the moment. That's how his surroundings felt in this moment.

When Gerald sat up, holding his head, the feathers that had been swirling around his head moved and caught an updraft. "What happened? Why are we in an oak forest?"

Pax looked around, confused. The trees around them were indeed oak, though some were clearly a kind of hickory as well. He was sure they were different when he had first woken up.

"Something weird is going on. I have no idea where we are."

"You got me. This may be another trap. If the people who constructed that tomb were able to keep a language enchantment going for centuries, I don't see why they couldn't do it with an illusion."

"I thought you said that'd be very difficult."

"Difficult, not impossible. And not outside the realm of possibility for someone with half a continent's worth of resources at their command."

"So, what do we do?"

"You heal bones rather quickly, right?"

"Yes w—ahh!" Gerald had twisted Pax's finger until it had broken. The Rage roused in Pax, and he smacked Gerald in the chest, sending him flying against a tree. The tree burst into a hundred white doves. Pax cradled his finger as it knit itself back together.

Gerald came back up to him, rubbing his chest. Pax was able to calm down enough to feel bad about what he had done. He opened his mouth to apologize but Gerald waved it off. "I should've warned you. That's my fault. But we did figure out a couple of things: firstly, we know that this is not an illusion. I assume that hurt."

Pax gave him a look.

"Right, if this was an illusion, you would've been pulled out of it by your mind when it felt real pain. True pain is the quickest way out of an illusion."

"So, we are actually in a real forest where the trees burst into a flock of birds when you hit them?" Pax had never heard of such a thing, but there was a lot about the world he didn't know.

Gerald shrugged. "That's the second thing we learned. You hit me into a fully grown tree, and rather than injuring me, the tree transformed."

The trees and feathers shifted again as Jiang woke up. They turned back into trees with pink petals. The spinning, shifting, petals reminded Pax of snow.

"What?" Jiang said as he started looking around. He gestured, but Pax was too far away to see what it could've been. He stood and walked over to Korivare. He shook the paladin awake, and Pax felt guilty for not thinking of doing the same.

They both walked over to where Pax and Gerald were standing. Gerald was studying the trees. "What happened?" Jiang asked.

"I am also curious. Weren't we underground when I fell asleep?" Korivare asked while looking around at the trees. It looked like they were shifting again. They seemed to become, somehow, more unsubstantial. When they didn't change, Pax wondered if he had gotten enough sleep.

"I'm working on it," Gerald said without turning around. "Wherever we are, it's not in our normal world."

Korivare opened his mouth, but Gerald continued.

"If you're going to ask how I know that, you can thank your large friend for that. I've seen people get thrown back by a hit, and I'm not just talking about Mr. Knight. All of them end up with something broken or worse. Pax, you're hit threw me against a tree and it didn't cause anything other than a small shock."

"Pax did what?"

"Hush my chivalrous friend. Your Master Storyteller is speaking. Anyway, that coupled with the fact that the same tree transmuted into a flock of doves, means that the laws of reality we are used to don't apply here."

Korivare's eyes began to move over the forest around them. He seemed to see it in a new way. "We're in the Dream World. The monks at my monastery told stories about a world of chaotic and shifting material that are not bound by any understandable laws. According to them, that is where our consciousness goes when we dream."

"So, a world made entirely of chaotic energy makes sense, but a world of endless skies doesn't?"

"I didn't believe what they said. It seemed ridiculous, but I can't ignore what is in front of my face. If that's really where we are, we are in great danger. There's no stability here and we could easily be ripped apart. We're lucky we've survived this long."

"How do we—" Pax began. Before he could finish the statement, however. He fell through the ground as it shifted into a clump of sand that dispersed under his feet.

Pax was able to turn around in just enough time to see the rest of the ground breaking apart under the feet of his friends. The ground broke into three pieces, one was carrying the two warriors, one holding the bard, and another holding a massive stone that appeared to have writing on it. It was too far away for him to read, but all of the pieces were falling incredibly fast toward a strange river of stars.

Pax stopped falling in the midst of the river. It wasn't a sudden stop like most landings. It was a gradual slowing until he was in the middle of the river and moving along toward something like a waterfall.

Cresting over the waterfall, Pax was deposited into a more normal river. The current was almost non existent, and it took little effort for Pax to swim to the bank of the river.

After he got himself onto the bank of the river, he looked up to see all three of his friends recovering from their own individual adventures that had led them to the bank of a river in strange valley nestled between several mountains.

The stone Pax had spotted at the beginning of his fall was also present. Approaching it, cautious about the ground beneath his feet, Pax was able to see what was carved into it. He couldn't read it, but that was nothing new.

DFINOUY ELORSUY AFINNNU AFIIILM EEHHMOR EFIORUY
ADEMNSS AEFGMOR ACENOTR EEOOSUY EEFLSR ADEEFLS
EHMOTRW DDFLOOR AEFIMSR ADEHMNT EFORSTT EEHHOSU
FHIOOUY EEEGHST M

-Granma A

"What the hell is that?" Pax asked the others as they approached as well. "Are those words?"

"No, these are just random letters strung together in an incoherent mess. Probably a result of this world," Korivare said.

"I... I don't think they're random." Gerald was examining the inscription. "Look at the byline."

"Granma A?" Korivare asked.

"Yeah. It's an anagram of... well anagram."

"So?"

"So, I think it might be encoded. Does anyone have any paper or something?"

Everyone gave Gerald a look. He looked embarrassed before two sheets of parchment made of vellum appeared in his hand. He looked at it. "I also need something to write with." A piece of charcoal appeared in his other hand, and he started working.

Korivare looked very deep in thought. Pax approached him and gave him a questioning look. He just shook his head before speaking, "everything I understand about the Dream World suggests that it should be more dangerous than this."

"Didn't you say we come here in our dreams?"

Korivare shook his head. "Our minds travel to this world while we dream. At least, that's what the monks taught me. It's entirely different than being here physically. When our minds are here, we are experiencing things, but they aren't happening to us in a way that can actively harm our bodies."

"Huh?" Pax said. He didn't understand exactly what Korivare was saying, but it seemed to disturb him.

"It's hard to explain, but basically the fact that our bodies are here, and not just our minds, means we are in great danger."

Pax's stomach growled and he realized he hadn't eaten for an entire day. This wasn't a new thing for him. He'd figured out a long time ago that it'd take several days before the hunger started causing him pain. However, he had gotten used to eating regularly with the caravan, so now his stomach seemed to be upset with him.

He looked up. Toward the rim of the valley, there were more of the trees with pink petals on them. He spotted fruit on the branches of one of them.

They were red, small, round fruit that grew in bunches among the petals. When he plucked one and ate it, he found the center hard like a pit. He noticed Jiang looking up and down the tree and making a slow gesture. To Pax, it looked like either confusion or intrigue.

"This is not right. This tree shouldn't have fruit."

"It seems to be edible," Pax said between, taking a handful and popping them in his mouth one at a time.

Jiang shook his head. "No. These trees come from my home. They don't make fruit."

"I don't think these are the same trees. Seems like wherever we are, Dream World or whatever, we have to get used to things being different."

Jiang nodded thoughtfully. He took his own bunch of the strange fruits and started eating. Pax saw his eyes light up in delight. Usually, he wouldn't notice something that subtle, but the warriors normally placid face highlighted the small expression. The pair had made a game of spitting the pits as far as they could and laughing when Gerald came over with what he believed was the correct message.

You find yourself in an unfamiliar home.
Here you find a message from a crone.
To see yourself released from the world of dreams,
find the Master of the House, you of high esteem.

"Well," Gerald said, "that settles where we are. I guess your teachers at the monastery were wrong about how dangerous the World of Dreams was."

"That is certainly one possibility," Korivare said.

"You have a different explanation?"

Korivare shook his head. "I don't know what to think right now. The only thing that matters is figuring out who this Master of the House is."

"If 'the house' in this metaphor is the Dream World," Gerald said. "I'd suspect we have to seek out the God of Dreams himself."

Korivare paled at that suggestion. Pax had never known there was a god of dreams, but he didn't know much about religion. "Who's the God of Dreams?"

"He is..." Korivare paused, "an unstable thing. Most of the stories I've heard that feature him depict all kinds of different things. I was never convinced that each of the characters were truly the same entity, but..."

"But he is the embodiment of existential chaos, and that means he is, fundamentally, unpredictable," Gerald finished.

Pax nodded and looked around at the trees around them. He sighed.

"I guess I wouldn't expect much else from someone who lives here."

As he said that, a huge ship sailed down the river, looking easily too large to be floating in such a shallow river. It had a full rigging and three masts of sails. It was far too tall to board from where they stood.

Pax heard a whistle from Gerald to his side. "This is quite the beautiful ride. What do you say gentlemen, shall we sail away to the great unknown?" The bard disappeared behind the massive ship.

"Is it safe?" Pax asked. He moved toward where Gerald had gone but the gnome had disappeared.

"It's the unknown. It is never safe. But," he popped over the railing on the deck of the ship, "no one discovered anything worth while by staying safe. C'mon Pax! We can either sail away or sit here in this valley waiting for eternity."

Pax didn't know how Gerald had gotten on, so how he was meant to completely eluded him. He moved toward the ship and the river until he was back at the bank of the river.

He heard Gerald shout from the deck, "get on the boat you big, green fool."

Pax walked along the hull of the ship until he found a rope that he could shimmy up. The moment he touched it however, it transformed into a set of stairs and he climbed them onto the top deck of the ship.

CHAPTER SEVEN

Dreams and Nightmares

The ship deck was much larger than it looked from the ground, and Pax had to keep reminding himself that space worked differently here. Trying to justify it in his mind made his brain hurt.

"This ship. Where?"

Pax hadn't noticed Jiang climbing aboard. The warmage was looking ahead to where the ship's prow was pointed. Ahead was merely a haze or some kind of fog. Usually, Pax could at least make out shadows or shapes through fog, but this fog seemed to be less concealing their surroundings and more their surroundings not yet manifest.

That gave Pax a nauseating feeling, and he looked over the side of the ship at the running waters of the river. He focused on his reflection to try and avoid all the things that were making him feel queasy: the fog, the weird spatial distortions, and the rocking of the ship.

The glassy surface of the water rippled and disturbed his reflection as something strange broke the surface. It looked like how someone once described a fish to Pax, but it was flat and looked like it was made of some kind of bread. He turned toward his friends and began to ask, "does anyone have a—" a net appeared on the ground around his feet.

He threw the net over the side and grabbed the rope attached as it almost went overboard. When the net became noticeably heavier, he started to pull it up and over the railing of the ship. The net was filled the strange creatures that flopped around on the deck. Pax picked one up, and it immediately went limp.

In fact, once he had picked it up it showed no signs of being alive ever. It was just a floppy piece of odd flat-bread. Pax took a bite, and found, at the center, a strange, viscous, sticky fluid. It tasted sweet and woody. It reminded him of his home in the forest. He smiled.

"Whatcha got there?" Gerald asked. He had been watching Pax from the bow of the ship.

Pax picked up another fish, and it immediately went limp like the first one. He tossed it, and it hit Gerald in the face. Gerald flinched. The flatbread fell into his hands, and he looked at it.

"I think I've had grain cakes like this before, though I haven't ever seen them in the shape of a trout before." He bit off the head and more of the viscous fluid spilled out. "Why is it filled with sap?"

He tasted it. "That's not sap. It tastes like maple candy, and, now that I think about it, it seems thicker than sap." He continued eating. "This is actually pretty good."

He finished his fish and practically sprinted toward the pile next to Pax's feet. He and Pax dug into to two or three fish each before they thought to call over the other two.

Korivare and Jiang walked over and took in the pile of fish. Korivare gave the other two men a curious look. When Pax held up one of the fish-shaped cakes to him, he took it and hefted it in his hand.

Korivare hesitated for a moment more before taking his own exploratory bite. The sticky maple sap poured out of the decapitated body, and Korivare spread it anxiously around his hand. A bowl of water and a rag appeared somewhere near by and Korivare used it to wash his hands between bites.

Jiang, for his part, ate a single fish before making a gesture that appeared to Pax like one of disgust. Pax shrugged. That left his share to the other three, and Pax dug into another fish.

When the net was empty the three men sat back with full bellies. Pax looked over to where Jiang had been standing and realized he had moved to the aft of the ship. Curious, Pax walked over to him. He was staring into the mist.

"There is nothing beyond."

Pax didn't say anything. He was trying to absorb the statement. He wasn't used to his friend being so dark and pessimistic.

"I see nothing. Fog is too thick." Pax let out a sigh that turned into a laugh. Jiang looked at him and gestured.

"I didn't think you were being so literal. I'm sorry."

Jiang nodded.

"I have to ask. Why do you speak the way you do? At first it seemed like you were struggling with the language, but now that I think about it, it seems like you understand the language just fine. So, what's the deal?"

"Where I come from, many words are not the way. You speak fewer words. It inspires thought. Your people speak so much and say very little."

"So, where you come from, everyone speaks like that?"

Jiang made a gesture like balancing scales with his hand. "In my language, few words carry much meaning. In this way, yes. But, the greatest of my people, they say still less. And many people see much in their few words."

"So, in your culture, a teacher would say what they wanted in as few words as possible and let their students take whatever meaning they found from those words?"

Jiang nodded. "Most teachers have many students. Each student has an idea. They begin to discuss."

"That seems rather… chaotic."

Jiang shrugged. "We learn in the world. World is chaotic." He gestured toward the surrounding mist for emphasis. As he did, the mist shifted.

Instead of a surrounding field of intangible mist, it coalesced into a writhing mass of black tentacles. Jiang eyes went wide in a subtle show of surprise that stood out stark on his normally placid face. "No. I didn't."

The tentacles lashed out at the hull of the ship. When they hit, the ship rocked, and Pax thought it would capsize. The tentacles retracted into the mass, and the ship stabilized. Pax turned toward the other end of the ship where Korivare and Gerald were.

He spotted them, but, at the same time, he got knocked to his knees by one of the sinuous tentacles. Pax felt the Rage welling up inside him again, and he stayed where he was. He had to focus on his breathing until he was certain he had it under control.

When he stood, he reached for his bow, but he couldn't find it. He wanted to go searching for it. This wasn't the time, though. He needed to help defend the ship. He spotted a spear leaning against the rail. When he went to pick it up, a part of him was certain it wasn't there before. The spear had an intricately carved willow handle that was mesmerizing.

Pax's attention was absorbed into a detailed carving of a dragon fighting with two warriors in armor. When he felt a cold muscley tentacle wrapping around his leg, he was pulled out of his hypnotic trance. The spear was already pointed down, so he merely stabbed down and the tentacle retreated into the black mass, leaving no blood or any trace it had been there.

Pax got ready to attack the next tentacle that came in range. "No!" He heard Jiang's voice off to his side. He looked, keeping his spear pointed toward the mass. Jiang was standing with his feet set apart. The side that held his sword was pointed toward the mass. "Like this."

Pax copied the stance, pointing his left side toward the mass and gripped the spear with both hands. When the next tentacle lashed out, Pax thrust toward it. He landed a hit on it, and it retreated, as the other one did, into the writhing mass. The next few attacks came in quick succession. Pax knocked one to the side, and thrust at the next. He ducked to avoid the next and stepped back as the last reached for him.

After that flurry of attacks, all the tentacles retreated back into the slinking black mass. Pax took in a breath. Then two. Then two dozen tentacles lashed out at the hull of the ship and it began to splinter. Pax felt the ship begin to sink under his feet. He grabbed Jiang's hand. Then he brought them both over to the railing and jumped. He twisted in the air, so his body broke Jiang's fall.

He stood and helped his friend off the ground. Gerald and Korivare had abandoned the ship as well, and were swimming to shore. The current seemed to bend around them, and they had an easy time of it.

When all four men were ashore, Pax looked back at where the ship had been. There was nothing there. No sign of the squirming mass of tentacles, no sunken vessel. Just clear water running swiftly downstream. This whole place was making Pax's head hurt.

"Now what?" Gerald asked. "We didn't even know where we were going, and now we're stranded."

"It seems reasonable to me that, if the ship was going to take us downstream, we could simply continue to follow the river," Korivare said.

Gerald pointed downstream to a fork in the river about half a mile ahead. "What do we do at that point?"

Korivare sighed and his shoulders slumped. "I don't know. Ask the river nicely to tell us where to go?"

"To the left." The voice sounded like tinkling bells. Pax looked around for the source, but Korivare just shook his head.

"Nope. Absolutely not. I am not taking directions from a river."

"Prejudice." The voice wasn't coming from the swift waters of the river. Instead, it seemed to be coming from the surroundings as a whole.

"You must excuse our friend Sir Knight. He is not used to talking to bodies of water. I assure you, we deeply appreciate your helpful advice," Gerald said.

He began following the river downstream. Korivare rolled his eyes, but followed. Pax and Jiang caught up with them, and Pax noticed Korivare was holding something.

"What's that? A spear?"

Korivare looked down where Pax was indicating. "It's a halberd actually. It's a pole-arm, like a spear, but more versatile."

He held it out for Pax to examine. It had a shaft that had carvings that looked like swirling wind. At the head was an axe blade that was made of a steel that looked like flowing waves. Finally, on the tip was a wicked looking spike with small, almost invisible barbs.

Korivare caught Pax's hand before his finger touched the spike. "It's sharper than anything I've ever wielded. I wouldn't do that."

Pax withdrew his hand slowly. "Where did you get it? I thought you left most of your weapons with the caravan."

Korivare shrugged. "It was on the ship. I found it when that tentacled beast attacked, and just picked it up. Not going to ask questions when my life is in danger."

Pax looked at his spear. The carvings on his shaft were very similar to the ones on Korivare's halberd. His was willow and depicted a dragon, and Korivare's was rosewood and didn't have a specific scene, but the details looked very similar. "Did it appear out of nowhere? I think my spear may have come from the same place."

Korivare shrugged. "Who knows? I don't seem to understand anything that is going on in this godforsaken place."

"Quite the opposite actually," Gerald said without turning around. "If this is the Dream World, which seems more and more likely with each passing moment, this place is the residence of a very specific god."

"Forgive me if I don't shout for joy."

The river lead deep into a dark forest that reminded Pax of his home. The sky, still covered in a massive white cloud, was heavily obscured by the branches of birch and willow trees that had to be centuries old. Still, Pax caught the occasional glimpse of the glowing cloud when the branches bent in just the right way.

Pax's stomach growled. He started thinking about the kinds of food that might be in this forest. He wished he had more of those small red fruits or those strange fish. Jiang stopped him silently with an arm out. Pax looked up and saw a wild boar. It was rummaging through the underbrush two dozen steps from where the group had stopped. It was six feet long and at least two hundred pounds. It's bristling hairs stood on end.

The boar stopped rooting in the ground and looked up. It huffed angrily at the group and dug in the ground with one hoof. Pax saw Korivare crouch and set the butt of his halberd against the ground. He gestured for Pax to crouch as well, and Pax mimicked his posture.

The boar charged straight at Pax and he leveled his spear at its chest. When the boar met the spear's tip, the haft shattered into splinters, and Pax, acting quickly, grabbed one of its tusks and shoved it to the ground. The boar wrestled its head away and pulled back for another charge.

Korivare stood to face it, but Pax waved him back. Those tusks were sharp and he didn't want his friend getting hurt. The boar came charging at Pax, and Pax tried to grab its tusks again. His hand slipped and one of the tusks pierced his breastbone and punctured his heart.

Pax took a knee as his heart began to fill with blood. The breastbone reknit itself painfully, and he knew the hole in his heart was closed.

The blood that leaked out, however, would take a while to get back where it belonged. The boar wasn't going to give him that time. It was already turning around to charge him again.

He heard whispering behind him and felt hands on his shoulders. Pax saw runes glow in a line between him and the boar, and when the boar charged, it stopped suddenly before crossing them as if it had hit an invisible wall.

Pax turned and saw Jiang with his eye locked on the spot where the runes were. The hands on his back were Korivare's and he could feel the blood that pooled in his heart being siphoned away quicker than before.

The boar paced back and forth on the other side of the rune-wall. Occasionally, it would hit the invisible wall with a tusk. When it did this, Jiang would flex as if he was catching the tusk in his hands. Each time he did this, the tusk would be stopped, but it seemed to take more and more effort from Jiang.

Something in the boar's overly intelligent eyes indicated to Pax that it came to the same realization. The boar turned and trotted back to where he was rooting. Pax felt the last of the blood drain from the pool in his heart. The boar circled back and came charging full force at the wall.

When it hit the wall, Jiang was thrown back. He fell to the ground and the boar continued to charge toward Pax, but he was ready for it. He caught the boar's tusks, and slammed it into the ground. Before it could react, Pax twisted and pushed with every muscle in his body.

He flipped the board on its back. He nodded at Korivare who didn't hesitate. He thrust the spike of his halberd into the boar's chest. The boar let out a long screech, jerked once, then stilled.

Korivare and Pax sat back, breathing heavily. It was only when the music stopped that Pax realize that Gerald had been playing any at all. He looked over to see his friend holding a silvery harp, much different from the lyre he normally played. Gerald set the instrument down and leaned against a tree, closing his eyes.

When Pax had caught his breath, he stood and walked to the boar's large body. Jiang handed him a knife. It had a brass hilt and the same swirling steel of Korivare's halberd or his broken spear. He cut into the fat at the base of the boar's belly and started to dress it.

He'd learned to dress wild animals from his mother, and Jiang began to help part way through. Between the two of them, the boar was ready to cook by the time Gerald and Korivare had a fire going.

They put the beast on a spit over a stone-lined pit. The fire in it had begun as a large bonfire, but Jiang explained that it would cook better and more evenly if the fire was allowed to burn down to hot coals and small flames. Gerald scoffed at having to wait longer for his meal, but Jiang was insistent.

Gerald relented and the group waited until the fire burned down properly before they started roasting the pig. Pax had to admit once he smelled the fat sizzling off the pork that he agreed with Gerald's impatience. His hunger reached deep inside him and mixed with his anxiety around the fire. The two were enough to rouse the Rage within him.

To avoid it awakening entirely, he got up and stepped away from the fire into the woods. There, he found a number of apple trees and tried some of their ripened fruits. They were sweet and juicy and eating them made his limbs tingle with energy. He decided to pick a few more and bring them to Gerald.

When he returned, he offered the fruit to Gerald. The little gnome took them and started cutting one up before he paused for a moment. Looking at the boar for a moment, Gerald smiled. He took the apple he'd been cutting and gestured for Jiang to pause the turning.

With the boar's belly turned up, Gerald picked up the knife they used to dress it. He cut the creature open and stuffed the apple pieces inside it before playing a light, simple melody that caused the boar's stomach to close around the fruit pieces.

The scent of the apples baking in the boar's belly mixed with the smell of roasting meat. Pax could hardly keep himself contained when Jiang declared the pork properly roasted. He used the knife a third time to cut pieces off the boar.

When the apples started falling out of the belly, Jiang caught as many as he could in a bowl that seemed to appear out of nothing. Korivare shaved a few thin sticks into skewers and the two started constructing a new dish out of the baked apples and roasted pork.

The group sat back after picking the boar clean of anything edible. Korivare brought the flame of their campfire up from glowing coals to a medium flame. Gerald plucked his harp absentmindedly, and a question arose in Pax's mind.

"You got that on the ship right?"

Gerald nodded.

"Did you summon it the same way you summoned the charcoal?"

Gerald moved his head from side to side. "Kind of. With the charcoal, I spoke my request and it happened. With this harp, it was more like I was looking for something and found what I expected.

"I assumed it was the same for yourself and the paladin. You found your weapons when you needed them because you were expecting to find them."

"That doesn't make sense. You can't merely summon things by expecting them to be where you look for them," Korivare said.

"Says the man holding a halberd he's never seen before. You picked it up on the ship as well I assume," Gerald responded.

"It was on the deck when that tentacle monster attacked us."

"Sure it was. And it's merely a coincidence that you didn't find it earlier than when you needed it."

"Are you saying that we can summon weapons through belief?" Pax asked.

"Yes and no," Gerald said. "It's more about what you expect rather than what you believe. A belief is something you choose, so it's more akin to a desire. Expectations are something you know to be true.

"It seems like this place can be influenced by our expectations. I was testing that theory with the charcoal request. It was hard to mold my expectations to do something I wasn't sure would work. Luckily for me, I had a great deal of practice when I tried to master lucid dreaming."

Korivare leaned back until he was lying down. He'd taken off his chain shirt. Pax wondered if he planned to sleep on the ground in front of the fire. Pax couldn't imagine being so comfortable around these chaotic flames.

"All of that," Korivare said from his position on the ground, "sounds as nonsensical as the rest of this place. I guess that means it makes sense as long as we're here."

"What?" Pax asked.

"It's simple. Nothing makes sense here. So anything that doesn't make sense, makes sense. Make sense?"

"No," Pax said.

"Exactly. Isn't it frustrating?"

"Have you never been in a dream before?" Gerald asked Korivare. "Weren't you the one that pointed this out as the dream world?"

Pax didn't hear Korivare's response. The fire and the unfamiliar place were making him anxious. It was hard to stay in the present moment when he saw the clouds above them darken and he felt sandwiched between burning flames and oppressing darkness.

By the time he was able to manage his anxieties, the rest of his group had fallen asleep. Pax, himself, was fighting the siren call of sleep when he heard a cackle from the trees beyond the fire light. Pax had a bad feeling that something worse than tentacles was moving to threaten them.

He kept his eyes open as the other three slept. He kept his eyes scanning the dark shadows beyond the firelight. He strained his ears to listen for the cackling again.

Nothing came out of the tree line, and Pax could feel himself slipping into unconsciousness. Jiang stirred as Pax was just about to give in to his exhaustion. The warmage stood and stretched out his muscles. He began moving in his slow methodical dance. Pax watched, letting the slow, practiced motions lull him to sleep.

CHAPTER EIGHT

Meeting the Master

Pax awoke to screeching. He jumped to his feet as Jiang and Gerald were stirring. Korivare was already awake and wearing his chain shirt. They all looked around for the source of the shrieking. It seemed to surround them and Pax started to get anxious about what was making it.

The sky was still dark and the light of the coals were better at casting dancing shadows around their makeshift camp than illuminating their surroundings. He felt uneasy with no weapon to use against the screeching creature. He balled his hands into fists. He had only one option: hope his strength would be enough.

The screeching stopped, and a light illuminated a path through the darkness. Pax looked up, but the sky was still dark. There was no visible source for the light.

Pax looked around to his friends and could tell they were equally nervous about following a strange light through shapeless dark. He nudged Jiang in the arm and gestured toward the bank of the river.

When Pax started to walk toward it, he suddenly found himself walking back toward the clearing where his friends were standing. He stopped and tried to walk out of the clearing in another direction. The same thing happened. He tried several more directions until he decided that their options were to approach the light or stand in the clearing forever.

"Well, on the bright side, if you'll excuse the pun, something in my guts tells me we're going to find out what was making that awful noise," Gerald said with a weak smile. His face was pale.

"Whatever it is," Korivare said. "We will face it. The gods have granted us victory up until now." He leaned on his halberd to emphasize his point.

"There's only one god that matters here, and there's no telling what he wants from us," Gerald said without taking his eyes off the lit path before them. He breathed in deep and took a shaky step forward. Pax put his hand on Gerald's shoulder and went ahead of him. As he was passing the bard, he saw him clam noticeably.

The trees parted and Pax saw a cobblestone pathway that led to a small cottage set in the middle of a gated garden. It was lit by a soft yellow light that made Pax look up and check to see if the sky was still dark. It was. The light simply seemed to exist around him. He turned to signal to his friends that he was safe, but they were already standing right behind him.

"I thought you would want to stay back," Pax said to them.

"Ground moved," Jiang explained. "We didn't follow. The ground moved."

Gerald nodded. His eyes were locked on the cottage. Pax gave him a concerned look, but Gerald just shook his head. He took a breath, put his head down, and marched toward the cottage his limbs shaking noticeably. Pax followed closely behind him, hoping his presence would soothe his friend's anxiety.

"Have you been wondering the same thing I have?" Korivare asked from Pax's side.

"I'm not sure. I don't know what you've been wondering."

"When we woke up here, the only thing from the tomb we left that came with us was that stone pool."

Pax remembered, and he wondered where Korivare was going with this thought. He nodded for Korivare to continue.

"Do you think that stone pool brought us here, or do you think this chaos god brought us here for some malevolent purpose?"

"I wish I knew," Pax said.

The four men walked through the garden gate and an old woman in a shawl and flowery dress woven of homespun greeted them from the front door.

"Ah my lovelies. I was wondering when you would be finding me. Honestly, what took you so long?" The woman coughed and leaned against the door post. "Come in, come in." She turned and slowly walked back into the cottage.

Pax looked around the garden. It was filled with colorful and fragrant flowers that all seemed to be in bloom. Pax didn't know any of their names, but there were several he recognized. There were pink ones with several petals and a large center, a clump of purple ones with five petals, and some pink one where the flowers drooped off the stem.

They reminded him of the meadows he used to explore at the edges of the forest he lived in. He remembered seeing for miles without anything in his way. He could still feel the wonder as he tried to reach the point where the sky seemed to touch the ground only for it to always be far away.

"Pax. Are you coming?" Korivare said from the doorway. The others were already inside. Pax nodded and followed him inside the small cottage.

The cottage had a single room with an oven in the corner that already had a pie of some kind baking inside it. A cat was drowsing in the window. The old woman was sitting at a table that took up most of the floor space of the cottage.

"Alright my lovelies. Now that you are here—"

"Hold on," Gerald said. The color seemed to come back to his face and he was speaking with an edge to his voice. "Who are you? Why are we here? I feel like we've been shepherded around since we got to this place with very little explanation as to why we're here or what's going on."

The outburst surprised Pax, who felt Gerald had been taking all of this in stride, but he couldn't say he disagreed. The old woman, for her part, nodded behind steepled fingers. She was quiet for a moment, and Pax thought she was going to simply ignore the question.

Instead, she took a breath and began, "you are here because the Master of Dreams has questions for the four of you. Many of the events you ran into while you have been here in the Plane of Chaos, Dream World, or whatever you insist on calling it, were influenced by myself in efforts to keep you alive long enough to get here."

"You sent that tentacled... thing, to attack us?" Pax asked.

"No. I'm not capable of making events happen or stopping them from happening. I am, however, able to dam the river, to borrow a phrase from you mortals."

She gestured toward the halberd that Korivare was leaning on. "I provided you with the tools you needed to defend yourselves. I ensured you didn't go hungry. I ensured you were always on the right path. But all that is beside the point. You are here now."

"And what exactly are we expected to do now?" Gerald interrupted.

The woman closed her eyes and took a breath. "Now I am going to explain what's going on. I—"

"Hold on. The note we got said we had to find the Master of the House."

The old woman gestured to the cottage around her.

Realization washed over Gerald's face. Then Pax could see the pieces fitting together in his head. "Then... that makes you..." The woman nodded. Gerald went pale again and swallowed.

"Now that we have all that out of the way, let's get down to the grain of things. Who are you four? You seem to have caught the eye of a lot of powers greater than simple mortals would normally warrant."

Gerald looked at the other three, but Pax spoke up first. "What do you mean?"

The old woman sighed heavily. "I loathe having to explain myself. Still, if I am to expect answers from you, I suppose I must."

Pax did not understand anything the woman was saying. He was waiting for her explanation when the cat on the window stood and stretched. It looked at him with huge, intelligent eyes and spoke to him with a rumbling voice.

"Some of the cosmic powers that govern this world have put a price on your head. Their followers will start trying to collect their favor by causing your demise. I am curious to know why."

When the cat stopped talking, Pax looked back at the old woman. In her place, however, was a young man with sandy hair and stormy gray eyes. He gave the group an expectant look, but Pax didn't know what to say. What was a cosmic power? Why would one want any of them dead?

There was a moment of silence where he could see the young man getting annoyed. Still, he had expressed annoyance at giving explanations, so Pax didn't want to ask further questions. This... god? Chaos spirit? Whatever it was, this young man made Pax feel uncomfortable. He was strange and otherworldly in a way that made Pax uneasy.

Instead, Gerald asked the most relevant question. "What would make a cosmic power want to put a price on our heads?"

"Yes. Precisely the question I am asking. Which of you is the god-killing monster or fate-changing hero that would get the attention of universe-defining entities?"

All four men looked at each other. They were all wearing their dumbfounded expressions plain on their face. It was clear to each of them and the god standing before them that none of them knew what was going on.

The young man let out a long and exasperated sigh. "I guess this entire venture was pointless then." He waved his hands between him and the group. Pax's vision became blurry. He heard the other three adventurers, but their voices came to him as if from a long tunnel. It wasn't long before he'd completely blacked out.

CHAPTER NINE

Meses

Pax woke on the edge of an oasis. It didn't have the same sand pillars from the one he had stopped at with the caravan, and he relaxed as he realized that meant there was no dragon to attack them again. It was night, and Pax was lying by a fire that was being tended to by a stranger with a snow-white beard, skin the color of a dark oak's bark, and bright blue eyes that seemed to shine unnaturally in the firelight.

Looking away quickly, Pax took quick stock of himself. He still had the cloak and the amulet he had taken from the dragon's hoard, and the pockets were still spilling over with coin. His bow and arrows had returned to him, and he was beginning to think everything he had just experienced had been a dream when he looked over and saw Korivare's new halberd and Gerald's silver harp.

"Well, at least one of you is alive. That's something I suppose," the man sitting by the fire said. His voice was quiet and clear, and it rolled around in Pax's chest like a distant thunder storm.

Pax continued to look around. The man seemed to have no supplies with him: No shelter, food, water, or any possessions of any kind. The man stood and walked over to Pax, taking the amulet into his hands.

"What you have here is very interesting. I have been looking for something like this for a very long time, and I would be very grateful if you allowed me to have it."

Pax couldn't tell if the man was threatening him or not. He felt very uncomfortable by the situation. He wished his friends were awake to help him, but each of them was still asleep. How did all of them get here in the first place?

He looked into the deep blue eyes of the man leaning over him. They seemed to shift slowly to a deep ocean blue to a pale sky blue, never staying one color for long. Something about this man seemed odd. He gave Pax the same otherworldly feeling that the Master of the Dream World did.

It was a long time before Pax realized he hadn't given the man an answer. "What do you plan on doing with it?" he finally asked.

The man smirked and stifled a laugh. "I suppose I shouldn't be surprised. I was hoping you wouldn't know what was around your neck, and that I could take it off your hands for a bargain. I guess my luck really has run out then. Very well, I need that to get home."

"Home? Where do you live?"

The man shook his head. "It's complicated. The point is, I need that to get home, and," the man looked around significantly "it would seem you're in a difficult position as well. My proposal is this, if you help me get home, using that little trinket there, I'll make it worth it to you by getting you somewhere less..." he paused for a moment "wilderness-y."

He held out his hand to Pax. Pax paused for a moment, but ultimately decided to take it and let the man pull him to his feet. "We are agreed then. You help me. I help you. Let's get your friends up so we can get out of here."

Pax and the stranger went around and shook the other three awake. After they woke up, Pax explained what he had agreed to. Korivare nodded along, and when Pax was done, he agreed without objection.

"Where did he come from, do you think?" Gerald asked.

Pax looked back at the man. He was wearing robes the color of the sand around them. He didn't appear to have much beyond what he was wearing. His eyes seemed far away as he watched the northeastern horizon.

"I don't know. Do you think he was the one who pulled us out of the Dream World?" Pax was still not sure what all had happened in that place. Everything felt really unclear now that he was back in the desert. "Dream World" seemed like an apt name, since it felt hazy like waking from a dream. Had it been real?

Gerald shook his head. "It was almost certainly the god of chaos that sent us back to the mortal world. I am surprised that we didn't go back to the tomb or the dragon's lair. I was certain that well we slept against was a portal or an anchor between the two worlds."

Pax was confused by everything Gerald had just said, but he heard Gerald say this strange man wasn't the one that had pulled them from the Dream World. Still, something about him reminded him of the god of chaos.

Pax approached Jiang. The man was standing as far from the stranger as he could without being considered outside of the group as a whole.

"That man is odd. He is…" Jiang struggled for a word.

"I'm still trying to get a read on him too. He still hasn't explained where he lives, and I'm not sure why he's being so cagey about it."

"God. The god. He talked about enemies. We should be careful."

"I hadn't thought about that. Do you think he's going to try and attack us?"

Jiang shrugged. He made a gesture that looked like brushing something away. "Just. Careful."

They rejoined the group as Gerald was interrogating the stranger. "What is your name?"

"My name is my own. But you may call me Meses." He looked at Pax. It was a different look than the one Pax got when he first woke up. He was examining Pax. It made Pax feel uncomfortable. "Do you have a name?"

Pax looked down at the sand and shifted his weight from foot to foot. "Kind of. You can call me Pax."

"But that is not your name?"

Pax shook his head. Meses looked like he was going to say something further, but then simply walked to the edge of the water. He took a vial out of the pocket of his pale brown robes. He filled it with water from the oasis and stoppered it before putting it back into his pocket. Then he gestured toward the horizon.

"Right then, we're burning starlight. Let's head out," he declared. He started walking out into the wilderness. He was already at the first sand dune that blocked the horizon before he looked back at the lingering group. "Am I leading myself? We had a deal, no?"

Pax looked around to his friends. He met Korivare's eyes, who nodded. Gerald shrugged a noncommittal acceptance. Jiang looked at Meses for a long time. Then he nodded once.

Pax was grateful to them. Meses was right. He and Pax had made a deal, and he was going to stick with it. Still, knowing he had his friends to back him up if things went sour made a bit of tension release from his shoulders. He didn't have to carry this worry all on his own.

The four men followed Meses for a few weeks, always being active at night and resting during the day. Traveling to wherever the strange man was taking them took up a smaller piece of their time than Pax would've preferred. The rest of the time he taught them how to forage in the dessert to ensure they had enough to eat. It wasn't a luxurious subsistence.

In fact, a great deal of their diet for those weeks were scorpions and snakes. When they found a thorn-bush, Meses took several branches off, not showing any pain as he handled the sharp barbs. Around the fire that morning, he showed them how to strip the thorns and prepare the branches so that they were edible.

They weren't tasty. To Pax, it seemed like the closest he'd ever get to eating a branch off a tree. It was clear to him that this man had been living like this for a while. It made Pax wonder even more what had happened to him.

Water never seemed to be an issue for them. Anytime one of them emptied their waterskins, Meses would trade his for theirs. His always seemed to be full, and by the time he needed to trade again, the skin he was holding was always full again.

Pax tried to keep an eye on him to see how he was doing this, but he couldn't watch the man all the time, and he never seemed to do anything out of the ordinary. Anytime he was asked about how he was doing this or where he was getting the water, he always had the same response, "I keep my end of the bargain, and you keep yours."

Eventually they saw a building on the horizon. It was a massive step pyramid reaching toward the sun just above it. When they crested a large sand dune, they could see the walls surrounding it and saw several people standing along the road just outside the gates.

"That's a city-state," Gerald said when he took it all in. He turned to Meses. "How long have we been in the Northern Territories?"

Meses gave him a confused look. "We've been in the Northern

Territories since I found you. Was that not where you were originally?"

Pax hadn't remembered where they were exactly when they lost the caravan. Only now did he realize how difficult it would likely be for them to find it again. Meses clapped Pax on the back.

"Chin up, my friend. We have an agreement to complete. I have you within sight of civilization, and now I will take my end of the bargain." He held out his hand for the dragon's amulet.

Pax still wasn't sure what was about to happen, but he had made an agreement with this man, and he wasn't going to go back on it without good reason. He handed Meses the amulet, and the man became visibly younger. Pax wasn't sure if it was a tired tension being released or... something else.

Meses began to chant in a language Pax didn't recognize, but he noticed Jiang made a gesture. Pax couldn't make heads nor tails of it. As he continued chanting, Meses' clothes changed dramatically. Originally he was wearing simple linen that was dyed a light tan color. That was what he had been wearing for the last month; however, before Pax's eyes, his outfit changed until it was the equal of anything worn by the leaders of House Morkae.

Meses was now wearing a silver circlet that held a small sheet of silk against the back of his head and neck. He was wearing a robe of linen dyed a deep, royal blue and was covered in embroidery that looked like clouds and blowing wind. Finally, he had a belt of silk rope that was dyed to looked like flowing silver. In short, he looked like he was steps away from being crowned the monarch of wherever he lived.

He opened the hand that was holding the amulet, which was now glowing a brilliant blue. Rather than falling to the sand, however, it floated up to sit feet above where even Pax could reach. What happened next was hard to describe. The only way Pax could understand it was to say that the air broke.

All of a sudden, the midpoint between the amulet and the ground began to open and expand. As it expanded, a fierce wind forced its way out of the opening that it created. The opening quickly took the shape of a doorway, and continued to expand until it reached the ground on one end and the amulet on the other.

The world beyond the doorway was one of screaming winds and

floating islands that seemed to be the only solid ground anywhere. Meses smiled openly, something Pax had not seen him do up until this point. He approached the doorway and Pax thought he was going to get caught in the sand that was spilling over into the new world and fall to... to what?

Pax didn't have to find out. The sand stopped pouring down the endless open air as Meses approached the doorway, and his clothes shifted again. Near where his legs would be under his robe, a bright white cloud formed. The sort of puffy cloud that formed shapes on a bright sunny day. The rest of the robe became a piece of sky, the embroidery becoming actual clouds.

By the time Meses had crossed the threshold, the only piece of him that was still somewhat recognizable was his face. The face itself was more cloud instead of flesh and blood, but the shape was the same and the eyes carried the same shifting blue color.

Pax noticed Gerald was nudging Korivare's arm and pointing past Meses toward the floating islands. Korivare glared at him and shook his head. Meses turned back toward the group, his cloud form shifting and rolling slowly.

"I do deeply appreciate you for helping me get back here. Our agreement is complete, but I'd like you to have this as a token of my favor." Something small launched through the doorway at Pax. Meses may have thrown it, but it was hard to tell in his current form.

Pax caught it and opened his hands to examine it. It was a ring of twisted silver with three pale blue stones set along its band. When he put it on, Pax was surprised to find that it fit him perfectly.

"If you need anything, just call on me," Meses said. His voice reminded Pax even more of thunder now that his body had become a mass of rolling white clouds.

The doorway closed, and the amulet fell to the sand. Pax walked over and picked it up. The storm it once held inside was gone, and now it was just a simple gem on a gold chain. Still, it seemed very fancy by Pax's measure, and he guessed it'd fetch a fair price.

The four men were left standing alone on a dune overlooking a sprawling city with a towering step pyramid at its center. Pax looked at each of his friends in turn. Each of them nodded their ascent and all four of them took sliding steps down the dune and approached the gates of the city.

CHAPTER TEN

City Charm

"That thing can't come into the city. It will have to sleep outside. Maybe it can find a cave somewhere closer to the mountains." The guard checking people in at the gate refused to speak to Pax directly and kept addressing Jiang. Apparently, he believed the warmage was some foreign noble with a bodyguard, a private minstrel, and a pet.

Pax was looking at the ground and trying to keep himself from shaking. He didn't feel much like talking to the guard. Still, it hurt deep into his heart to be treated like an animal.

"No. We will pass. Pax comes." Jiang was playing into the guards expectations well. With Gerald's improvised support, he was appearing to all as the incredibly privileged, put upon noble.

The guard just shook his head. "We don't need that thing going on a rampage inside the city."

"Maybe you didn't hear him," Gerald said. "His Majesty said that Pax is coming with us into the city. Consider yourself lucky that we aren't asking for an escort directly to the City Lord himself."

He looked around to the other guards keeping the line in order. "Not that we'd really trust a bunch of deputized brutes to offer a proper escort for his Royal Greatness. If you don't want to let us through those gates, perhaps your superior would have a different opinion."

The guard smiled smugly. "You'll probably have to wait awhile to get an audience with him, considering, as the captain of the wall guard, I answer directly to City Lord Emir."

Gerald's face was unreadable, but, from where Pax was looking at the ground, he caught a shift in his stance that said this was an unexpected development. His friends were really sticking up for him and he hated that he couldn't help them. He had faced a dragon, fought a tentacle monster, and talked to a god. What was so intimidating about this guard that it made him practically mute?

He clenched his fists until his knuckles went pale. Before he even realized he was speaking, the words came flooding out of his mouth. "I am a bodyguard for House Morkae! This man is their guest in this land. You will allow me to accompany him into the city or there will be consequences."

There were gasps and excited whispers from the crowd behind them. Some hadn't expected Pax to be able to speak, but Pax heard others whispering about House Morkae employing such a "monster" as a bodyguard for a foreign dignitary.

Pax summoned every ounce of courage he could muster and looked up at the guard who was blocking their way. His face was stunned and pale. Either he too didn't expect Pax to speak, or he had heard the words "House Morkae" and became concerned about his position as Captain of the Wall Guard. As a merchant house with a great deal of wealth and legacy, their name carried weight all across the deserts of Maskohma.

"I... you... I didn't... which is to say I..." the guard stammered to a halt. He paused for a moment, probably trying to decide if Pax was lying. He apparently decided finding out wasn't worth his job because he stepped aside and the four men entered the city.

The streets of the city were bustling, and vendors were calling out to passing customers. There was all manner of interesting things being sold: spices, coffee, weapons, jewelry. Pax also noticed that many of the commuters stared at him longer than would usually be considered polite.

However, most of them went quickly on their way afterward, apparently too busy to be bothered by the fact that there was some kind of monster roaming the streets. They did give him a wide berth, but Pax just pretended that was because they too believed Jiang was a noble that was above things as trite as being in a crowd.

"We should head to a money changer first." Gerald said. "I doubt any of these vendors are going to be able to make change for gold.

Unless we buy their whole shop that is." He looked at one of the coins he'd carried off from the dragon's hoard. "Especially if it's Aruhdaban gold."

Pax wanted to ask what that meant. Jiang and Korivare were already nodding their heads, however, and Pax decided to agree and hold his question for later. They made their way to a building made of carved sandstone that stood out among the plaster and cloth buildings around them. Pax looked around at the stares he was getting from the citizens and decided he didn't want a repeat of what happened at the gate.

He caught Jiang's arm and handed him a handful of gold coins. "I'm going to wait for you guys out here. If you could get these exchanged for me—" Jiang nodded before he finished. He pointed to a nearby square that had a small acacia tree growing at the center of it. Pax nodded his understanding and went to browse the open-air market near the square.

It wasn't long before Pax found a stall selling jewelry. There were a few bracelets, a necklace or two and several dozen rings. None of the gems looked all that interesting, but they were pretty. When the copper-skinned khaldabri running the stall turned around, he jumped at the sight of Pax looming over his shop.

He started to shake and stutter out an apology while wringing his slender six-fingered hands. Pax tried to give him a friendly smile, but by the way the man paled and widened his already big eyes, he guessed it didn't work. Pax closed his lips and his shoulders slumped. Then, he took off the amulet and handed it to the man. "What would you give me for this?"

The man took out an eyepiece Pax had seen some of the Shatka merchants using. He guessed it was for examining gemstones. The man took a minute to look the gem up and down, running the chain through his dexterous fingers. When he was done, he didn't meet Pax's eye.

"To be honest, master," the vendor said. "I don't know if I could give you a fair price for this piece. The gemstone alone is so exquisite I'd want to know the name of the jeweler that cut it." He took a long, deep breath and gave a shaky laugh. "Though I wouldn't want to pry into your business, of course."

"That's OK. I got it off a dragon in the desert. A friend told me lots of dragons have things like these." That didn't seem to calm the merchant. If anything, hearing that Pax took on a dragon seemed to put him more on edge. "It attacked me first. I don't usually go out looking for trouble."

The merchant shook his head quickly. "Of course not, master. The setting isn't terribly special, but if this is pure gold than it's also worth something. In short, I'd like to buy it from you, sir, but I couldn't offer you a fair price and wouldn't dream of trying to swindle someone like you."

Someone like me, Pax thought deflating. "Well," he said, sighing, "if that's the case, maybe we could trade. Some of what you have looks interesting."

The merchant gave a sickly grin and nodded. "Th… this here is one of m—my finest pieces." He pulled out a long flat box and opened it to reveal a silver pendant with a large emerald hanging off it. "I could give you this and ten silver marks to cover the cost of what you're offering."

Pax paused to look at the pendant. The merchant hurried on after a moment, "and this ring to match." The ring he proffered was bright gold with a teardrop shaped emerald in the setting.

The offer seemed rather generous by Pax's standards. He gave the merchant a smile that didn't show his teeth, and it seemed to relax the poor man slightly. Now, rather than looking like he was going to faint, he just looked like he was going to be sick all over his merchandise.

"Sounds like you've got yourself a deal. Thanks for all your help." He took the pendant and, after realizing the chain wouldn't go over his head, he undid the clasp and put it around his neck that way. It was a bit tight, but not uncomfortable. The ring was too small for any of his fingers, so he put it in his pocket. Maybe Jiang or Korivare would like it.

On his way to the tree, Pax found a beggar laying on a mat with a small tin cup in his hand. He looked like a mat of skin pulled taught over a skeleton and he didn't seem to have the energy to speak, so he held up his cup, wordlessly, to passersby. Pax remembered the difficulties he had when he came to the first city he was allowed in after being lost in the wilderness. Was that only two years ago?

Well, he had money now. He had lots of money if the exchange with that merchant was anything to go by, and he wanted to make sure this man got the care he deserved. He approached the man.

When he saw Pax, the man looked like he wanted to run, but couldn't muster the energy or will to get off his mat. Pax took out one of the gold coins he still had in his pocket. After he was sure the man saw it, he placed it in the man's cup. Pax was surprised by the reaction he got out of the man. There were equal parts surprise and terror in his eyes.

"Do you need help?" Pax asked.

The man propped himself up on his arm, it looked to be very difficult for him, shook his head once, then lay back down. Pax didn't believe him, but he didn't know what else he could do. He walked away toward the tree he agreed to meet the others at, all the while trying to think of a way to help the man.

He heard Gerald's delighted laugh before he saw the group sitting by the tree. "Did you see the look on that money changer's face when he walked up to her with handfuls of gold and said 'we need this broken up please'? I thought she was going to faint. Oh, hey Pax. Nice necklace. Where's the amulet?"

"I sold it."

Gerald nodded. "Figured wasn't worth keeping now that the arcane energies are completely drained from it?"

Pax shrugged. "Do you guys know what that building is?" He pointed toward the step pyramid that was looming over the city. They were still a few blocks from the center where the base must be, but its height dominated the landscape."

"That's the Sun temple. Every major city has one. The priestesses there offer religious rites, accept donations and feed the poor when times get tough. I was actually thinking of talking to some of the priestesses there. Since the Master of Dreams made it seem like we were being hunted down by some kind of god, maybe one of them could offer us some insight."

"They help the poor?" Pax got an idea, and he started heading toward the pyramid without another word. The three friends jogged to catch up and asked him what he was doing.

"If they help the poor," Pax explained, "then that means they can help someone I found when you guys were in the money changers' building. He looks like he's going to die any day now and he barely has the energy to move. He needs help."

The other three nodded and their steps became determined. The crowd still parted around Pax, but this time it was to his advantage.

CHAPTER ELEVEN

Those in Need

The pyramid was larger than he'd anticipated and much further away, so it took them a half hour to get to the base of the temple, and Pax's breathing was noticeably more labored when they did.

The temple was a massive stone building with tiered terraces that were filled with lush greenery. Even from the ground below the first level, Pax could smell sweet fruit and blooming flowers. It was surrounded by men with wicked spears and chain shirts that were a stark contrast to the leather cuirasses and banded clubs of the city guard.

There was a woman standing next to a collections box at the foot of the steps. She was wearing bright white linen and wearing a brass disc hanging from a braided cotton cord around her neck. When she saw Pax, she paled for a moment, but she stood firm.

"How did this beast get into the city?" she asked to no one in particular.

Pax swallowed the first words that came to his mouth and simply held up two gold coins. The woman's eyes locked on them hungrily. He put one into the collections box, and held the other one above. "I have a friend that needs help. This one is for after you see to his needs."

She nodded once and turned toward the steps of the pyramid where a group of younger women wearing similar pendants of copper and twine were standing. "Nasira, you and Thana go with these men.

Bring back whoever it is this creature is talking about and see they are tended to."

The two women nodded and hurried off. Pax and Jiang led them to where the beggar was laying on his mat. The beggar looked confused as he saw the women accompanying Pax. They knelt over him and examined his body. He looked like he wanted to protest but couldn't muster up the ability.

"He's extremely malnourished. We'll have to get him to the healers in the temple quickly. Creature—"

"My name is Pax."

The woman shrunk a bit at Pax's hard tone, but continued. "Pax, would you be able to carry this man for us?"

He nodded and took the beggar gently in his arms. As he did so, he saw the merchant from earlier talking animatedly toward one of the guards and gesturing at Pax. Pax had the beggar in his arms, and Jiang had put his tin cup in his hands, the gold coin was still in it, before the guard approached them.

"'Scuse me. Is this your pet?" he asked Jiang.

"No." Jiang moved to follow the priestesses back to the temple, but the guard held out his hand.

"We got word that this thing has been shaking down the locals for extra coin. Would you know anything about it?"

One of the priestesses sighed. "These men are on official temple business. If you would like, you can follow us to the temple and question them until your heart's content there."

The guard went silent and the five of them went back to the temple, practically jogging through the city. As wide a berth as the citizens gave Pax out of fear before, it was nothing compared to the reverence they showed the priestesses as they passed by. Many of them made slight moves as if they would stop the women, but then thought better of it when they saw the busy looks on their faces.

They made it back to the temple and one of the priestesses went to fetch a healer. The other explained that men, and especially monsters, are not allowed in the temple proper. Pax didn't make an issue of it. The beggar was being helped, and that's what mattered to him.

When the healer arrived, and they had taken the beggar away, Pax made good on his promise and dropped the second gold coin into the collections box. He wasn't sure the priestesses deserved it after their comments, but he wanted to keep his promise. The priestess with the brass pendant nodded her thanks, and the guard approached him again.

"Right, now that you've gotten me ran all through the city, I have some questions for you."

As Pax came down form the adrenaline of getting the beggar to safety, his anxieties started to creep back to the forefront. He took a breath and looked the guard in the eye while he still had the courage to do so. "What?"

"You threatened a merchant on my block. We can't have scum like you trying to intimidate people. Not 'round 'ere."

"I… I didn't… he…" Pax stammered. His anxiety was coming back and he knew he was about to be completely tongue tied. He looked around at his friends, and Gerald took the hint.

"Look," Gerald began. The guard gave him a withering glare, and he paused for the space of a single breath. Then, he looked at Pax whose eyes had gone to his feet.

"Pax said he traded for these pieces from that shill fair and square. I saw the amulet he got in return and its worth at least twice as much as this tin-and-glass garbage. If he has a problem with the trade, he can talk to my friend himself. Otherwise, you can piss off and go kick a beggar for standing too long or however you occupy yourself when you can't find something useful to do."

The guard's face went hard. He nodded to the men standing at attention around the temple complex and two of them approached Pax and his friends.

"I'll make this easy for you," the city guard said. "Come with me quietly, or we'll skewer you right here on the temple grounds." The temple guards looked at each other as if they would protest, but said nothing.

Pax put his hands up, and Gerald whispered in his ear, "we'll get you out one way or another. Don't worry." Pax nodded and the guards put him in manacles and escorted him away.

The city guard brought Pax through the city. Pax didn't know how many jails tended to be set up in a city like this, but this guard took a while to find one to put Pax in. After a while it occurred to Pax that the guard may be taking him to the furthest jail as an excuse to parade him through the city.

They finally made it to a building that was built up against the wall that surrounded the city. The sun was well past its zenith and was sinking behind the tall pyramid temple at the center of the city. The sky was far from the pink and oranges of a desert sunset, but Pax could tell the day was waning as he was led into the jail.

Pax had to duck to fit through the door and the gate of his cell. The cell itself was a little cramped, and it reminded him of the smaller chambers of the cave he lived in as a child. All told, it didn't seem as bad as he'd feared. He lay on the bare stone and looked up at the ceiling.

CHAPTER TWELVE

A New Perspective

Pax was snoozing in his cell hours later when he heard the door being flung open. "Who the hell do you think you are?" The voice was hard and fierce. When Pax looked up, he saw a woman wearing the same white robes and disc-pendant of the priestesses from the temple. Hers was a polished bronze and hanging from a strip of velvet.

"Ma'am? Priestess… miss… umm," the guard that was watching the jail cells stammered. Pax had guessed he was a low-level recruit, and that was further reinforced by the way he prostrated himself before the priestess.

"You will tell me immediately who had the audacity to arrest anyone on the temple grounds. Do you want the High Priestess to hear about how you guards aren't respecting the temple's authority?"

"No! Never your Holiness. I'm sorry. This thing was accused of intimidating—" he was cut off by a slap across his face.

"I don't care if he cut someone's heart out in front of the City Lord. He was on temple grounds. He was to be dealt with by us and our guards. Now let him out. Maybe the shame of having to release such a monster will teach you some respect." There was that word again.

"But… ma'am… what if—" he flinched as the woman brought her hand up again. The guard nodded and grabbed the keys from the desk. When the guard opened the gate to Pax's cell, Pax was still trying to decide if he was more hurt by being called a monster or more confused about why he was being let go.

He decided he had time to decide later. He walked out of the building after the priestess, but she didn't acknowledge him. She merely walked back toward the temple muttering something about stupid men.

Pax looked up at the sky. It was painted with the reds and oranges of late sunset. He couldn't quite remember where he was, so he started walking perpendicular to the wall. He hoped that going toward the temple would lead him to more familiar territory.

It was well into the late evening when Pax found his friends. Korivare and Jiang were both out of their armor and in simple traveling clothes, and Pax found them talking to the thinning crowd of patrons.

When he shouted for them, the relief of seeing him was plain on Korivare's face, and Jiang made a gesture Pax guessed was his version of the same. They came up to him, and they both grasped his forearm and threw their other arm over his broad back. The feeling of having friends who were excited to see him was foreign to him. It felt like a warm broth sitting in the pit of his stomach.

They found Gerald and they each took part in explaining what they'd done after his arrest. Korivare knew that the temple grounds were sacrosanct, and that the city guard had no authority over anyone standing on temple property. He'd spent the day convincing the priestesses that what had happened was an affront to their authority.

Gerald, for his part, had been sowing rumors about how the guard had tried to command the temple guard to attack Pax right in front of the Sun temple. That affront to common decency coupled with Korivare's nudging had created enough of an outcry that one of the assistants to the High Priest herself had gone to confront the guards that had arrested Pax.

"So, that's who that woman was," Pax said out loud.

"The priestesses here are very protective of their authority," Korivare pointed out. "It still took longer than I would've liked to find you. Did they really take you all the way to the city wall to put you in jail."

Pax nodded.

"That must've been one of the furthest jails from the temple. I wonder if they were trying to hide their insubordination."

"I had assumed he wanted to parade me through the city for his own glory," Pax said.

They made their way down the street toward the market square. Gerald continued explaining what else he'd been doing with his time. In addition to the guards overstep, Gerald had been talking about Pax's donation to the temple and how he'd helped the priestesses save a beggar's life.

This had convinced most people in the city that, far from the monster that the merchant and guard claimed Pax was, he had to be some sort of pious servant sent from the wilderness to the city. The gold had obviously been a gift from the Queen of the Sun herself, and Pax simply deserved better treatment than that.

"All of that in half a day?" Pax asked.

"I work quickly when I'm properly motivated," Gerald explained with a significant look down at his silver harp. "And have the proper tools."

Pax grinned, and he noticed the people around him were giving him significantly different looks than before. Now, they were looking at him like he was... a hero. This kept him grinning like a fool while he followed his friends to an inn whose innkeeper was just putting out a lantern as the moon was coming out.

"Ah. My fine patrons have made it home safe for the night," he declared.

He walked right up to Pax and gave a deep bow. "And the Holy One is here as well. I was surprised when I heard your story. The Lady of the Day does not often choose men for her callings, let alone one such as yourself. It is good all the same. I am happy to serve."

The innkeeper led the group inside and up into an open room with a few straw-stuffed mattresses on the floor. "I do not get many traveler's here. Most of my business comes from the tavern downstairs. I hope this is to your liking Holy One."

"This is perfect. I tend not to sleep well on mattresses though. I'm always worried I'll tear or crush it. Is it OK if I sleep on the floor?"

"Oh yes, whatever is to your liking." The man bowed again and backed out of the room. "If you need anything, do not hesitate. I will be downstairs with my wife and daughter. We are all happy to have you here."

"He seemed nice," Pax said when he was gone.

Gerald gave a single laugh. "He ought to be. He charged us three silver for the room. I was going to tell him to bite it, but..."

"But Gerald saw that the tavern had his favorite whiskey downstairs, so we just had to stay," Korivare interrupted.

"It's from the other side of the mountains. It's made from melted snow and nectar from the Silatri flower. You'll understand when you taste it tomorrow morning."

"In the morning?" Korivare asked disgusted.

"It's a breakfast whiskey. The dwarves drink it with their mushrooms and sausages. According to them, if you have a tumble of that whiskey at the beginning of the day, you'll have the luckiest day you've ever experienced."

"And you believe this?"

Gerald shrugged. "Couldn't hurt. It's just one tumble. At worst, I'm out a copper or two and had a nice drink."

Korivare just shook his head and rolled his eyes. He took off his tunic and threw it over his chain shirt. Jiang stripped down to his underwear and started doing his slow, methodical dance. Pax realized as he watched it that it was more like a mock fight. Jiang moved through the motions of a punch like he was suspended in molasses. Then he balanced on one foot and kicked out with the same slow deliberateness. Pax watched his friend move through the motions and let the slow motions lull him to sleep.

CHAPTER THIRTEEN

New Clothes

Pax woke up to a call from the innkeeper for breakfast. He looked out the open-air window and saw the first rays of dawn peaking above the horizon. He thought long and hard about going back to bed, but Korivare shook him and started getting dressed.

Pax sighed and stood up. His cloak fell to the floor and he picked it up, draping it around his shoulders. A thought occurred to him then, and when he went down to join the innkeeper, his wife, and their teenage daughter for breakfast, he asked about the tailors in town.

"Ah," the innkeeper said, touching the bridge of his nose. "I had wondered if you would ask about that. Your..." he paused for a moment, "look is good for making you seem like a wild man. However, if you have words for us from the Sun Queen, I would expect you would want to look presentable when you stand next to the priestesses."

"Oh, I don't—"

"That's it exactly kind sir," Gerald interrupted. "Our great green friend here wants to look his best when we present ourselves to the priestesses. Alas, he had to give up his worldly possessions when the Sun Queen told him to follow her rays into the wilderness."

The innkeeper nodded as if this was what he expected. "I have a friend a block or two from here who may be able to help. When we are done eating, I will show you to her."

Pax nodded, and most of the rest of the meal was filled with Gerald's stories. He told one about a beggar who found the crown of a king and used it to rule better than the king who lost it. By the time he was finished, the innkeeper's daughter was wide-eyed with wonder, and the wife was smiling warmly at the storyteller. When his belly was full, Gerald requested a tumble of the whiskey, and the innkeeper gave only the slightest raised eyebrow at the request.

After the rest of them finished eating, the daughter took the dishes into the back, and Pax followed the innkeeper and his wife down the street to the tailor's shop. They made introductions. The tailor's name was Sadia.

Afterward, the couple said they had to go back and tend to chores before anyone stopped by. That left Pax alone with Sadia. Her brown eyes were quick and discerning, and her shiny black hair was pulled back in a tight braid. She wore a tight linen dress with a slit cut into it for easier mobility. Her sepia skin was smooth, and her hands were firm but gentle as she pressed Pax into an upright stance.

Her hands turned to quick and diligent when she took Pax's measurements, and it was hard for him to not be nervous when she wrapped her arms around his waist. She measured him twice and put him in a simple cotton tunic and matching trousers. The fit was a little tight, and she scowled at the clothing. She looked him up and down and then stripped him back down without a word. She gestured to a cushion near the far end of the workshop, and Pax sat down as she began to shear and sow.

As quick as her hands were in measuring and dressing him, they were like lightning with a needle and thread. Pax sat silently for roughly an hour before she rose triumphant. He stood with her and she dressed him again.

The feel of the fabric against his skin was unlike anything he could remember. His cloak was great, but having such a soft feeling all over his body was incredible. The clothes hugged him and accentuated curves and lines of his body he didn't realize he had.

"Thank you. These are perfect. I've never had clothes like this before."

"You are too kind Holy One. Surely there are many quality tailors where you are from. I am humbled by your compliments."

Pax realized she had misunderstood what he meant, but she seemed to appreciate it either way. He didn't see a need to correct her. "How much do I owe you for such fine work?"

"The materials and the fitting come out to about seven silver marks."

Pax pulled out another of his gold coins. Based on what Gerald said about the exchanges between the different coins, Pax was sure this was about twice what she had asked for. The woman raised an eyebrow. "Do you think you could make me a second set?"

She looked at him. "You wouldn't need to pay for another fitting."

"Two sets then? And you can keep the rest as a gift. It's been a while since I've had money like this, and I'd rather it goes to people worthy of it."

"Two more sets it is then. I'll have to get more cloth. Do you have anything specific in mind? A robe, cape, shoes?"

Pax shook his head. He put the coin in the tailor's hand and told her he'd be back by the end of the day for the other two sets. She agreed, and he left.

He found Jiang and Gerald haggling with a merchant over a scroll case and asked Jiang about it.

"Map. To find the caravan."

Pax looked suddenly excited and the merchant caught the look. "Ah! You want? This tiny man is trying to crack me, but I'll sell it to you for five marks," the merchant's voice was gruff.

"Don't bother Pax. A map like this is worth no more than three, or I'm the Hero of Nighthall."

"It's worth five! My wife drew it herself after a long caravan expedition. She surveyed the land herself while fighting off a mad raving beast."

"If your wife can fight off a dog while doing proper survey work, she'd be working for one of the Merchant Houses, not shilling from a twig stand in some nowhere city. Three marks or we walk."

The merchant looked for a long moment like he was going to punch Gerald in his nose. Then he threw the case at Gerald instead, and Gerald paid him. When they walked away, Pax was very confused.

"What was that all about?"

Gerald shrugged. "Some merchants just like being aggressive. They think it's manly to yell and bully their customers into paying outrageous prices for things. Probably why that merchant yesterday thought you were trying to swindle him. You're big, and he took everything you said as a threat."

"That's ridiculous. You shouldn't treat people that way. Especially not if they're trying to buy things from you. Anyone with an ounce of self-respect would just leave."

Gerald laughed. "Maybe some. Others would just yell back." He gave Pax a knowing wink. "Let's have a look to see if this map was worth a bent copper." He opened the case and unrolled the map.

It was more detailed than the ones he had seen the Caravan Master using, but that's all Pax could say about it. He didn't know much cartography, so he'd be hard pressed to tell the difference between a good map and a bad one.

"Nine hells," Gerald whispered. "Maybe this map was worth five marks. Probably more."

"Why wasn't that man insistent then?" Pax asked as Gerald rolled up the map.

"Probably because he doesn't know anything about maps."

Pax looked confused.

"Men here aren't craftsmen or scholars. You haven't noticed? Any man who is running a merchant shop is either running the selling end of things for his wife; who is doing the actual crafting, scholarship, and the like; or he's basically a pawn broker. Men don't create things here. Women are the educated and skilled labor in these parts."

"What about the innkeeper we're staying with? He's a man."

Gerald nodded. "Inn-keeping is seen as a domestic job. Most domestic duties are things both genders are expected to do, so it's one of the few areas where you'll find a mix of both. In fact, I'd bet gold that most inns in this city are run by couples like ours."

Pax thought about that until they made it back to the inn. There, they grabbed a table with Korivare who had been visiting with the priestesses and asking after the beggar. He was doing well, but the healers said he would take at least another week or two to recover. Pax nodded, glad that he was being taken care of.

"So, let's see this map you found," Korivare said. Gerald unrolled it, and Korivare whistled appreciatively. "Well, that certainly is helpful."

He pointed to a spot on the map. "This is the city we are in now." He pointed to another spot closer to the middle. "This is the oasis where we fought the dragon. Based on the scale down here," he gestured toward the bottom of the map, "it's about a hundred miles away."

Pax's face went stricken with worry.

"The caravan," Korivare continued, "was on its way here." He pointed to a place near the coast labeled Cerna. "That was about a month ago at this point, so I'd say it's safe to assume they made it.

"If they miss us, they'll still be there. If not, we'll ask around until we find out where they went. Either way, we'd ought to get moving. It's going to take us a week to get that far. More if the roads are bad."

Pax nodded. He was worried what the Caravan Master would say when they finally caught up with him. Would he tell House Morkae that Pax had abandoned his duty? Would they take away his bow? Realization flashed on his face and he stood.

"What's wrong?" Gerald asked.

"My bow. The guard took it when he put me in jail and I—"

Gerald waved him off. "I got that covered. Your bow and arrows were the first thing I grabbed when you went off clothes shopping. They're upstairs safe and sound."

"How?" Pax asked.

Gerald strummed his harp. "Turns out the guard watching the jail got a bit sleepy. So, I had to help myself to the chest where all the confiscated goods are kept. I also got a bottle of something tasty and this neat ring." He held up the ring Pax had traded for.

"That's the one the jeweler gave me. Does it fit you?"

"Not really. I was going to pawn it, but if you want it back..."

"Nah. It doesn't fit me either. It just looked nice."

Gerald threw it up and caught it in his other hand. "We'll trade it for supplies then. We'll be needing plenty of those if we're headed toward the coast. Not many oases between here and there."

CHAPTER FOURTEEN

Leaving for New Adventures

They ordered lunch from the innkeeper, and after they ate, Gerald and an indignant Korivare went about gathering supplies. The group agreed that Pax and Jiang should find a caravan or traveling group headed in the direction of Cerna. Pax agreed, and he followed Jiang out into the street.

After spending most of the afternoon searching and asking people in the market square, Pax and Jiang met a group of Wanderers performing an impromptu play near the city wall to a crowd of gathered onlookers. When they finished, Jiang approached the group and gave them a gesture of greeting.

"Greetings strangers," A young man with the shadow of a beard on his chin said. His tawny skin and homespun clothing marked him as a stranger to the city and most of the other places Pax had seen since he'd been in the desert.

"Hello," Pax said. His breath caught at the sight of the woman moving through a fluid dance with a grace and expertise that Pax had never seen before. His mouth went dry when he caught her eye.

"Did you enjoy the performance?" the young man said, pulling Pax's attention back to him.

"Yes. It was very funny," Pax said dumbly. He was still trying to get his thoughts in order when Jiang stepped in on the conversation.

"You are traveling? To Cerna?"

"I don't see any reason we can't head that way. What say you?" The young man said turning to an older man standing near him.

The older man grunted indifferently, and that seemed to be agreement enough for the younger man. "Sounds like we have a new destination. Are you two trying to catch a ship back to Techarae?"

Jiang shook his head. "Finding a caravan. We lost them."

The young man nodded. "I see. And you want a group to travel with. Safety in numbers and all that?"

Jiang nodded once. The two shook hands and that seemed to be all the exchange the issue required. Pax followed Jiang back toward the inn to meet Korivare and Gerald.

They found Gerald and Korivare outside the door of the inn with four bags nearly bursting with the sort of dried fruits and salted meats that would keep for extended periods of time on the road. Gerald waved them over and asked about how the search for a traveling group went.

"We found a band of Wanderers. They said they'd be willing to modify their travel plans to come with us to Cerna," Pax said.

Gerald's face lit up with excitement. "Real Wanderers? How could you tell their troupe was authentic?"

"Are there fake bands of Wanderers in the world?"

Gerald shook his head. "The word band implies they are all musicians. A traveling group of Wanderers are, more generally, called a troupe.

"To answer your main question, though, there are traveling performers that aren't real Wanderers. I was trained to spot a fake by a group I traveled with a few years back.

"If these people are genuine though, we are all in for a real treat. Wanderers always know the best stories, and they always tell the best jokes. I can't wait to meet them."

"Oh. I'm glad I didn't call them a band to their face," Pax said.

"They weren't likely to get offended," Gerald said. "They are fairly accommodating because they're used to being strangers wherever they go. That's why a lot of them travel in groups. How many did you say there were?"

"We talked to two of them, but there was at least twenty of them participating in the performing."

Gerald raised his eyebrows. "That's a pretty big group for a troupe to be. I wonder if they have the patronage of one of the Merchant houses. That would certainly attract more members to them."

The four men walked back to the inn and explained that they would be leaving. They took their possessions out of the upstairs room. The innkeeper made a comment about the "Holy One" having other cities to visit, and they made their good-byes.

They were already on their way to meet up with the troupe, the sun sinking behind the city wall, when Pax remembered something. "My clothes!" he said, and, without another word, he hurried to the tailor's shop.

"You are back. Good. I worried you had forgotten." She pulled out a richly dyed purple linen tunic and trousers that where a royal blue. The second was a silk robe and Pax looked up at her confused. Silk was a luxurious fabric; the kind only high-born nobles wore.

The woman looked embarrassed. "I had a commission from a wealthy caravaner some time ago. He gave me a good deal on silk in trade. I thought you might like it."

Suddenly Pax wondered if she really needed to measure him twice. Based on the shy look she was giving him, he thought maybe it was just an excuse to get close to him.

"I... have to leave the city. I'm on important business. If, however, I ever come back around this part of the world, I'd like to stop in and visit. Is that OK?"

She looked excited and nodded vigorously. Pax smiled. She was sweet when she wasn't all business. He put the clothes in a backpack Gerald had bought him, took Sadia's hand and kissed the back of it. She smiled, and he left with a new confidence in his stride.

#

"Well, well, well. Someone is cutting quite the confident figure. Did you get your new clothes?" Gerald asked when Pax made it back to the group. He was sitting with some of the Wanderers and swapping stories when Pax strolled up, the spring still in his step.

"You bet. And I have something I can wear when I present myself at House Morkae."

The Wanderer who sat next to Gerald spat on the ground. "Damn bastard Merchant Houses think they own the sky. Don't know why anyone would want to associate themselves with those high-born cretins."

Pax's surprise was plain on his face. Most of the people he knew thought highly of the eight Merchant Houses. He supposed there were bound to be people somewhere that didn't like them, but he had no idea what this particular Wanderer would have against them. Pax doubted this man had ever met anyone from House Morkae.

"Don't look at me like that. There's no reason everyone needs to fall over themselves for those houses in the first place. A man's blood runs as red no matter where he comes from."

Pax nodded slowly, not sure what point the man was trying to make. He looked at the man's hard expression, and thought better of making an issue out of it. "Are we leaving soon? It's getting dark out and I don't want to have to run into any scorpions if I can avoid it."

The Wanderers nodded. Jiang looked at the sky. "The sun sets in four hours."

Pax considered that. "We can get a fair distance in four hours, right?"

"Why so eager?" one of the women asked him. She was the one that made Pax feel very nervous when we first spoke to the group. She was sitting on one of the troupe's wagons with her bare feet and calves dangling in the air.

"We need to meet up with a caravan as soon as possible. A particular one. I don't want to miss them."

The woman nodded, and they started packing. Gerald asked Pax to make a round of introductions, and Pax realized he'd forgotten to ask the Wanderers for their names. When he told Gerald, he just laughed.

"We were wonderin' when you'd get around to that," the younger man said. "The name's Jeremy. The lovely lady with which you were just speakin' is Rose. The hard-faced man is Graham and—"

"For godsake Jeremy, if you try to introduce us all right now it'll take the four hours we have left. Let's just do the rest later."

Jeremy went quiet at Graham's rebuke. His eyes went to the ground, and Pax wondered if there was some tension between them. The group finished packing and they made their way through the gates of the city out into the open wilderness. Now, there was nothing but the roads and their map to guide them.

CHAPTER FIFTEEN

Wandering the Desert

It didn't take long for Gerald to become fast friends with most of the troupe. Graham was particularly stand-offish, but the rest of them appreciated his knack for storytelling. The troupe as a whole had heard a version of all Gerald's stories, but they were enthusiastic about hearing his version of the tale. They clapped delightedly when he told them.

"Don't take it to heart," Jeremy said after Gerald failed to find a story he didn't know the first week they traveled together. "It is a rare story that this troupe doesn't know. Still, a new version of an old tale is often just as good as a new tale."

Gerald considered that as they traveled over the sand dunes. When Pax next heard his voice, he was asking Jeremy about his personal favorite story to tell to a crowd.

The young man thought for a long moment. When he did answer, Gerald seemed surprised. "The Copper Wishing Well. It's a good story to tell to an unfamiliar crowd."

"The Copper Well? What makes you say that?" Gerald asked.

Pax didn't recognize the name, but, then again, he didn't know many stories. He wanted to ask Gerald what the story was about, but he didn't want to interrupt the conversation.

Jeremy shrugged casually. "The Copper Wishing Well is all about a community coming together. A whole town spends all this time wishing in the well, and at the end they realize their neighbors had the key to their happiness the whole time. It's not likely to tear open old wounds, but it does make people think fondly of the other people in their community."

Gerald nodded. "I never thought of it in that way. The way I always heard the story told, the focus was on the old crone and her odd spells."

"Why would you focus on that? Sure it's the catalyst for the conclusion, but she's hardly a main player in the story," Jeremy said.

Gerald shrugged. "I guess we have heard different versions. I wouldn't mind hearing yours though. Maybe we could compare notes. I wouldn't mind having a couple of versions to tailor to different audiences."

Jeremy clapped the small gnome on the back and let out a loud laugh. Rose and Graham looked back at the sudden outburst. Rose smiled at the two story-tellers getting along, but Graham just rolled his eyes and went back to telling Jiang one of his risqué jokes.

Jiang and Graham had become well acquainted when Graham discovered Jiang was a bit of a dirty joke connoisseur. He'd been spending most of their week traveling together telling Jiang his best jokes and receiving ratings from the placid warmage.

After this latest round of jokes, Graham was scratching his head and looking confused. "I gotta say," Graham declared. "I can't make head nor tail of your sense of humor kid. I still don't know what kind of jokes punch your gut."

Jiang made a gesture, and Pax guessed it was either one of resignation or nonchalance. "These jokes are good. Ones in my language are better."

Graham nodded and tapped his nose knowingly. "I understand now," he said. "A joke is difficult to translate between languages. The humor doesn't always move over right. That's why we're having so much trouble with this."

Pax wasn't sure why Graham was using "we" when it seemed to him that Jiang was mostly indulging the old Wanderer. From his perspective, Jiang didn't seem terribly interested in the part of the exercise where Graham would try and guess his taste in humor. Still, the two seemed to get along well enough through most of the trip.

Korivare, for his part, was suffering through another story of sexual conquest by a member of the troupe named Trick. The man seemed entertained by the paladins distaste for such stories, and Korivare listened to what he was saying without paying him much attention. Instead, he'd watch the horizon for threats to the troupe and respond at semi-regular intervals with a noncommittal grunt or "is that so?"

Then there was Rose, the woman who made Pax feel unsettled every time she caught him staring at her. She would simply giggle and give a girlish wave, but it always made Pax's mouth go dry.

When they stopped during the middle of the day or after a full day's of travel, she would pull from their trail rations and make an exquisite meal for the troupe and their temporary companions. She would always sit near Pax, who would find a spot away enough from the fire to feel comfortable, but near enough to be a part of the conversations and stories.

At the moment, she was practicing a few of her dance steps with a few of the other dancers in the troupe. Their lithe and dexterous movements allowed them to keep up with the pace of the rest of the troupe as they moved along the dunes. Watching Rose move entranced Pax and he realized too late that he had been staring.

Rose spotted him looking at her and wiggled her fingers in his direction. Deciding there was nothing else that could justify what he was doing, Pax walked up to the dancers and asked them if they could show him what they were doing.

"We're practicing our routines," Rose said. "Would you like to join us? I can show you how to do it."

Pax started shaking with nervous energy. Rose giggled, and she pulled him closer to herself. She gestured to her feet as she started making a slower version of the steps she'd been moving through.

Pax tried his best to follow the movement. He was still shaking with nervous energy, and he misstepped a number of times. He was starting to feel bad about it when Rose nudged him. She smiled up at him. "You're doing great. I know how hard it can be the first time you try it. We can keep practicing with you if you want," she told him.

Pax smiled back at her. He wanted to thank her, but he couldn't get his mind to form the right words. Instead, he nodded and spent the rest of the day practicing the moves that Rose was showing him.

Another week went by like this: with Gerald learning as much as he could from Jeremy about storytelling, Rose teaching Pax about her dancing, Graham and Jiang exploring the finer points of translating humor between languages, and Korivare suffering Trick's endless stories. Pax had a lot of fun learning from Rose, and he noticed it was easier to keep his nerves in check when there was something to do with the energy. After that week, however, disaster struck, and it struck with spears.

CHAPTER SIXTEEN

Captured

Everyone was lounging around a campfire, having eaten their fill of Rose's cooking. Jeremy and Gerald were taking turns telling a story about a giant that lived under the sea, when a chittering sound came over the dunes around them. A spear dug into the sand next to the group. Everyone looked around for a moment. The shadows beyond their fire covered the spear's origin, but everyone knew what was happening: bandits.

Pax jumped up and ran to grab his bow. It was unstrung near his backpack, and he had to dive out of the way of another spear before he got to it. As he strung the bow, Jiang and Gerald began to chant and balls of light appeared all around the dunes. Their light didn't reveal anything, however, and Pax began to wonder if the attack was over.

It wasn't. Another volley of spears came over the dunes and Jeremy let out a yelp of pain. Pax took an arrow from the quiver he got from the dragon and drew back. He tried to aim where the arrow would arc over the dune, and then he let loose and prayed. The arrow lit in mid air and by the time it went over the dune, it was nothing but a tongue of flame.

An explosion behind the dune sent sand flying everywhere, and the ground shook. Pax had to blink the sand out of his eyes, but when he did, he saw the dune was gone and what had been hiding behind it was revealed.

Pax remembered knocking over an anthill when he was younger. The ants had crawled all over him in a chaotic swarm. He got a very close look at many of them and still remembered the feeling of their many tiny legs on his body.

He shivered when he saw a similar group of creatures stream out from the collapsed dune. They looked like ants, but they were five feet tall and the upper halves of their bodies were upright like a person's. Some of them still had spears in their upper claws and the others were drawing fierce-looking curved broadswords.

They crawled toward the group of travelers on two sets of legs while brandishing their weapons with one. When they got close to someone, they threatened them into submission, and used their middle legs to tie them up. When one threatened Pax, he punched it in its mandibles and sent it sprawling to the ground. Half a dozen more came scrambling to their ally's defense, and Pax picked up the creature's fallen spear.

He jabbed and slashed as best he could, keeping the creatures back. Out of the corner of his eye, he saw Korivare making a similar effort. One-by-one the other ant creatures tied up members of the troupe. When they finished, each of them came toward Pax and Korivare. A bolt of lightning bounced through several of the creatures as Jiang moved to stand next to Pax, but for each one that fell to the sand, two took its place.

There were too many to fight off, and still more were coming as others gave up the fight. Pax was knocked to the sand from behind, and felt a swarm of claws and legs hold him down as he was tied with several different ropes. By the grunts and annoyed clicking, Pax guessed Jiang was having similar troubles putting up a fight. The butt of a spear hit the back of Pax's head and he passed out.

Pax woke up to him being hauled to his feet. He was used to recovering quickly from wounds, so he wasn't surprised that he'd only been knocked out a few moments before. The others had stopped fighting and were being rounded up with severe efficiency.

The ant creatures collected their prisoners and forcing them to their feet. They spliced the ropes that held everyone together to make a long chain and they led their new captors away from their camp, and away from all their weapons and equipment. Pax had lost his bow again.

The prisoners were forcibly marched through the desert for the rest of the night and well into the next day. Many of the Wanderers were so weakened by the ordeal that the ant-creatures had to whip them bloody to get them to stand up and keep moving. It reminded Pax of how he was treated by the ringmaster that led the circus he escaped.

When they finally came upon their destination, Pax thought it was just another sand dune. Getting closer, however, he realized it was a mass of piled and congealed sand that formed a structure honeycombed with openings. The group of prisoners were forced into one of the ground-level tunnels and the ropes on their midsections were released. Their hands were bound to small posts on the wall made of the same congealed sand as the wall.

Pax was tied next to Jiang and across from Gerald, who gave him a weak grin. "What's going on?" Pax asked. "Do you know what those things are?"

"Formains. They're a race of insect-like creatures with a hive mind. I thought they were just a myth, but I guess that's what I get for doubting a story," Gerald said.

"Don't be stupid." The voice was Jeremy's and it came from deeper in the tunnel. "Formorians are from the Fae-Realm. Do those things look like fae to you?"

"Not Formorians. Formains. Most of them look like ants, though I've heard of some that look like beetles too. I'm guessing this group got tired of doing their own work and decided to pick up a few traveler's when they can to act as slaves."

"Wait. Gerald?" the voice was new but familiar. It sounded like the voice of the Caravan Master's son.

"Farhan? Is that you? Where is your father?"

"I don't know, sir. Those devil-creatures took him and many of the others when we got here. What did you call them? Formains?"

"Yeah. How many of you do they have?"

"The whole caravan was attacked just before we got to Cerna. We thought you died during that dragon attack. Is anyone else with you?"

"I'm here Farhan," Pax said. "I'm sorry I wasn't there to protect you guys like I promised."

"Sorry? You were taken by a dragon. That is not your fault. Besides, if you are here now, that means you probably would've been captured if you were with us anyway."

"The boy has a point," Gerald said.

That did not make Pax feel better. He was trying to think of a way out of this mess when he heard Jiang from beside him. "The ring. Call Meses for help."

"I forgot about that," Gerald said. "Pax, do you still have it?"

Pax nodded and shifted his hands around in his restraints and touched the ring on his finger. He thought of Meses and how he needed help.

Suddenly, a flash of light and a sound like rolling thunder filled the tunnel. Then Meses was standing, or rather floating, in front of Pax. He wore a silk vest and his circlet. His bottom half was still a bright white cloud. He smiled down at Pax. "Miss me?" he said.

"I need your help. We found the caravan we were looking for but we've all been taken captive by things called formains. Can you fight them off and get us out of here?"

"Hm. I'm not much of a fighter. Don't you guys have your weapons?"

Pax shook his head. "We left them at camp when we were captured."

"I'll get them for you." Before Pax could protest, Meses had disappeared with a *pop*. Moments later, he appeared again holding an armload of weapons: Pax's bow and quiver of arrows, Korivare's halberd, Jiang's sword. He set them down at Pax's feet. "There now you can..." He trailed off looking at Pax's hands. "I guess you'll need me to free you as well." He untied Pax's hands. When he went to untie Gerald, Gerald stopped him.

"If we all get released, they'll just capture us again. I'm sure the group that attacked us is just their raiding party. There's probably hundreds more patrolling these tunnels."

"What do we do?" Pax asked.

"We stay here. You need to find the queen that's controlling the hive mind. If you kill her, then everyone will be disconnected from each other. Chaos will ensue, and we can use the confusion to escape."

"Are you sure?"

"No. But, it's the only plan I've got, so we have to try. See if you can find the rest of the caravan as well."

Pax thought about protesting. Anyone else would be better suited to this task. He looked at Gerald and saw he was right. This was something Pax had to do. He had to be a hero.

CHAPTER SEVENTEEN

Slavers

Pax had gotten two dozen steps down the tunnel when he spotted a pair of formains coming his way. He looked around. He needed to hide, but there was nothing but bare walls around him.

He pulled up his hood and pressed his body against the wall. The formains passed him, and he was certain he would be spotted when their candlelight illuminated him. When they didn't, he stood confused for a moment.

He looked down. His cloak had turned from its normal pale, sandy brown, to a dark black. He looked at his hands and they were covered in a shadow that was unnaturally deep. Pax put his hood down and the shadows became natural again. He touched the fabric of the cloak, which had also turned back to its original color.

This wasn't the first time Pax had pulled his hood up, and nothing like this had ever happened before. Now that he thought about it, though, he couldn't remember a time when his hood was pulled up in shadows. Even at night he kept it down so it wouldn't block the beautiful starlight.

He breathed a sigh of relief. If this cloak could make shadows around him deeper to help him hide, this may not be an impossible task. It was merely a hideously difficult one. He continued down the tunnel.

Pax ran into his next problem when he hit the intersection of several tunnels. It was a large chamber that dropped down several feet from where he stood and ended in a domed roof about a story above him.

The curving wall that surrounded it was honeycombed with

openings to other tunnels. Each one was marked with a small glowing candle that covered the whole chamber in a dim, shadowy, light. Pax could see bustling forms moving from one tunnel to another below him, but none of them came close enough for him to make out anything but vague shapes.

After a moment of observation, where Pax stayed back from the ledge as much as he could from both a fear of falling and of being seen, he noticed something interesting. The shapes moving through the ground-level tunnels here human shaped.

They definitely had two legs and a normal human silhouette. He reasoned that must be where the slaves were being kept. It made sense since, based on the buzzing going on around him, it was normal for formains to fly. If your slaves can't, make them do the ground work.

If Pax could get down there, he may be able to find out where the rest of Farhan's father's caravan were taken. It was at least a twenty-foot drop, and simply jumping and letting his bones heal would leave him vulnerable to the formains while alerting some, or all, of them to his presence. He thought for a long moment. Then a plan started to form in his head. Gerald had said the formains had a hive mind.

Pax picked up his bow and drew an arrow out of his quiver. He nocked the arrow and aimed for a tunnel one level above where he stood. This was an insane idea, and would probably get him killed but...

He loosed the arrow and it sailed out of sight. A moment later, a loud boom shook the chamber. The formains that had been buzzing through the various tunnels began to swarm the tunnel where the sound came from. Pax chose his moment, jumped, and he landed on one of the buzzing formains.

In its momentary surprise, Pax grabbed its belt knife and jammed it between the creature's wings. A blue-green liquid spurted out of the wound and covered Pax's face. The wings stilled, and they both fell.

When they landed, Pax pulled up his hood and dove for a particularly shadowy part of the chamber. A small group of the swarm that had been going to the exploded tunnel broke off and went to investigate their fallen comrade. Pax heard human voices from the tunnel opposite his hiding spot, and a new group of formains came out from that tunnel and met the investigators.

All of their antennae flicked wildly around the corpse. Pax hadn't thought of the possibility of them having a sense he didn't know about. Did they already know he was the culprit? Hopefully the humans in the tunnel wouldn't get blamed for this.

The formains seemed to come to a consensus and the investigators broke away. Some went back into the tunnel with the humans, while others started moving from tunnel to tunnel, their antennae flicking in various directions. Pax stayed along the wall as he tried to move toward the opposite end of the chamber. He slipped by the formains as they returned from whatever investigation of the humans they had been doing, and dashed deeper into the tunnel.

When he got to where the humans were working, he saw they were carving out cubbies for some kind of huge larvae. Farhan's father, Abdul-Tajir, was one of the people working, but he didn't look well. His face was ashen and his limb were shaking. The strong, stern man that led Pax's caravan was a shadow of his former self.

Pax approached him. "Tajir?" The man flinched, but perked up at the sound of a familiar voice. He turned.

"You! Did house Morkae send you?"

Pax shook his head. "We were captured trying to find you. What's happening? What is this place?"

"I believe it is some sort of nursery. We've been building it ever since we got here. Every day they come in with new larvae and seal them in some sort of sticky residue. Do you know where my son is?"

Pax nodded. "He's tied up in one of the entrance tunnels. Gerald and the others are with him. Do you know where the queen is? We have a plan."

"I do." Another voice said. It was a tall slender khaldabri woman. She looked malnourished like Tajir, but her back was straight, and her bearing was proud. She almost appeared to be a noble of some sort.

"Can you lead me?"

She nodded.

"If you are going," Tajir said, "you should do so now. Our overseers will be back any moment, and they seem agitated."

Pax nodded, but then a thought occurred to him. He looked at the several dozen people working on the nursery. "Can you pass word along to as many slaves as possible?" he asked Tajir.

The elder Caravan Master gave him a questioning look.

"Gerald says once the queen is dead, the formains will lose their hive mind and become confused. You should try and lead a revolt when the moment comes. If this works, we'll all get out of here."

Tajir nodded and waved him away. Pax gave the Caravan Master a solemn nod, and followed the woman through a small tunnel off to the side of the one he had come through.

They moved quickly, avoiding main tunnels that had groups of formains. They didn't speak to each other, the woman seemed determined to stay as silent as possible, and Pax didn't mind. Her noble bearing made him nervous, and he'd rather avoid embarrassing himself anyway.

When they found a lone formain in a tunnel, without a word, the khaldabri grabbed it and twisted its head until Pax heard a crack. He looked at her, surprised, as she picked up its spear.

"Don't worry. If you kill them quickly enough, they can't send a distress signal. It took a lot of trail and error to learn how to do that, but I've gotten good at it since I've been here." She stooped and grabbed a limb and snapped it off. Then she sucked the meat out of the carapace. The same blue-green liquid dripped out of the place the arm was torn off and pooled on the ground.

When Pax gave her a surprised look, she shrugged. "They feed us enough to keep us alive, but if you want to be in fighting shape, you need some way to supplement your diet. Their larvae are a better source of protein, but they guard them viciously. The last person who tried to steal one got pulled apart at the limbs."

Pax shook as the terror of this place began to settle on him. "Don't go catatonic on me. We're nearly there." The woman got to her feet and started moving quietly toward a tunnel and Pax couldn't think of anything to do but follow her.

CHAPTER EIGHTEEN

The Queen

She led him to a chamber that, at Pax's best guess, was the center of the entire structure. The vast majority of the structure was taken up by the biggest formain Pax had seen since he had gotten here. Her back half was engorged to the point that Pax could see through her carapace.

It was filled with a mass of squirming and undulating maggots. Moments after they entered the chamber, one was forced out her back end and taken up by one of the swarms of formain workers that were tending her.

"Well," the woman who led Pax to the chamber said, "we're here. I hope you have a plan for how you are going to kill her."

Pax hefted his bow and chose an arrow. The woman raised an eyebrow as he nocked the arrow and drew it back. He aimed for the engorged backside. He hopped the explosion would kill a large amount of the workers as well. If it didn't, they'd have a difficult time getting out of here. He let go of the string, and the arrow sailed, turning into a tongue of flame.

It made contact with the queen. There was a flash of fire and Pax heard a pop and a ringing in his ears. The flames burst out around him, engulfing the chamber in an inferno that sent Pax back in time. He saw flashes of his past. Tents burning. People shouting and screaming. A woman in his arms that was covered in blood.

Someone shook him. He looked up to see the ringmaster. His lips moved. "Are you OK, lad?"

Pax couldn't hear the voice over the ringing in his ears, but he could read lips. Except, no, the ringmaster never called him lad. He never addressed Pax at all.

Pax blinked. He was back in the chamber with formains running around in a chaotic mess. Meses was standing over him trying to get him to stand. He took a breath. His heart was still racing and his throat felt tight, but he could stand. He ran, trusting Meses to lead him away from the hellish inferno he had created behind them.

They ran through tunnel after tunnel. Eventually Pax's ears stopped ringing, and he heard the frantic clicking that filled the tunnels. None of the formains they passed seemed to give them a second thought.

Pax entered a chamber that looked similar to the first one he found: a tall dome with several tunnels leading in different directions. There, the khaldabri woman was commanding a group of slaves.

They were fighting a group of formains armed with broadswords. Most of them were human, but there were several khaldabri and a pair of gnomes. Some of them had spears that were clearly stolen off the already fallen formains, but some were simply grappling, scratching and biting as best as they could to kill their former masters. Pax didn't see Tajir among them. He turned to Meses.

Meses touched his arm, and Pax felt his body shift into something less substantial. He felt lighter. When he looked down, he saw he was already floating up toward one of the top most tunnels. He got into the tunnel and his body became mottled-green flesh again. He saw his friends, including Jeremy and Farhan.

Between him and the group, however, were a group of formains brandishing their spears toward his friends. Korivare was bent over something, Jiang was slashing at the spears, trying to keep their tips back. Gerald had one of the formain's broadswords and was doing his best to keep Jiang from getting flanked.

Pax stepped up behind one of the formains and grabbed it by the back of the head. He pulled it back and tried to yank its broadsword out of its hand, but he misjudged their grip. Instead, he tore the thing's arm clean off and it fell to the ground clicking violently as what Pax suddenly realized was blood poured from the wound.

The other formains turned around, creating an opening for Gerald and Jiang. They both slashed their blades across the backs of two formains, and they fell to the floor. The four standing up looked from Pax to his two friends. Back and forth. Back and forth.

Pax watched them for a moment before realizing they were trying to figure out what to do. They had acted so mechanically before with near perfect tactics. Without their hive mind, however, they were just a bunch of confused bug-creatures.

Pax brandished the sword. Two of the formains dropped their weapons, but the other two jumped at him. Before they landed, Jiang took one in the back-side, and Pax slashed the other across its midsection. They both fell limp to the floor. Pax looked at the two that surrendered and pointed into the tunnel where he'd come. They scurried away, clicking rapidly.

That's when Pax saw who Korivare was bent over. Tajir was bleeding heavily, and Korivare had a sheen of sweat on his forehead. Pax had seen that look of concentration before on his friend, and he knew Korivare was doing everything he could to keep the man alive. Now that things were safe enough for him to approach, Farhan knelt beside his father and took the hand Tajir raised to him.

"My boy," Tajir said.

"Don't speak father. You need to save your strength."

"Listen. The knight is doing his best, but it will not be enough. The rest of our people are gone. I held on in hopes that I would see you again. You have to begin again. Make me proud my son."

Farhan's eyes welled up with tears, and he clutched at his father's hand. "No! Father don't leave me. Please hold on."

It was too late. The hand Farhan clutched to his face went limp and Tajir's eyes went glassy and lifeless. Farhan sobbed and Jeremy put a consoling hand on his shoulder.

"He's gone friend. We have to get out of here if we don't want to join him."

Farhan shook his head but didn't say anything. It took Korivare and Jeremy both pulling to pry him from his father's corpse. Pax picked it up with all the care and reverence he could, and the seven of them walked out of the tunnel into the harsh light of the desert.

CHAPTER NINETEEN

Mourning a Loss

Meses met them outside and led them to a small river that Gerald guess flowed from one of the large oases into the ocean. They spent the rest of the day and that night burying and mourning Tajir. It took a long time for them to get enough sand out of a hole that they were sure his body would be covered. The rest of the time they spent in quiet meditation.

When the sun was setting on the third day, Meses explained that he had to return home, and Pax asked if he needed help again.

"No, my circumstances are much different this time around. I will be able to get home on my own. Thank you for your concern."

With that, he disappeared into a gust of wind. Pax raised his hand in farewell and noticed that one of the pale blue stones on his ring had faded to a dull black.

"Where did you meet an Eruan?" Farhan asked. The amazement was plain in his voice.

"Who Meses? We helped him get home while looking for you," Pax explained.

"Is he an Eruan?" Gerald asked. "I had my suspicions, especially after seeing where he lived. But I only know one story that has one, and it plays a very minor role."

Farhan shook his head. "I can't think of anything else that could do the things he did for us, then disappear in a gust of wind."

"What's an Eroo... whatever you guys just said?" Pax asked.

"An Eruan is a wind spirit," Farhan explained. "They act as guides and heralds of mighty heroes, but they can also be terribly deceptive at times. You seem to have gotten on one's good side. That is a place

98

you would want to stay."

"Heroes? Really?" Pax thought back to the people in the city they had left. The way they looked at him. Did Meses see something in him?

He thought of all the times his Rage had made him do terrible things: the knight he almost killed, the circus, hurting Gerald in the Dream World. Meses probably made a mistake. Or maybe he meant for Korivare to wake up first, and Pax had been the mistake.

Gerald sat down next to Pax. The rest of the group had dispersed to prepare for their long journey to the closest city, so they were alone.

"A coin for the words that you hold?" He held out a silver coin to Pax.

Pax looked at it. He didn't take it, but he started speaking anyway. "I think Meses made a mistake." He thought back to Korivare healing Tajir in the tunnel. "If he was supposed to guide a hero, it should have been Korivare, or maybe Jiang. Not me." He remembered how his two friends had defended themselves and the others during the chaos.

"What makes either of them a better hero than you?"

Pax just looked down at the sand.

Gerald waited.

When he didn't continue, Pax sighed and said, "I'm just a monster. I'm strong, but that gets people around me hurt as much as it seems to help. When I get mad, I can barely control myself. I'm just... broken."

Gerald waited to see if anything else was forth coming. When Pax didn't continue, he took a breath and let it out in a slow exhale. "Pax, of course you're broken. We're all broken. That's what life does, it breaks us.

"Some people crack. They're the lucky ones. Some of us shatter into a million tiny pieces. But those pieces can be put back together into a beautiful mosaic, and the great thing about cracks is, the more there are, the more the light shines through."

Pax nodded, but he didn't say anything. He wasn't sure he understood what Gerald was trying to say, but he could tell his friend was trying to help. That was enough to make him feel better.

Gerald clapped the troll on the back and stood. "We should get some rest. I'm not sure how far we are from the nearest city, but I feel a long walk is in our future."

He walked toward a tree near the bank of the river and put his back against it. Pax lay down and used his cloak as a blanket. It took a lot of tossing and turning before he was able to get his dark thoughts out of his head long enough to sleep.

Pax could feel himself falling through a dark-violet void. It reminded him of being in the Dream World flying through a sky of unfamiliar stars. He saw a floating island near his falling form.

With great effort that made his movement feel strange and clumsy, he swam toward the floating island. When his feet finally touched ground, he felt much more stable. He saw the same trees from the Dream World with their odd pink blossoms.

"Have you gained your answers yet, little troll?" A disembodied voice said to Pax. "You and your friends face threats on all sides. Have you discovered which of you is offending the powers of the cosmos?"

"All I want is to protect the caravan. I just want to make House Morkae proud," Pax shouted. His voice was like a sapling bending in the gust of a storm. He felt the hairs on the back of his neck stand on end as he felt the gaze of the incarnation of primal chaos on him.

Storms crackled around him and the wind picked up. Pax felt his feet shifting under him. The wind flung him off the floating island, and Pax fell into the waiting void.

CHAPTER TWENTY

Long Road Ahead

Pax woke and stretched out the stiffness in his muscles. Gerald and Farhan were gathering figs from the trees growing on the banks of the river. The group ate their fill, guessing it would be a long time until they had access to food. They also used two water skins to settle and filter the sand out of some of the river water.

It took most of the morning, and by the time they were ready to set out, the sun was too high in the sky for them to travel. This meant they spent another couple of hours eating figs and discussing what they were going to do when they found a city.

"I must carry on my father's legacy," Farhan said. "He asked me to begin again. Someone has to preserve our people's traditions."

"I thought you were just caravan merchants," Pax said.

Farhan shook his head solemnly. "I am a Shatka. We are no more caravan merchants than Jeremy is merely a minstrel."

Jeremy nodded at that. Pax wanted to ask if he knew what had happened to his troupe, but he didn't want the man to be reminded of his despair if he believed his troupe was lost as well.

"I'm sorry for your loss," Jeremy said to Farhan. "I will do everything I can to help you get back on your feet while I search for the rest of my family."

Farhan looked at him with a tilted head and a curious expression. "Do you believe they made it out of the lair of those creatures?"

Jeremy smirked and moved a coin across his knuckles. "My people are not fighters, and those bugs didn't have enough time before our hero of the battle killed their hive mind to kill all of them." He winked at Pax. "I suspect plenty of them made it out safely."

"If they were injured at all, or were unable to find a source of water as we did," Korivare said, "they would not survive the desert heat for long. I do not want to crush your hope, Jeremy. However, it seems prudent to be realistic about the situation."

"My people are survivors," Jeremy insisted. Pax wasn't sure, but he thought he saw a flash of worry on Jeremy's face as he said it.

Pax could tell he was choosing to hold hope in his heart for his troupe, and Pax hoped along with him. He thought of Rose out in the desert with no food or water. He thought of her being bitten by a snake and succumbing to its venom. There were too many ways to die out here, but still, Pax hoped.

The sun sunk lower in the sky, and the group decided it was time to move. Gerald took a guess at which river they were by, and said that following it was their best chance to find a city. Everyone else agreed, and they walked along the bank of the river until the moon rose high in the sky.

The river bank was a lush strip of green that was a stark contrast to the sandy wasteland around it. Subsequently, there were a number of different fruit trees and edible plants along the bank. They ate melons that were sweet and so watery their juice ran down Pax's face like pink streams, and they roasted dates over their evening campfire.

After they ate, everyone traded stories, Jeremy and Gerald making a competition out of who could tell the best one. By the time they were on their third round, everyone was too tired to continue and they all fell asleep.

Each day after that was roughly the same. They walked along the bank of the river; ate what they could get their hands on. Meses' tricks proved useful when they couldn't find fruit to eat. They rested when continuing was too dangerous.

It took several days, but they finally saw the high point of the temple that marked a city-state on the horizon. It was still another day of walking ahead, but knowing they had all but made it released a tension that had been quietly building up in the group since their journey began.

When they began approaching the city gates, Pax remembered what happened the last time he tried to enter a city. He didn't think his friends and him would have as much luck with the same trick here.

According to Gerald, this city was the last one before the coast, which was too dangerous to build on because of storms. This meant that this particular city had gotten rich enough to enjoy a great deal of autonomy, and the City Lord didn't cater to the eight Merchant

Houses the same way others did. If Pax was seen as a monster here, there was no one to vouch for him.

"Next." The guard at the gate was looking at a clay tablet when the group approached. When he looked up, Pax was the first thing he saw, and Pax braced for what was to come. "Do you have travel papers?"

Farhan produced a folded piece of vellum parchment. It was one of the only things he had left from before his capture. The guard read it over. Then he looked up speculatively at Farhan. "You're the son of a Shatka Caravan Master? Where is he? Don't you people normally stick together?"

"There was a raid on our caravan. I am the last one alive. These men have been escorting me here, so I may find people to help me rebuild."

The guard looked at each of them in turn, and he looked like he was going to protest. Pax's heart began to pound in his ears. His mouth got dry. The guard nodded, then waved them through the gate. Pax took a breath and tried to ease the shaking in his legs enough to walk forward. It was difficult, but he managed. They were all through the gate of the city.

CHAPTER TWENTY-ONE

Skulks

"The first things I need are more sleds and sturdy pack animals. Camels would be ideal, but I was never good with them. My father..." Farhan paused when he mentioned his late father.

"Anyway, what else could survive the desert wilderness?" Everyone, aside from Jeremy, had stopped at a tavern near the city gate to discuss what to do next. Jeremy, for his part, had disappeared into the crowd with not a word to the others.

Pax was sitting on the floor. The chairs in the inn didn't appear sturdy enough to support him, so instead he sat on the floor. Luckily, he was tall enough that his head still appeared over the table.

"Not many large animals that are good for carrying burdens," Korivare said. He thought for a long moment.

"It's too bad," Gerald mused, "that dragon decided to try and kill us. I'll bet it could carry a whole ton of stuff for you. Then you could fly on it from city to city instead of walking."

"Elephant?" Jiang suggested.

"Elephants are good in the savannas south of here, but they don't do as well as you'd think in deep sand," Farhan explained.

"What's an elephant?" Pax asked.

"It's a big gray creature with tusks like a boar and a really long nose it uses to grab things," Gerald explained.

Pax had trouble picturing anything that matched that description, but didn't make an issue of it.

"Donkey?" Gerald suggested.

"Almost as stubborn as camels, but I suppose those are our options." Farhan sighed. He put his head on the table next to his mug. Pax laid a hand on his shoulder.

Surviving the desert wilderness had kept him occupied until now, but that was over. Now he had to wrestle with the idea that he'd never see his father again. All of the people he'd known his entire life were gone, and it was hitting him hard.

Jeremy burst into the tavern, startling the man behind the bar and gaining several sour looks from the patrons scattered through the room. He paid them no mind as he walked briskly to the table where the five men were discussing things.

"I've found them," he declared triumphantly. "The first thing Farhan will need in his effort to rebuild is a set of sturdy steads to cross the sea of sand."

Everyone gave him a questioning look. "We are already discussing this fact," Farhan said.

"No need to discuss it. I've found your new pack animals," he insisted. He beckoned the group to follow him and strode out the door.

Everyone else looked at each other confused until he popped his head back in.

"You're supposed to be following me. They're not likely to meet us in a tavern." Seeing no other option, the five men followed Jeremy out the door into the afternoon sun.

He led the group to a menagerie of sorts in a square near the city temple. It held all sorts of brightly colored birds, screeching monkeys, and a few larger animals as well. Jeremy went past all of them and straight to the back where a pair of light-colored, short haired creatures were pacing a large cage. Jeremy made an expansive gesture in front of them.

"Gentlemen, may I present to you, a breeding pair of desert skulks." They were almost cat like, only as big as a horse and with fierce, intelligent eyes. Pax wondered if the things were on some level sapient. He could feel them sizing him up.

Gerald's jaw dropped. Pax had never seen him so amazed before. Farhan's face split into an excited grin. The remaining three men just looked at each other, confused.

"Ok. I'll ask. What's a desert skulk?" Korivare looked at Gerald, but he was too enraptured by the creatures to speak.

Jeremy explained instead. "These beauties used to roam the sands around these parts. They were the kings of the desert, discounting the great dragon, of course. Alas, between shepherds defending their flocks, hunters trying to prove themselves or get their pelts, and general human activity, their numbers dwindled. These days there are maybe a few hundred out in the wild."

"And they can pull sleds?" Pax asked.

Jeremy made a gesture with his hand as if balancing a scale. "Yes, technically, but their proud beasts. You can't force them to do what you want, and training them is rather difficult. I think we can manage it though. Maybe not pull a sled right away, but if we get them to relax while we strap some packs on to them, they are stronger for their size than anything else north of the Nahrett river."

Korivare looked at the merchant running the menagerie. "And you are willing to sell them to us?"

The merchant nodded. "As your friend stated, these are exceptionally rare creatures. Anything less than five gold marks would be insulting their worth."

Pax looked in his pocket. After all the expenses in the other city his pockets were noticeably lighter. He looked at his companions, but Korivare had already handed the man his money. The man went into the back and brought out a large wagon with a smaller cage nailed into it. Pax had seen one of those before, and even ridden in it. He didn't like what happened next.

The man took out a whip and started cracking it until the two skulks were inside the smaller cage. Then he rolled the cart over to where the six men were standing. Korivare noticed the dark look Pax was giving the cage. He approached the man. "You don't bring your animals through the city, do you? That would be exceptionally dangerous."

The merchant nodded.

"How do you get them to your shop?"

"I have a tunnel I carved out of the bedrock. It opens up just beyond the walls of the city."

"We'll be using that to transport our new friends out of the city. No need for the cage."

The merchant paused as if he would protest, but Jeremy already had his hand on the lock. The merchant paled at the idea of the skulks being released in his menagerie. He nodded once, and led them to a door that opened onto a ramp down into a dark tunnel carved out of sandstone.

Pax and Farhan coaxed the skulks into the tunnel, and the other four joined them soon after. Once everyone was inside, without a word, the merchant closed the door with a *thump*. That left them in complete darkness. The skulks soft purring was the only sound, until Gerald strummed his harp, and a ball of glowing light appeared before them.

The group started down the long tunnel, and the skulks followed close behind Pax. One of them even placed their head under his hand, and he scratched behind its large ears. The scratch turned into a pet that went down its muscular neck, and its purr became louder.

The other head-butted his backside playfully, and he yelped in surprise. Gerald turned around, startled, but his shoulders relaxed as he saw what was going on.

"They seem to have taken a liking to you. I wonder if it's because of that look you were giving their cage."

"Would they be able to sense something like that?"

Gerald nodded. "They are very intelligent. No doubt, they also appreciate us freeing them from that merchant's care. I doubt that man even knows what to feed such noble beasts."

"What do we feed them?" Farhan asked. "I can't have pack animals that cost me everything I make. Meat isn't cheap around here."

Jeremy approached and gave a dismissive wave. "They aren't that picky. Remember, they're native to these parts and cleverer than anything else you'll find out in the desert, including most people. Now that they're out of that cage and headed into the desert proper, they'll be able to hunt for themselves mostly. Although, supplementing their diet with a tasty morsel."

Jeremy pulled out a bit of dried meat and waved it in front of one of the skulks before tossing it down the tunnel. The beast chased after it, pouncing as it reached the food. "It will make them more passive towards us, and make them easier to train."

"Do they have names?" Farhan asked.

Jeremy shook his head. "Not that I know of." He gestured toward the one that chased the meat. "That one's the female."

"Iris," Farhan declared. "She is clever, cunning, and watchful. Just like the Lady of Skies. She is Iris."

"That feels right," Pax said. "I was thinking something similar."

Jeremy nodded. "That makes him..."

"Fertul." This time it was Pax who spoke.

"A dwarvish name?" Gerald asked.

"I don't know any dwarvish, but that's the name that comes to mind when I see him."

"I think it means 'strong protector,' so it's not a bad one."

"Fertul." Farhan repeated the word, tasting it. "I don't know if I like its origins. These creatures belong to the deserts, and shouldn't have foreign names. However, if you say it means strong protector, then I will call him Asim, but his name will be Fertul."

Pax nodded. It was a reasonable compromise. They continued walking until the light of the orb was washed out by the sun shinning into the tunnel from outside. At the first smell of the fresh, sandy air, the skulks sprinted forward. When the group caught up with them, they were rolling in the warm sand with their massive paws flailing in the air. Pax smiled. These magnificent creatures were home at last.

CHAPTER TWENTY-TWO

Learning and Teaching

The next few days were spent on the outskirts of the city, getting Iris and Fertul used to the idea of carrying bags around on their backs. The group slept outside with the cats to get them used to their new owner and to keep them from wandering into the desert where they'd be lost forever.

On the third day of training, Iris was bounding around, not paying any attention to Pax's instruction. He was getting more and more frustrated with her. Soon, he shouted at her, "Iris, stop."

Her muscles tensed in midair, and she fell to the sand like a brick. She didn't seem hurt, but she was rigid as if she had been turned to stone.

Pax looked at her confused. "Come here," he said in his best commanding voice. She obeyed. Pax gave her a piece of dried meat. She chewed it happily.

Gerald came over, giving Pax a questioning look. "That was... odd. Has she ever done that before?"

Pax shook his head. "I must have frightened her."

Gerald sneered. "A loud noise isn't going to scare a beast that can tear your arm off without a second thought. She may have looked at you curious if that was the case, but she wouldn't have suddenly become obedient."

"What then?"

"Not sure. Whatever you did, you should figure out how to do it again. Maybe you could teach Farhan."

They both looked at the man as he tried to strap a sack onto Fertul's back. He cursed as the great beast made a sudden movement.

109

Farhan jumped back and fell on his butt. Fertul's posture looked amused, and Farhan tried to look sullen before bursting into a good belly laugh. It was good to see the young man getting along well with his new traveling companions. Pax hoped his new budding friendship with a couple of great desert predators would ease the loss of his father.

On the fifth day of training, a couple of people came over to where the group was teaching the skulks to follow them and not get distracted by all the interesting smells and sounds.

They watched as Farhan led the two of them in a wide circle, while Pax, Gerald, and Jiang tried to get their attention using anything but their names. The handful of people became a crowd, and the crowd grew larger as the group tried to get the skulks to sit, and roll over for tummy rubs.

The crowd cheered when the beasts finally got it, and Pax could sense a bit of showmanship coming from Iris. She liked the attention she was getting, and she became much easier to work with. It wasn't a practical way to get a creature to do what you want. There isn't always a crowd willing to cheer when you strap a pack on, but it worked for the time being.

After they were done training for the day, and the skulks were fed from some provisions Jiang had gone into the city to buy during the midday break, several people came up to Farhan. They talked for a while, and Farhan was smiling as he said good-bye to them. He approached Pax excitedly.

"Those people want to join the caravan. They were silk caravaners, but their supply was stolen by bandits on their way here. They have a couple of camels that they are good at handling."

"Does that mean you don't want Iris and Fertul? I mean, Asim."

Farhan waved the mistake away. "Call him by his name. I merely want him to remember his heritage. But no, I still need them. The bandit attack left them wary of traveling. They said they'd only feel safe if they had skulks to protect them."

"Fertul is very protective. Should we introduce them."

Farhan shook his head. "Not until tomorrow. They have business in the city, and I'd prefer the skulks well rested before meeting new people."

"There's wisdom in that." Pax turned toward the setting sun. "We should get a fire started. How much wood do we have left?"

"Not enough for the whole night. Enough for dinner, but stories will be told under starlight."

Pax shrugged. They moved toward where the others were gathering for the evening. The pair of skulks passed, Iris rubbing up against Pax as she did so. Pax scratched behind her ears, and her tail flicked in appreciation. The pair of beasts lay down near the pit where Jiang was building a fire. When it was lit, he lay back against Fertul's side waiting for the rest of the group to gather for dinner.

They ate, and Farhan told the rest of the group about the people looking to join his caravan. Jeremy clapped him on the back. "Sounds like you'll be a Caravan Master in your own right soon enough. Your father would be proud."

Farhan gave a small smile. Mentions of his father still plainly hurt, but knowing that he was doing what his father wanted seemed to help.

After everyone had finished their meal, Jeremy and Gerald told stories, and everyone joked late into the night. The fire went out hours before anyone was ready to stop, but no one seemed to notice. Jeremy taught them a new drinking song, and Gerald started to improvise new verses by the end.

By the time the moon was at its zenith, everyone was wearing a tired smile, even Jiang. He'd decided that, just this once, his emotions need not travel as far as his hand. Pax fell asleep against Iris' broad side and dreamed of the shadows, rustling leaves, and quiet coolness of his forest home. It was the most pleasant night he could remember.

CHAPTER TWENTY-THREE

A New Path Forward

The next morning Pax and Gerald went to the market to buy more food and meet up with the new additions to their growing caravan.

"I was also hoping to see what I could get for this." Gerald pulled out the broadsword he'd taken from the formains. "I don't much care for swords. Getting that close to anyone who is likely to be violent is simply not in my nature."

Pax looked at the small man and couldn't help but agree. Gerald wasn't weak, necessarily, but his small stature did give him a disadvantage in a fight. Pax mentioned this to him and he laughed. "No kidding. I've been thinking of trying to learn a bit of Gera-dul for that reason."

"What?"

"It's a martial art common among halflings. The name roughly translates to 'beat up the big guy', but it's basically about taking as many advantages as you can and fighting dirty. It's pretty much designed for guys like me."

Pax chuckled. "Well, maybe you and Jiang could spar a bit when we get back. He might be able to teach you some of the moves he uses."

Gerald shrugged. "Jiang seems to be pretty guarded about that. I don't know if he's very confident in his abilities, and he might be afraid of giving someone bad advice if he tried to teach them."

Pax nodded. Another thought occurred to Pax in that moment. It was almost too difficult to give it voice, but he felt that he needed an answer for it. When he spoke, there was a slight catch in his voice, "what do you think you all will do now that we found the caravan?"

Gerald gave Pax a confused look. "I was planning on helping Farhan with his caravan. Were you thinking of leaving?"

Pax shook his head quickly. He felt a weight lift off his shoulders. Gerald couldn't speak for Korivare and Jiang, but Pax was glad to hear at least one of his friends was sticking around.

"I," he said, "think my charge to protect the Shatka caravan isn't done until I ensure Farhan is taken care of. After that, I'd like to bring all of you to House Morkae when I announce that my quest is complete."

They got to the square they were walking to, and their conversation lulled as Pax watched Gerald negotiate with merchants. He noticed a couple of commonalities in what Gerald was doing at each stall, and wondered if he could replicate them. He thought about asking Farhan to let him practice while he was with the caravan.

When they were done, Pax's pockets were noticeably lighter in coin and they had several sacks of food. Gerald had gotten two silver marks for the sword, and he was muttering about how hard of a sell it was.

They passed by a fletcher and Gerald stopped. "Pax, do you have any arrows besides the ones we got from the dragon hoard?"

Pax shook his head.

"Thought so. Why don't we get you a quiver of normal arrows, so you don't have to worry about causing a huge explosion every time we need cover fire."

Pax rolled his eyes at Gerald's pun, and they walked into the shop. A woman with the dark complexion of the Southern Countries was at the counter. How had she gotten north of the River-Line?

Her black hair was wrapped in tight coils that outlined her smiling face in a halo, and her eyes sparkled with cleverness. When she looked at Pax, he could feel himself blush, and hoped his mottled green skin hid it well.

"Good morning," she said. "What can I do for you two handsome men?" Her accent was faint, but noticeable. "Are we looking for anything particular today?"

Gerald nodded. "I think you may be able to help us. My friend here is in dire need of your fine work." He gave her a sly wink, and the shopkeeper giggled girlishly.

"I hope your talking about my craftsmanship. Otherwise..." she paused significantly.

"Otherwise, I'd have to spend the rest of the day treating you like the queen you clearly are. To prove I meant no disrespect."

She smiled again. "Otherwise, you'd have to be the one to explain it to my husband."

"I'm sure he knew what he was getting into when he married a little mink like you."

She giggled again. "'Little mink is what he calls me as well."

"It suits you. He's a wise man. As it is, my friend does need arrows. What will it take for me to take them off your pretty hands?"

Her smile turned sly. Pax was reminded of the look Iris gets when she's ready to pounce. "Well, as you can plainly see, the arrows I have here were made by my own hand. I've been in this business long enough to know what I have. How many do you need?"

"A full quiver if you can spare it." Gerald gave her his own wry grin. They seemed to be playing a game, but Pax couldn't keep up.

"Ah. That is a might plenty. Going hunting, are we?"

"We'll be on the road a while. Bandits. You know how it is."

She nodded her head. "I have been hearing about traveling merchants and caravans going missing out here. Some people are even spreading rumors about bug-creatures."

"I heard a similar rumor, but it was that the problem had been taken care of."

"Well, the worry has been good for business, so why don't I make you a deal?"

"I'm listening."

"If you can do your best to keep that rumor of the problem being solved from spreading, I'll let you have the quiver of arrows for just one silver mark."

Gerald raised an eyebrow at that. "A silver mark for twenty arrows?"

"Crafted of the finest woods money can buy."

He nodded and pulled out one of the coins he'd gotten for his sword. "I'll see what I can do to pull people this way. You have my thanks."

The woman grabbed a wooden quiver from behind the counter. It had a leather strap buckled around it with a brass buckle. She went around the shop, inspecting her arrows, and choosing each carefully. When the quiver was full, she handed it to Gerald, who took her hand, kissed it, and passed the quiver to Pax. The shopkeeper gave them another warm smile, and they walked out of the shop.

On their way back to the city gates, Pax heard a voice that set his stomach churning and his spine tingling. "Pax? Gerald? Is that you?"

Pax turned, and his face lit up with excitement. Rose was pushing through the crowd toward them. Pax forced his way toward her, getting a number of scowls from the people he jostled out of the way. When she was close, Rose jumped into Pax's arms and hugged him tightly. He hugged her back, careful not to hurt her. They were just letting go of each other when Gerald reached them and gave her a much more modest hug.

"I can't believe you're alive. How'd you survive the desert?" Pax asked.

She waved the question away. "My people are survivors. We aren't afraid of any wilderness." Her face went dark. "Unfortunately, not everyone was as lucky as me. Graham and Jeremy are still lost out there somewhere. I don't know if they made it."

"I don't know about Graham," Pax said, "but Jeremy is with us. C'mon, he'll be so happy to see you."

He and Gerald led Rose to the gates of the city where they met up with the silk merchants. When Pax tried to introduce everyone, he realized he didn't know the names of their new caravan members. The woman didn't hesitate though.

"I am Nasira, and my husband is Jabir. Your friends are very kind to allow us to join them. Ever since we were attacked, we haven't been certain of our future. When we saw Master Farhan training those beautiful beasts, we couldn't believe anyone could command such wild power. We knew he'd be able to protect us."

"I'm sorry? Beasts?" Rose asked. Pax hadn't realized he'd failed to mention the skulks. He stepped in to explain, but Rose waved him off. "I'm sure I'll find out soon. When are we leaving?"

"My hope is sooner, rather than later," Nasira said. "My husband and I have sold what we can to buy food and stock for Master Farhan, and we don't have money left for lodging."

"Where are your camels stabled?" Pax asked. "I can get them for you, and we can head out after introductions."

They told him. He agreed to meet them all back at camp and went to go fetch them. The man they were stabled with insisted Pax pay for the lodging. Pax hadn't realized that Nasira and Jabir hadn't paid for the lodging in advance, but he didn't have any money left after buying supplies.

He took the necklace he traded for off his neck, and offered it to the man. The man became very confused, but he accepted the offer and showed Pax to the camels. Pax touched his neck as he led the camels away from the stable. It was his first piece of jewelry, and he didn't like how it pinched his neck. He decided there was no love lost out of the transaction.

CHAPTER TWENTY-FOUR

Setting out

When he got back to camp, introductions had already been started. Jeremy gave rose a quick embrace before promising they's speak later. He helped Nasira approach Fertul slowly and calmly. Fertul was stand-offish and suspicious, but Iris was curious about Rose.

She approached the dancer immediately and sniffed at her outstretched hand. Rose giggled at the feeling. Iris licked Rose's hand. Rose scratched under her chin and soon had Iris' head in both her hands. "You are the most beautiful thing I have ever seen. Look at this face."

Iris closed her eyes and stood proud with her head still in Rose's hands. Fertul came over to investigate, leaving Jeremy and Nasira standing with hands stretched out toward him. Jabir made a move off to the side, and Fertul jumped between him and Iris.

Without thinking, Pax said "Fertul. Calm." The words came out like a commandment, and Fertul's muscles relaxed immediately. His eyes were still locked on Jabir, but he didn't look ready to pounce.

Jabir stayed completely still. His eyes were locked on the skulk. They were wide and full of fear. Pax brought Iris over to him, and she pushed her head into the palm of his hand. He looked down at her slowly, glancing up at Fertul on occasion. Iris rubbed at his side and her long tail flicked him on his nose. He blinked and scratched at the spot the tail had touched him.

Fertul stalked over to Farhan, keeping one eye on Jabir as he did so. Farhan took Fertul's head in his hands and pulled his gaze away from the other man. He searched deep in the cat's large yellow eyes.

When he finally spoke, he said, "you are a protector aren't you?

Well, these people are a part of our caravan now. That means they are as much family to you as I am. They are not enemies. Do you understand me?"

Fertul turned and licked the man's hand. His tongue was flat and wide. The skulk's mouth was largely dry, so his tongue didn't leave much on Farhan's hand.

Farhan nodded and stood. "He seems to understand now. If he gives you anymore trouble, talk to me. I will set this foolish creature straight again."

Jabir nodded slowly, but he didn't say anything. Instead, Nasira asked, "is there anything else left to do before we depart? You have food and water for everyone?"

Farhan nodded. He went about checking the packs on the camel's backs and storing everyone's most precious items in the packs he strapped to Fertul and Iris. Pax took everyone's waterskins into the city for one last fill, and by the time the sun had past its zenith, they were ready to move on.

Before they could leave, however, they heard a gruff new voice from the line that formed everyday into the city. Graham was pushing past the crowd and holding up a three fingered greeting to his fellow Wanderers. Jeremy let out a yell of surprise, but Rose's swift dancer's strides made it to their old guard first.

They both wrapped him in a tight embrace. Rose began to weep quietly into his shoulder as she recounted the harrowing escape her and the rest of the troupe had to face. Graham held her in an embrace that was more gentle than Pax thought possible from the hard and gruff guard.

Nasira and Jabir listened to Rose's story with growing concern. Neither Farhan nor the adventurers had told them the details of the Shatka caravan's fate. Rose, on the other hand, spared no detail about the formains and how difficult they were to route long enough for the troupe to escape.

"The rest of the troupe is with you then?" Jeremy asked.

Rose nodded. "Most of them anyway. We lost Trick, Marion, his wife, and Theo. The rest are performing in one of the market squares. I came out here because Pax said you were with him."

Graham said, "It was good that you did. I heard your giggling when you were with that great beast of a cat. I always told you I could pick your laugh out of a crowd. Jeremy, here, just sounds like every other whiny youngin I've ever met."

"I missed you too, Graham. Well, at least our family is back together again. Tonight we can sing Trick and Theo's favorite drinking songs to send them off. As for Marion and his wife, maybe I'll have a go at their puppets and see if I can get their ghosts to come tell me off one last time."

Rose giggled and shook her head. She tugged the two men by the arm back to the group of onlooking adventurers and caravaners. "I'm eternally grateful to you all for helping Jeremy find us again. I can't imagine what would've happened to him without the five of you to keep him sensible."

She turned to Nasira and Jabir. "You two are in good hands with these men. I wish you the best in restoring Farhan's caravan, and I hope your roads are easy and that they meet with mine soon." She shook hands with the two newcomers. She gave the others a quick kiss on both cheeks, and when she did so for Pax, his stomach did a somersault.

Jeremy grasped Pax's forearm in farewell, and Graham did the same. Gerald told Jeremy that the two of them will have to meet again at a tavern. "That way," Gerald said, "I can show a lot more people how much better I am at storytelling."

Jeremy laughed and agreed that a larger audience was needed to be certain who was the better bard.

Graham approached Jiang and told him one last risqué joke. Jiang gave it a slow gesture like brushing something from his nose. Afterward, he held up four fingers to Graham, declaring the joke a four out of five on the scale they'd developed.

Graham laughed and declared he'd finally cracked the warmage's humor. Pax, however, saw another smaller gesture from Jiang. He'd pressed his thumb and forefinger together and twisted his wrist in an overhead arc. It seemed to be one of regretful longing.

Pax put a hand on Jiang's shoulder as they all watched the Wanderers make their way back into the city. Pax hoped he'd see them again one day, but somewhere deep inside, he knew he was hoping in vain. Rose, Jeremy, and Graham were out of sight before anyone turned around. It was time to leave this city behind and cross the waiting horizon.

CHAPTER TWENTY-FIVE

Out in the Wilderness

During the next few weeks, Pax stayed near Farhan and the skulks to ensure that they didn't make too much of a fuss at the other members of the caravan. "I wonder if they will ever be comfortable with welcoming strangers into our caravan," Farhan said one morning while he and Pax were giving water to the camels and watching the skulks hunt for their morning meals.

Pax thought for a moment before responding. "That's a tough one. I am certain Iris has no issue with strangers as long as they give her lots of praise and attention. Fertul, on the other hand..." Pax paused for a moment.

Farhan nodded his understanding. "Amir is a protector before he is anything else. Strangers upset him, I suspect. I still think he is wary among Jabir, but he at least understands that Jabir is one of his family. The idea of having people come and go out of this caravan without giving him time to know them..." Farhan shook his head.

Pax watched the male skulk as he paced wide circles around his mate. They had been bought as a breeding pair, which meant that a litter of kittens were likely on the horizon. If Fertul was protective of Iris, Pax couldn't imagine what he'd be like around his own young.

"Why do you need them comfortable around strangers?" Pax asked. "I know that some join your caravan every once in a while, but I always assumed that they were hired guards. If you have these skulks, would you still need caravan guards?"

Farhan looked at Pax with an appraising look. "You aren't from around the deserts of Maskohma, are you?" he asked. There was no accusation or suspicion in his voice the way many people sounded when Pax was prompted of his past.

Pax merely shook his head, offering no further explanation.

Farhan simply continued, "the Shatka are a tradition of people going back many generations. According to our oral history, our culture predates the fall of the Araka Empire. The fact that Shatka caravans are the only people allowed to cross the River-Line supports this as well.

"It is because of our mobility and our expertise in so much of Maskohma's landscape that we are so highly valued. Shatka caravans not only carry exotic goods from far away places, but we are the carriers of knowledge and wisdom from place to place. That's one of the reasons the Eight Great Merchant Houses work with our people so often."

Pax nodded. It seemed like a lot for him to understand, but he got the gist of it. The Shatka were a culture of caravaners, not just people who do it for their living. It was Farhan's living. Now that he was the last of his father's caravan, it was up to him to not only rebuild the caravan, but do his part to keep their culture alive.

"Are Nasira and Jabir Shatka now, too? I mean, they weren't before, right? They were just normal merchants."

Farhan nodded. "They were normal merchants traveling from town to town, but not as far as Shatka roam. Still, they are a part of my caravan now. I am Shatka, and so is everyone who is a part of my caravan. Even you and your friends are part of the Shatka people while you travel with us. That is our way."

Pax thought about Rose and the other Wanderers they had met. They were also a nomadic culture. Both the Wanderers and Shatka seem to be built on the families their people choose, on one level or another. He asked Farhan about his culture and what makes a Shatka.

Farhan considered that question for a long time. When he did speak up, it was slow and deliberate like he was choosing his words carefully. He said, "firstly is the Caravan Master themselves. The Caravan Master is the one who holds the papers and legal authority to travel as we do throughout Maskohma. When we buried my father, I had to ensure that I retrieved those before anything else.

"Other than that, a Shatka caravan is largely made of people who choose to be Shatka. We are very much like Wanderers in that sense. Our culture is not one that is inherited by blood, but instead by ability and skill. No matter who you were born to, when you join a Shatka caravan, you become our family for as long as you travel with us.

"It is not exactly that simple. I hardly think any culture is. There is the understanding that anyone who joins our caravan, but is not a merchant, is not the same kind of family member as a Shatka merchant. I still consider you and your friends to be a part of my family, but you should understand that it is not normal for us to extend such considerations to our guards. They usually have greater loyalties to the house they work for."

"I'm confused. Didn't you just say that anyone who travels with you is Shatka as long as they travel with you? But then you said caravan guards aren't part of your family."

Farhan nodded knowingly. "It can be confusing at times. It is, after all, a culture like any other. It is best to think of it like this: a Shatka merchant belongs to the caravan as a family member. We treat each other as brothers, fathers, mothers and daughters.

"When someone decides to travel with us, they become Shatka. We accept them as a part of our caravan and, therefore, they are our family. But, we are not fools. We know when someone's loyalty lies with someone or something that is outside of the caravan. When you join the caravan knowing that you will leave soon, we treat you as more distant family."

"Like cousins. You're still family, but you aren't part of the same household."

Farhan nodded. "Many Shatka caravans believe that all people are part of one great family. Not all, but some. That is why we do not treat anyone, no matter where they are from, as strangers. Still, we remember who has accepted our culture and who is only joining us temporarily."

Pax asked more and more questions of Farhan as they traveled. He and the other adventurers spent a few weeks traveling with the burgeoning caravan before fate would pull them away again. In that time, Pax did everything he could to understand Shatka culture, and he hoped to continue asking questions and learning more, but they were ambushed half way through their journey.

CHAPTER TWENTY-SIX

Marching Under Rays

The ambush didn't come like the dragon, bursting out of the sand and throwing Pax from a great height, nor did it come like the formains, throwing spears and clicking maddeningly. This time, the ambush was silent. Before he even woke up, Pax was paralyzed.

At first, he'd assumed it was merely the paralysis that sometimes plagued him when he first woke up. It had been an off and on thing since his childhood in the cave. This paralysis didn't go away, though. The dark figure that stood above him wasn't a figment of his half-dreaming mind. She was real, and she was chanting a soft prayer over Pax's inert body.

Pax couldn't hear anything other than that prayer, and he worried that he was the only one awake. Was everyone else paralyzed too? Were they all being quietly slaughtered right next to him with him unable to turn and see it happening? He couldn't tell.

Soon the woman's prayer changed and Pax felt his body move. It wasn't his command, though, that drove his motion. His body moved of its own accord. He stood. He could see that Gerald, Korivare, and Jiang were awake and being given the same treatment as Pax. Pax's anxiety rose and he felt his chest tighten.

He was no stranger to being forced to do things. Most of his life seemed to be spent in service to one person or another, but his own body was always his to command. If he was made to lift heavy things, he chose where to grasp them and hoist them up. If he was made to perform in front of a jeering crowd, he decided how he'd move and when. This was a new kind of horror. He saw the same fear in the stricken expressions of his friends. Each of them was terrified of what was happening.

Each of the four friends had their own praying woman who led them to a group of more women wearing similar clothes to the priestesses in the city temples: the same white robes bound at the waist with a cord of rope. Theirs were dirtier and wrinkled, and their hair was wild and unkempt. They were every bit the wilder cousin to the clean and polished women that lived in the city.

When the praying stopped, the four men were bound in iron manacles and hitched by a hemp rope to a donkey. One of the women hissed a command, and the donkey started moving, pulling the men along with it. They walked until the glowing embers of the caravan fire disappeared behind a dune, and they came to a different camp.

This one had large tents like the ones Farhan's father had for his caravan. They were set up by a large bonfire, not the small campfire Farhan had made. When Pax looked closer, he saw the tents were well worn and had many stitches where a hole had been torn or cut through the fabric. These tents were luxurious, but not new.

"Tie them up in my tent. I will watch over them tonight. The rest of you have earned a night of rest." The speaker was the woman who had led the donkey. The other women did as she commanded without word or hesitation. Soon, Pax and all three of his friends were tied to a post in the largest tent. They sat there. Waiting.

"Who are those women?" Korivare finally asked. "What did they do to get us here? I felt like someone else was in charge of my body."

"Some kind of wilderness priesthood based on their clothes," Gerald said. "The body hijacking was almost definitely some sort of divine magic."

"What kind of god would give favor to such an action?" Korivare demanded.

"There are more gods out there than just the kind ones. Don't forget what the Dream Master said. We're being hunted. I suspect, whoever is patron to these women, that it's one of the cosmic powers who are plotting our doom."

Pax shifted uneasily. If the gods that were coming after them had priestesses that can make you their puppet, what else did they have at their disposal? What kind of horrors could a god bring down to smite someone? He thought of plague, famine, and... fire. He tore his mind away from the thought before his anxiety could dwell on it.

The woman who'd been giving the orders walked into the tent. She stood smugly in front of the group bound in her tent. "I guess we managed something neither a dragon nor those bugs could do. The Lady of Rays will be most pleased when we gift her with your hearts."

"Lady of Rays?" Korivare asked. "That's an old one. The Sun Queen hasn't been worshiped in that capacity in..." He trailed off trying to remember.

The woman spat on the ground. "Her names are like ash in your mouth. You should be ashamed to have spoken them. Perhaps before we give you to her, I will cut out your tongue to teach you some respect."

She brandished a knife she hadn't been carrying when they were brought here. "Luckily for you, your capture was a tiring chore. Tonight, my sisters and I will rest, and tomorrow we will begin the long march toward the ritual site and your doom. Pleasant dreams." She sneered and wiggled her fingers, exiting the tent. Pax was asleep again before she came back.

Pax was awoken by a swift kick to his stomach. His hands were already bound in manacles, and the tent was taken down after they were dragged out of it. Jiang, Gerald and Korivare were awake and manacled as well. They were tied to the same donkey, and the group of women lead them away from the rising sun, deeper into the desert wilderness.

They were forced to march all day, even while the sun was at its zenith. The women kept themselves cool and hydrated through plenty of water and a great deal of praying that Pax was beginning to understand as their version of Jiang's chanting or Gerald's music.

Their prayers were spells, and Korivare explained as they marched that the power behind the spells came from the Sun Queen. That meant that any spell that went against her wishes simply wouldn't work. It didn't lift Pax's spirits to think that the Sun Queen approved of them being marched to death in the hot sun or controlled like dolls.

When evening came, the priestesses set up camp and tied the four men to a set of posts, this time outside the entrance to one of the tents.

Since their hands were bound, when the call came for dinner, the woman in charge gave a woman, barely more than a girl, the task of feeding their prisoners.

She took a bowl of porridge and a spoon, filled the spoon and held it up to Pax's mouth. He didn't feel like eating. He was hot, tired, and just wanted to rest. The woman gave him an angry scowl and approached one of the other priestesses. The priestess nodded and began to pray.

When the young woman brought the spoon up to Pax's mouth again, his mouth ate without his permission. The porridge was bland and watery, but Pax's throat swallowed. He ate like this, each action forced on him without his consent, until the bowl was empty.

Jiang looked at him stoic from a post across the tent's entrance. His face was pale and clammy. His hand moved from behind his back, but Pax couldn't see the gesture. Pax let his eyes fall to the sand. He felt oddly ashamed about his lack of control over his own body. He wanted to cry, but he was just too tired to bother.

The next several days passed in much the same way. Pax was kicked awake, tied to a donkey, and made to walk under the hot desert sun until it fell beneath the horizon. He was force fed, and left to sleep. Wake. Repeat. Again. And again.

The first couple of days saw the men trying to lift each other's spirits or come up with an escape plan, but soon that ended. Everyone was too tired and sullen to speak. When one of them did, someone else would snap at him, and they'd all go back to silence.

Near the end of the first week, Jiang became delirious. He had difficulty standing, and wouldn't talk except in what Pax guessed was his native language. The priestesses decided it was heat exhaustion, and when they stopped for the night, they took him into one of the tents. When he came out again, he was back to being stoic and sullen. They tied him to his post, and the next day everyone was given twice as much water as they were forcefully marched through the hot sand.

It took three weeks of marching before something came into view. When Pax first saw it, it looked like one of the step pyramids that sat at the center of every city-state in the desert. As they got closer, however, he began to realize it was a large red sandstone plateau. It looked odd, however. One side of it was perfectly smooth like a giant had cut a piece of it off. The other sides were craggy and looked like the formed naturally, which made that one side stand out all the more.

The sun was still high in the sky. It was a surprise, then when the group of priestesses stopped the forced march at the base of the plateau. The head priestess stepped in front of the group and turned to face them with her back toward the red sandstone wall.

"Sisters and honored guests," she declared with a sneer at Pax, "welcome home."

CHAPTER TWENTY-SEVEN

Under the Shadow of the Sun

The lead priestess touched the bare red-brown stone and a large *crack* startled Pax and made him jump. The face of the stone split to reveal a dark stairway leading up into the plateau. Pax was shoved inside by one of the women, and he climbed the stairs to an entrance hall. It was largely featureless save for the seven doors on either side of the room. The doors seemed to be made of... was that oak?

He was forced through one of these doors and it led to a square room no more than a half dozen steps big on a side. There were no windows or furniture save for a clay chamber pot, but when the woman said, "get comfy," and locked the door behind her, Pax understood this was his new prison cell.

He sat in the dark, waiting. Soon he heard the faint echoes of music through the door. "Gerald?"

"Hey big guy. You get your own cell, or did they make you room with Jiang?"

"I'm alone. You have your harp with you?"

"I do now. Not sure how though. I know I left it with Farhan's caravan, but when I got in this cell, it was just lying on the floor."

"Do you have anything else in there?" Korivare asked from beside Pax.

"Nothing but air and my endless charm. You?"

"No. My halberd is back at the caravan as well. I'm wearing my chain shirt now. I found it when they forced me in here, but I doubt that will be of any help."

Pax heard a faint laugh from Gerald's cell. "Maybe your halberd will appear in your cell by tonight. Might take extra time for weapons and such."

"No. The harp is magic. The chain shirt was a gift." Jiang's voice was the faintest, and Pax wasn't sure if he was far away, or feeling weak.

"What do you mean gift?" Korivare asked.

Jiang didn't respond.

"Sounds like you're our only hope Gerald. Know any songs that can unlock doors?"

"And get us in trouble with the ladies who can tell our bodies what to do without our permission? We need a whole plan before we try anything like that. You know of any way to separate a crazed cult from their bitch of a goddess?"

"Hey! Some of her followers may be... cracked, but the Sun Queen is still one of the gods. Show some respect."

"Respect? I just spent the better part of a month being forced to eat porridge against my will because her followers think it's acceptable to puppet people around, and then kill them for fun."

Korivare went silent at that. Pax wondered if he felt as violated as the troll, and apparently Gerald, did. Did being a servant of the gods mean that he was more used to doing things at someone else's command? Pax remembered his life of servitude again and guessed that wasn't the case.

Pax quickly lost track of time in the small, dark cell. He slept most of the time, listened to Gerald play when they were both awake, and sometimes a woman wearing simple road clothes would bring him food and switch his chamber pot. He wasn't sure if they were doing this more than once a day, but it happened about ten times by his count before someone came into his cell unexpectedly.

He had just finished his porridge, and thought it was the woman in road clothes coming back for his dishes, but the woman wore the robes of the priestesses. None of the women who brought him food wore anything but road clothes.

"You are quite the specimen," the priestess said with no preamble.

"What?" Pax asked. His voice was weak from lack of use.

The woman closed the door, cutting off the candlelight of the hallway, and Pax felt her get closer. Her hand went to the lace of his trousers.

"I have been waiting for the right opportunity to get to know you."

Pax didn't understand what she meant until she undid the knot and his trousers fell to the stone floor.

He pushed her away, but she whispered something and his body went rigid as a stone. His legs felt weak, but they were held up by some invisible force that also kept them from shaking. He felt her hands on his cock and she sighed when she felt the length of it.

No. No. Not this. Please, Pax thought. He wanted to say it, but his mouth felt like it was inside of a vice.

He felt himself become erect at the stimulation. *No. Damn it. Stop.* He felt something warm and wet touch his tip. *Please. I don't want it. Stop.*

The flashes came then. He heard the voice of the ringmaster. "She's paid a lot of money to get you alone. You play nice with her, or I'll see you whipped bloody every night for a week."

Pax didn't understand what he meant by "play nice," but he knew better than to disobey the ringmaster. The circus was his, and, according to him, the only law it followed was his will. Pax may be the strongest one in the circus, but the ringmaster knew other ways of controlling people, and he'd realized quickly that the whips the fire benders used scared Pax more than anything.

The ringmaster led him to a private tent where a half-dressed woman was waiting for them. "Here it is ma'am. The beast itself."

The woman approached Pax and looked him up and down. He didn't feel particularly vulnerable being naked. He had been most of his life. When her eyes fixed on his crotch though, the hungry look she gave him made him want to turn and walk out of the tent. He felt dirty just standing there.

The ringmaster left, and he was alone with the woman. She grabbed at him and he stumbled back.

"Oh, you sweet creature. Did I startle you?"

Pax moved along the wall to stand at the opposite end of the tent. She hopped over to him in three quick strides.

"There, there. This will all be over in just a few moments. Those big, strong hands of yours will have me finished in no time, then you can go back to your cage where you belong." Her tone was soothing, but nothing about what she said made Pax relax.

She grabbed at him again, and he threw her back. He was shaking with anxiety and anger. What did this woman want with him? Couldn't she just leave him alone? He saw her excited eyes when she stood back up.

"My, you really are the strongest beast in the world aren't you. I bet those arms of yours could crush a little thing like me."

She put a hand on his chest and he knocked it away. Why didn't she understand he didn't want this?

She scowled at him. "Look, you ignorant monster. I paid good money to have you tonight and if you think I won't get what I want, you have no idea who you're dealing with."

Monster. That word rang in Pax's ears. *Monster.* That's all he was. *Monster.* All he'd ever be.

She grabbed him and threw one of her legs around his waist. He felt her against him and he flailed in a desperate rage.

One of the lamps that had been lighting the tent fell to the ground. Pax didn't notice until the flames were tickling his back. It felt like the burning whips and he stumbled forward, knocking them both to the ground.

He felt a crunch, and his chest came back bloody. He looked down at the half-dressed woman. Her eyes were bulged and lifeless. She was covered in blood. Pax picked her up in his arms and started to shake.

The fire burned his skin, but he couldn't think. He couldn't move. He just sat there staring at the woman he had killed. When one of the acrobats came to pull him out of the blazing inferno, he didn't put up any resistance. He just left the woman there to burn.

Pax was pulled back to the present by his beating heart and the feeling of built-up pressure being released through his groin. The strange woman who had invaded his cell took her mouth off his cock. She pulled something out of her pocket. It clinked like glass, and he heard her spit. She stood and walked out the door, and when she was gone, he could move again.

Pax curled up in a ball feeling very small and helpless. He cried. He cried harder than he had since that night in the tent. The scars on his back tingled as he cried for the woman he killed. He cried for a body that was no longer only his. Mostly he cried because he didn't know what else to do, and when no more tears came, he was exhausted. So, he slept.

CHAPTER TWENTY-EIGHT

Friends to Mend the Aching

Pax woke up to Gerald playing a song he knew. It was the drinking song Jeremy had taught them all when they were training Iris and Fertul. The verse he was on finished and Jiang, Korivare and Pax came in on the chorus.

"Over rivers and under mountains
We march through marshes
We walk through woods
To home and hearth
Throw back our hoods
Til adventure calls again"
The music paused. "You awake big guy?"

"Yeah."

"Everything ok? I heard you shouting last night. I thought they were finally killing us. Then you started crying, and I didn't know what was going on."

"I'm fine," Pax lied. "Can we keep singing?"

"Sure thing, pal."

The music started up again, and the four kept singing. The music helped Pax put some distance between him and the memories from last night. Tears welled up in his eyes again, but, at least this time, he was with friends.

After the song was over, including the improvised verses, Gerald spoke, "hey Korivare."

"Hm?"

"You said the name the priestesses used for the Sun Queen was an old one, right?"

"Yeah, very old. She hasn't been worshiped as the Lady of Rays in living memory."

"But what does that mean? Isn't it the same god?"

"Technically yes. The Lady of Rays and the Sun Queen are epithets. Basically, replacement names for the sun goddess' real name, the one that encompasses her entire being.

"Each epithet describes only a single aspect of the overall god. The Sun Queen is the name given to the aspect of her that is the bringer of life and civilization. The story of her sending her son to teach people how to farm is her acting as the Sun Queen. The Lady of Rays is an epithet that comes from the God Wars."

"Oh. That make sense." Gerald's tone was grim.

"What's a god war?" Pax asked.

"The God Wars was an era of untold brutality. Centuries of war and conflict that spread all over Aragore, from the Coasts of Kermal all the way over the Great Divide into Lukor.

"Actually, if you believe the legends, the Great Divide came after the God Wars. It was supposed to act as a dividing line for the two main factions of gods that would allow them to come to a sort of truce."

"Kind of like a chalk line down a house," Gerald said. "You stay on your side, me on mine, and ne'er the two shall meet."

"Exactly. The Wars became so bloody and all-encompassing that civilization crumbled, and people stopped living in cities. They were too dangerous. Instead, they formed loose bands of travelers for protection, or started small villages in out-of-the-way places like hills or desert oases. Any community big enough that not everyone knew everyone else was just too risky with the constant waring and pillaging."

"Most of the stories I know are from the God Wars. It was supposed to be a time of epic heroism and great battles," Gerald said. "What a lot of people forget is heroes don't come from prosperous times."

"The oral traditions are the only record we have of a lot of that era," Korivare added. "Like I said, civilization crumbled, and things like writing and agriculture went almost extinct except for a few pockets.

Every language we have today came from the few surviving scraps."

"And what about the Lady of Rays?" Pax asked. "You said she came out of all this." This was a lot for Pax to take in, but he thought he understood most of it.

"The Lady of Rays is the warrior aspect of the sun goddess. She is violent and fierce. She's seen as a protector by most, but that epithet emphasizes her marriage to the war god and the tendency for the desert sun to be somewhat merciless.

"In short, if the Sun Queen is her creative side, the Lady of Rays is her destructive side. That's why I'm none too keen on letting whatever these women have planned for us go through. Anyone think of anything yet?"

Gerald spoke up. "I think I have something that may interrupt their prayers long enough for us to gag them. Still working on getting this door unlocked though. I can't seem to do much from this side. I wonder if our big green friend might be able to wrestle a key from one of these women."

Pax put his hand on the oak door in front of him. It didn't seem that thick. "Maybe. I could try to break down the doors too. That would be loud and attract attention though."

"Leave that to me. I'll let you know when it's time."

"If Pax can break down his door, why not just have him break down our doors too?" Korivare asked.

Pax answered, "I don't know how easily I'll be able to take down my door. No matter what, it will be loud. If we want to get everyone out of their cells, I don't think we can rely on my strength alone."

Korivare went silent, but Pax sensed that both he and Gerald were in agreement with him. Jiang had been abnormally silent, even for the normally stoic warmage. Aside from singing along with Gerald's music, he didn't speak. It made Pax worry about him.

CHAPTER TWENTY-NINE
The Deep Magic

The next few days passed as normal. Sleep. Food. Change chamber pots. Sing.

After Gerald got tired of playing through his whole repertoire each day, he began telling stories of the great heroes that arose during the God Wars. He told them about something called the Libras Univertas. The name meant "Book of all Truth," but it was in fact, not a single book, but an entire library.

"It was founded by one of the old True Namers, though stories disagree about which one," Gerald said.

"What's a True Namer?" Pax asked.

"They were extra powerful users of the Deep Magic."

"I see," Pax had further questions, but he wanted to allow Gerald to continue.

"The library quickly became the largest collection of books and scholars in the world at the time. It was named by Terralf the Young, one of the High Kings of Lukor, and the King of the Desert at the time, Ejiro the Wise, as a cornerstone of all civilizations. It became such a storehouse of knowledge that people began to teach there. Well-read scholars taught lectures and the True Namers, who had mentored people all around the world in Naming, started to focus their efforts there.

"In fact, the word university, as well as many of the traditions of modern education, came from the practices started at the Libras

Univertas. A lot of people think the University Arcanum in Lukor is trying to build itself up as a modern version of the Libras Univertas. It might be true, but they have a long way to go if that's the case. I don't think they even have a Master Namer anymore."

"What happened to the old Libras Univertas?" Pax asked.

"Some idiots thought that; since they gave away knowledge, largely for free, to anyone who asked and was willing to put in the work; the whole place was a detriment to their side of the Wars. They burned it to its foundations, and most of the people there died. Some got away and carried away some of the books. Others were actually clay tablets that just got baked and buried when the building collapsed."

Pax absorbed that for a moment before asking another question. "Is Naming a kind of Deep Magic?"

"Naming is the most basic form of Deep Magic and the foundation for the rest of it," Korivare explained. "Knowing the Name of something reflects a true and complete knowledge of it. When you have that, you can move on to Calling it, Binding it, Shaping it, or Restoring it.

"Most Namers were merely Adepts, or people who knew one or two Names of things that were close to them. A full-fledged Namer was fluent in Truespeak, and could learn the Name of almost anything with a few days or weeks of study."

That was a lot of new words for Pax, but he was pretty sure he got the gist of it. Naming was a kind of magic, and the people who practiced it were powerful because of it. A thought occurred to him then.

"If names have power, why can't I use your name to make you do what I want? Your name is Korivare, and I know it. Can I get you to dance for me?"

"Names and names are different. A name like Korivare is what we call each other so we don't have to call everyone 'you'. They are, however, shadows of real Names. I call you Pax because I suspect you want to be peaceful, even if sometimes you…" Korivare trailed off, not wanting to mention Pax's Rage.

"Anyway. Our names have an effect on our identity, and our identity forms the bedrock of our Names. If I just kept calling you 'that troll over there,' it would be easy for you to start to believe that's all you were. You'd start acting like just a troll, and then that would be your identity."

"Instead, you give me a name and treat me like a person."

"And you rise to the occasion. You accept that there is more to you than a mere monster, and thus," he snapped, "your identity, and by extension your Name, change to fit."

"So, Names can change?"

"In ways. It's like gold. A gold bar is not the same as a coin, but they're both just gold. Your Name encompasses everything you are and everything you have the potential to be. Some of that potential is realized and some abandoned. That changes a piece of who you are, and opens up new potentials. The core of your being, on the other hand, is consistent. That core is also in your name, and is the piece that doesn't change."

"This sounds very complicated."

"And now you know why there haven't been any real Namers since the end of the God Wars and the burning of the Libras Univertas. Once all that knowledge was lost and civilization was fragmented, there wasn't enough left for anyone to learn how to do it."

"What about the True Namers. You mentioned they were naturally good at Naming, right? Couldn't they go back to teaching people the way they had before?"

"They did. If I remember correctly, one of the last True Namers was the first Master Namer at the University Arcanum. Once he died, one of his students took his place, but they were barely more than an Adept.

"Soon, everything we knew about Naming faded into legend. Some of the monks that raised me knew enough that they had the potential to be Adepts, but I doubt anyone else in the world knows a single Name."

Pax got sad at the thought of an entire magic art dying out because someone burned down a library. It seemed so violent and unnecessary. He didn't know how to read, but he saw the way some people treated books. They were like precious treasure, and those people just lit it on fire. Just one more reason Pax did not like fire.

CHAPTER THIRTY

Get Out

Pax awoke one morning to a woman praying before him. It was hard to tell exact numbers of days without access to the rising and setting of the sun. Still, Pax had counted ten full meals since his last encounter with a priestess of this wicked place.

At first, he stared at her wide-eyed and terrified, wondering if she was going to treat him as the other priestess did when she... But no, she finished her prayer and Pax could still flex his fingers and move his jaw. When his fear subsided, he saw that this woman wasn't wearing robes like the other priestesses. Instead, she wore the road clothes of the women that brought their meals, but she was the first one he'd seen perform the magic of the priestesses.

She looked up at him. "We can speak freely now. The other priestesses are watching, but I have placed an illusion around us. As far as they know, I'm examining you, making sure you haven't found a way to hurt yourself while you are staying with us."

"Ok." Pax didn't understand what she was talking about.

She continued, "you and your friends only have a few days left before the solstice. Our Lady's day is when they intend to sacrifice you at the top of this plateau. Your souls will be given to the Lady of Rays, and she will have successfully stopped you."

"Stopped us from what?"

She looked at him puzzled. "You don't know why she's after you?"

"No. No one has told us what she wants with us. The—" He

stopped. He didn't feel like mentioning his adventures in the Dream World to a stranger.

She waited for him to continue.

He didn't.

"I don't know either. I heard what my sisters were planning and it just... didn't feel right. They say you are just a monster and the men with you are going to use you to do terrible things, but..."

"Yes?"

"I've been listening to the four of you. My room is on the floor above this one, and I can hear you singing with each other, telling stories, and laughing... when you do laugh that is."

Pax nodded. Gerald usually tried at least a handful of jokes to lighten the mood each day, but they only worked occasionally. It became less effective as the question of when they were going to die loomed larger and heavier.

"I want to help you escape. I've been thinking of a couple of ways to get you out of here, but the desert outside is harsh, and I don't know how to get you somewhere safe."

"Can you get us water?"

"Of course. That's not the issue. I—"

Pax raised a hand. "If you can get us enough water for us to survive, we can take care of the rest once we are out of here. This isn't the first time we've had to do this."

The priestess chuckled. "Does that mean what Madam says is true?"

"What do you mean?"

"She claims the Lady of Rays has sent a dragon and an army of bug-creatures out to hunt you down. According to her, you thwarted both attacks and have even gained a small following within one of the city temples. Madam claims the Lady of Rays is furious with that temple for assisting you and their prayers are going unanswered."

"Your goddess, this Lady of Rays, is she really after us?"

The priestess nodded.

"And you don't know why?"

She shook her head. "Like I said, according to Madam, you're a monster bent on destruction."

Pax scowled at the word. "Whose this 'Madam' you keep mentioning? It sounds like her and I need to have a few words before we make our escape." Pax's thoughts were turning dark.

"She's the one who leads our group. She was called by the Lady of Rays to go into the desert and begin a new generation of her worshipers."

How would Korivare act? Perhaps he could ask the paladin when he next got the chance.

The woman glanced over her shoulder. "They're coming with your meals. I have to go. I'll be in touch with details of how to get you guys out before the solstice." She turned and walked out of the room before Pax could respond.

#

"The solstice?" Korivare said. "That's what they're waiting for? I should've known. Of course, they'd choose the most important day in the Sun Queen's calendar."

Pax had just finished telling his friends what the woman told him about Madam's plan. He didn't mention the escape plan. She said they were being watched, and he didn't know if he could trust her anyway. As far as he was concerned, their own escape plan was the one they were going with. If she helped, fine. If not, they'd get to safety on their own.

"What did she mean our souls would belong to the Sun?" Gerald asked. Korivare was still kicking himself from not realizing the day they were to be sacrificed, so it took him a minute to realize Gerald was talking to him.

"Hm? Oh! Posthumous Claim is a common belief among cults that practice human sacrifice. The idea is that if your death is dedicated to a power, usually a god, and the ritual is done in the proper way, that god gets first claim on your soul, or whatever eternal version of you the cult specifically believes in."

"Is it true?" Pax asked.

"I doubt it. It seems entirely unjust to have someone's whole-life dedication to one deity be erased or ignored because someone else killed them. The gods of justice would never allow such a farce to pass into cosmic law."

"It would," Gerald noted, "explain why gods with small cult followings often see rises in power."

"Inspiring fear of your god works as well as genuine faith in the short term. It's not as sustainable if you want your god to have a more permanent place in a pantheon, but fear still has its own powers."

"Isn't there a similar rule with kings?" Pax asked. "I think I've heard something similar before. 'To be feared over loved is folly, for a short time...'" Pax trailed off.

"'To be loved, rather than feared, is difficult enough, but it will not pass when you grow old. To be feared instead, will bring you folly, and a crown of bronze rather than gold.' It's from a poem by Hart the Piper. That man had such a way with words. It's no wonder his songs are favored among the Wood Elves," Gerald said.

"I don't really understand the crown thing, but it stands to reason that the same would be true of gods. People don't like things they're afraid of. I would know," Pax said.

"They only fear you because you're bigger than their horses. If they took half a second to speak to you, they'd know you're practically harmless," Gerald told him.

"Not harmless," Pax said. He thought of all the times he'd hurt someone because of his Rage.

"Ok not *harmless*, but I've never known someone who holds back like you. I see the way you calm yourself when you start to get mad or anxious. It doesn't always work, but I'm amazed at how often you make it work."

Pax's mouth split into a smile. He'd never realized how much Gerald had been watching him. It was nice to know some people understood how hard he worked to stay calm.

"We're getting off track," Korivare said. "You said this woman told you she thinks Madam is wrong about us being evil?"

"Yeah."

"Seems like a convenient excuse. I suspect this 'Madam' knows why we're being hunted. If she hasn't told the rest of the women here, or even lied to them about it, she's playing a dangerous game."

"What do you mean?"

"You said this woman lives on the floor above us. I'll bet gold to copper she isn't the only one. If a bunch of these priestesses think they are ridding the world of a great evil, and they hear that great evil under their feet singing and telling stories..."

"Then many of them would come to a similar conclusion to the woman who visited you. Add to that the fact that many of them are being told to come in to our cells while we are unrestrained and feed us. These women can't possibly think we're as cruel or evil as is being claimed."

"Exactly," Korivare said. "I think this might be a trap of some sort. This woman gets you to trust her, and we reveal whatever escape plan we have. Then they shut it down."

"Speaking of which," Gerald said. "I think I have the counter song that will confuse them enough to stop their prayers. All we need is a key and Pax's muscles. Then, we're out of our cells, and out the door."

"What about water?" Pax asked. "We know how to find food in the desert, but we don't know any water sources around here, and we wouldn't know where to start looking."

"Kist!" Gerald cursed. "I hadn't thought of that. Maybe we could use this woman to our advantage then. If she comes back, Pax you have to get her to believe you don't trust her."

"Shouldn't be too hard. I don't."

"Right. Then, she'll ask you what she can do to change that. Tell her to show you where their water is. We can fill up before we go. After that, well, they have to be getting water somewhere, right? I'm sure we can find it too."

"How?" Jiang spoke up. It was the first time in days that he had spoken.

"I was beginning to think they'd gotten to you already. How ya feeling?"

"Cold. But hot."

"Like a fever?" Korivare asked.

"What?"

"It's when your body gets hot because you're sick."

"Oh. Yes. It is a fever."

"Have they given you any medicine?"

"Yes. I'm not taking it. It's probably poison."

"They aren't going to poison us. If they were, they'd put it in your food first."

Pax stopped listening to the conversation. Jiang was sick? And he wasn't taking his medicine. Was his first friend going to die before they could get him out of this horrible place?

CHAPTER THIRTY-ONE

Helping Freinds

Pax spent the rest of the day worrying about Jiang's illness. When the woman in charge of bringing their food showed up, Pax listened as she tutted over Jiang. He heard the door open and the woman grunting and encouraging someone to "keep going." Where was she taking him? Hopefully it was to be healed, but could they take that chance? They should escape now, water or no water, his friend needed help. "Gerald."

"Yeah?"

"You have a key?"

"I'll get hers when she comes back."

They waited. Pax began pacing his tiny room with anticipation, and, more than once, kicked his clay chamber pot by accident. By the third time he'd done this, he felt his Rage boil up and threw his back against the wooden door in frustration and pain. The door creaked under the weight of his strength as his Rage swelled. Pax felt the oak of the door splinter and shatter under the strain.

Gerald shrieked. "What was that? Pax did you knock down your door? I don't have the key!"

It was too late to worry about that. They were escaping. Now. Pax took two quick steps and was in front of Korivare's door. He pushed with all his might, but the door stayed firm. He backed up a few paces and charged the door, and he was thrown back when the door didn't budge.

"Hold on," Korivare said from the other side. Pax heard a *thump* and Korivare cursed. The sound of footsteps echoed from the stairs leading up into the plateau.

Pax had one last thing to try. He bent down and grasped the under side of Korivare's door. He pulled. When the wood started to bend, he also pushed up with his legs. Every muscle in his body went tight, and the bottom half of the door cracked and splintered.

Korivare slid out under the opening. He was wearing his chain shirt, and it made a scraping and ringing sound as it scraped against the stone. The footsteps came more frantic.

Pax looked at Korivare. There were a few candles on the walls, so he was mostly in shadow. Still, Pax caught it when he pointed at Gerald's door.

"On three," he said. "One. Two. Three." They both charged the door. It flung open immediately. Gerald was on the other side playing his harp. Pax and Korivare tumbled through the open doorway and crashed against the opposite wall.

"Turns out one of the songs I know is also an unlocking spell," Gerald said sheepishly. His allies stood and brushed themselves off.

Korivare gave him a dark look, but the footsteps were getting closer. The three friends huddled in the tiny room together and Pax closed the door just enough so he could still see outside.

The woman came back with a tray of bowls. The tray clattered to the ground when she saw what had happened to the two doors, but before she could do anything else, Pax jumped out and grabbed her.

He put his hand over her mouth and whispered in her ear, "we aren't going to hurt you. We just want to know where you took our friend. If you lead us to him, we'll take him, leave, and you won't have to tell anyone you helped us."

The woman nodded and he let her go. "You aren't going to be able to get out of here. That door," she pointed toward the way they'd been brought in, "stays locked unless Madam herself unlocks it. The only other way outside is to the top of the plateau. Unless you plan on jumping to your deaths, you're stuck."

"Just lead us to Jiang. We'll take care of the rest ourselves."

She shrugged. She led them up the stairs and through a handful of hallways. Occasionally, they ran into others in the hallway, and the woman leading them would shove them in a closet, or gesture around a corner for them to hide.

She brought them to a room that had a strong anti-septic smell. The room was about the size of two of their cells pushed together and had a clean linen bed; a cabinet that was open to reveal all sorts of bandages, needles and jars; a wash basin; and an unconscious warmage with his clothes thrown in a heap in the corner.

"What did you do to him?" Pax demanded.

"He was fighting too much. We had to treat him and this was the only way that he'd stop moving."

"How are you treating him?" Korivare asked. "Have you diagnosed him?"

"No. I had to go feed our other prisoners, so I didn't exactly have time."

Korivare didn't say anything else. He merely walked to the unconscious warmage and put his hands on Jiang's temples. A soft gold light appeared around him as he began whispering. He closed his eyes for the space of three long breaths.

When he opened them, he looked Pax in the eye. "Desert flu. He most likely picked it up while his body was weak with heat exhaustion. He's been fighting it ever since." He looked at the woman standing in the room with them. "His living conditions didn't make it easier either. It gets warm in those cells you know. I'm surprised he lasted this long."

"We gave him medicine," she said, but her voice was quiet. She knew that wasn't good enough.

Korivare rolled up his sleeves and looked through the cabinet. "Go outside, close the door and turn away anyone who tries to come in here. I'm going to do what you should've done when we got here."

She gave him an angry look, but she obeyed. Korivare took out several jars, one at a time, sniffed them, shook his head, and put them back. He got to one that, when he opened it, he raised an eyebrow. He sniffed, then put a small amount of the green paste on his fingers and spread it around. He closed his eyes for a moment, then nodded, taking the rest of the jar to where Jiang was laying down.

"Pax. I need you to hold his shoulders. I don't know how he will react when he wakes up, but I need him against this table while I work. Gerald, I need some extra healing magic."

"I have a song for that."

"I know. Start playing. This may end up being a long process, but I'll be damned to the Nine Hells if I let Jiang succumb to a preventable disease like this."

Gerald started strumming and a quiet, lilting melody filled the room as Pax held his friend to the table. Korivare began to spread the paste on his chest, and his eyes flew open. He pushed against Pax's hold. Then he looked up at Pax, and Pax could see no recognition in his eyes.

Confused, Pax looked at Korivare, but he just shook his head and continued applying the paste, muttering under his breath. Jiang continued to struggle, but Pax held him down. It broke the troll's heart to see his friend in so much fear, and he didn't understand why he looked at the men around him like strangers.

"It's the fever," Korivare said when he saw Pax's eyes welling up with tears. His forehead glistened with sweat. "I expect that's also the reason he's been so quiet lately. At least, why he's been more quiet than usual. The fever has started to make him forget things, including us."

"Can you fix it?"

"I don't know. Minds are harder than bodies to fix, Pax. I'm doing what I can, but there are only a handful of people in the world that truly understand that sort of thing. I, unfortunately, am not one of them."

Pax struggled to come to terms with that. He wasn't sure if he could stand Jiang looking at him like this for the rest of their lives, even if they did end on the solstice. He thought about what Jiang must think, seeing the great green monster holding him to a table while a stranger puts his hands all over the warrior's naked body. Pax knew what that was like, and he tried to think of some way to get Jiang to understand that they were helping him. Could he understand through the fever?

Jiang continued to thrash, but Pax held firm. Whether or not Jiang knew they were helping, they were. He was going to get better. Korivare promised he'd do everything to help Jiang, and Pax trusted him. Korivare was a hero, and heroes helped people in need.

Korivare moved back to Jiang's head. The golden light appeared around his hands again. He began whispering, and Jiang stilled. His eyes closed and his breathing became steady. He was asleep.

CHAPTER THIRTY-TWO

Escaping Fate

Korivare nodded to Gerald, who stopped playing. "He needs rest now," Korivare said.

"We don't have time for rest. If that woman out there decides to give us up, we have nowhere to hide."

Korivare sat on the floor and put his head against the cabinet. He was breathing heavily. Pax wondered how much his healing magic took out of him. He decided he ought to ask. "Why are your healing spells so exhausting?"

Korivare looked at him with tired eyes. "Life for life. Blood for blood. That's the ancient law. Our bard friend gets around this by reinforcing existing life force, but that has its limits. I..." He started breathing heavy again.

"He gives his own life force to the person he's healing. A lot of people believe this shortens the caster's own life in order to extend the one of the patient's, but..." Gerald trailed off.

"But that assumes we all have a discrete amount of life to give," Korivare finished. "Only fools who believe in destiny, like me, think that way. Right Gerald?"

"I didn't mean it like that."

Pax looked from one to the other. They seemed to be having a moment, but Pax didn't know what they were talking about.

The three friends waited a long time for Jiang to wake, but a hard knock came from the door first. "We know you're in there. Don't make us use our magic to get you back in your cells. If you do, it will end badly for all of you." Madam banged on the door again.

"What do we do?" Gerald whispered. "I told you we didn't have time for this. This was our one chance to get out of here and we blew it."

Pax put his head in his hands. Then he felt something. He looked down at the ring on his finger with the two pale stones and one dark one. "Meses. Of course. He can help us."

"He said he can't fight. What is he going to do, tousle their hair in a breeze?"

"He can get weapons for us. We've fought our way out of worse situations than this. Meses. Help us."

There was no answer. The stone didn't turn. Meses didn't come. Pax's last hope for salvation died as quickly as it had risen.

The banging came again. "I won't ask again."

Pax's thoughts turned dark. They were all going to die, but he wasn't going to die in a cell or on some altar as an offering. "Get your song ready Gerald."

"Pax, what do you mean?"

Pax stood and walked toward the door. He wasn't going to succumb to these priestesses again. He was going to die fighting. Gerald saw there was no arguing with him, so he started playing a discordant sound. It sounded nothing like music, and it made Pax's brain itch.

Pax threw open the door, and as soon as the women on the other side heard the horrible sound coming from the harp, their brows knit in confusion, and their hands, moments ago folded in prayer, covered their ears.

Pax charged the woman called "Madam" and threw her to the floor. The other priestesses looked at the two on the floor, confused. Pax wrapped his hands around Madam's neck and squeezed. He thought of the fear he felt when they puppeteered him around and squeezed tighter. He thought of the woman that had forced herself on him and squeezed tighter. He thought of Jiang and squeezed tighter.

His muscles tensed, and he was thrown back and to the ground by an unseen force. Madam stood, rubbing her throat and breathing very carefully and coughing. Some of the priestesses around her moved to aid her, but she waved them off. Pax stood, Rage burning like hot coals inside him.

"How could you follow this bitch?" he demanded of them. "Look what she's done to my friend. She let him get sick, and now he's either going to die or forget me." His voice cracked with rage and pain at the last words.

The priestesses looked at each other. They wore expressions of open surprise. "The beast speaks?" one of them said. She must not be one of the priestesses that could hear them singing. Pax wondered what other information was kept from these women.

"It's a trick. You saw how it attacked me. It needs to be put down for the safety of all people," Madam said. She stood. Her throat seemed to be largely healed, and Pax wondered if he'd overestimated the force he'd used, or if she'd used healing magic.

Pax grabbed Madam's head and shoved her back to the ground. He stood over her, and she looked up at him. For the first time since she'd captured them, he saw fear in her eyes. The other women just stood and watched as Pax picked up Madam and threw her against a wall. "Why? Why does your whore goddess want us dead?"

The fear was gone from her eyes now. She sneered at him and spat. Saliva landed on Pax's cheek, but he didn't flinch. He pulled her away and slammed her against the wall again. Her head smacked against the stone, and she started blinking.

One of the priestesses started doing her chanting prayer, and Pax's hands opened without his permission. Madam fell to the floor in a heap, and Pax went to his knees. He tried to fight it, but he knew it was of no use. He was going to be taken to another cell and killed on the solstice.

Then, Pax saw a flash and heard a crack of thunder. The prayer turned into a gasp, and he was able to move his own body again. He turned to look, and he saw Jiang sitting up on the table, hand outstretched toward the priestesses. He had an angry look in his eye, but he was breathing heavily.

Korivare looked stunned, but Gerald was grinning from ear to ear. He started to play the lilting melody again, and Jiang drew up to his full height, jumped off the table and stood in the doorway. He didn't seem to notice or care that he was naked. His eyes were locked in a white-hot fury on Madam.

"No. Not my friend. You stop."

Pax's heart soared at the words. He remembered. The sickness was gone and Jiang hadn't forgotten him. The pair was ready to fight.

CHAPTER THIRTY-THREE

Facing The Sun

With Jiang giving him support, and Gerald filling them both with extra energy through his music, Pax fought with a vigor he hadn't felt since they took on the dragon. He threw priestesses off him, punched some in the stomach and sent them crumpling to the ground, and got to Madam again in the space of a few breaths.

Before Pax could lay a finger on her, however, she spoke a couple of words in quick succession, and a flash of light blinded him. He flailed about wildly searching for Madam's arms, neck, or clothes. He'd take any part of her, if it meant he could work out his Rage on her. At the same time, he tried to blink away the dots floating in his vision.

Unfortunately, they didn't go away before he felt hands on his back and he felt his knees give way as the priestesses began their prayer. Apparently, they had gotten over the confusion of Gerald's song. When the dots finally did go away, Pax couldn't turn his head, but he was sure the others had been captured again as well.

Madam stood over Pax, and his head was forced up so he could meet her eyes. They both gave each other venomous glares. She did not mask her unrelenting hatred for Pax, but he didn't care. He was tired of being afraid of her and her priestesses.

He had almost lost his best friend to sickness because of her neglect. In a few days he'd lose his life because of her goddess' prejudice. He hated this woman, and her hating him back suited him just fine.

"Clearly we cannot wait for the solstice," Madam announced. "The Lady of Rays will simply have to accept her sacrifice early. Sisters, go prepare the altar." Several of the priestesses bowed and walked away as others put Pax in chains.

Pax's heart dropped out of his chest. He expected to have a few days left of life, not a few moments. All the rebellious hatred he felt for Madam wilted at the idea that, by the next sunset, his life would be given over to the most aggressive aspect of the Sun Queen.

He and the other three were marched up to what Pax guessed was the last floor before the top of the plateau. It had several stone benches that were too low and narrow for sitting. The stone was smoothed out, and had divots carved into them in pairs. Each of them was roughly a hand span across.

All the rows were under a skylight that let in the sunlight. The sunlight created a circle around the stone benches, and it made the rest of the room look shadowy.

The four men were brought to thick wooden spikes that looked like they had been driven into the stone fairly recently. Their chains were attached to the spikes, and they were left hanging by their arms and sitting on the cold stone outside the circle of sunlight.

Then, a sound like a large temple bell began to ring. Pax looked around, but he couldn't tell what the source of the sound was, or where it was coming from. As it rung, several women, some in the dirty white robes of priestesses and others in road clothes, filed into the room.

Pax realized that this must be the whole of the population of the wilderness cult that had trapped them. He searched for the woman who assaulted him, but he could barely remember her face. All the priestesses here wore the same disheveled white robes, and he couldn't be sure who had done it.

They each stood before a pair of divots. When everyone was present, they all simultaneously knelt, their knees fitting easily into the divots. Each of them bowed theirs heads, and, from where Pax was sitting, the sunlight shone down on them like a spotlight.

They began chanting:

Oh! great Mother of Light

We beseech you, grant us might

Before you our enemies fall

You who hear our call

You are the Mighty Warrior

who slays the Shadows of Night

Nothing can be hidden

from your sight

We give you our lives

You give us peace

> Our faith in you
> Will never cease

The unity of their chant gave Pax an uneasy feeling. It reminded him of the chittering and clicking of the formains with their hive mind. They started humming and chills went down Pax's spine.

Madam stepped into the center of the circle of light, and they all stopped at once. "Sisters, fellow daughters of Her Majesty. I come before you today, Her humble servant, to announce our victory over evil.

"About a month ago, I lead many of you on a pilgrimage of sorts. The Lady of Rays sent us to capture a great beast and the evil men who were controlling it. These evil men have been locked in our humble temple ever since our return.

"As many of you know, our original plan was to send these evil souls to Her Majesty on her most sacred day. This was going to be part of a great many ways we would celebrate how the Lady of Rays conquered the evil Night King and ushered in a new age of peace for all who follow her.

"Alas, some of you have proved disloyal to Her Majesty, and allowed the agents of evil to escape. Many of you sitting here witnessed the savagery with which the beast attacked me. He nearly killed me.

"Even now," her hand went to her throat, "speaking to you is difficult. It is no matter. Our goddess watches over me, and I will heal. However, the disloyalty shown by some in our midst cannot be healed." Madam stopped and allowed the crowd before her to stir.

She began to move through the rows of kneeling followers. Each person she passed looked stricken with fear. "Her Majesty is, of course, merciful to those who struggle with their loyalty to her. If you confess and repent, your punishment will be swift and, afterward, you will receive forgiveness." She paused and waited.

A woman stood. "I'm sorry Madam. I gave one of the evil men an extra piece of bread the other day. He looked like he was suffering and I wanted to help. I thought if I showed him kindness, I could turn his heart."

Madam approached the woman and struck her on the face. Then, Madam promptly took the woman's head in her hands and cradled her like a child. She kissed the woman's forehead. "You are forgiven for your trespass." She turned to the rest of the room. "Would anyone else like to confess their sins?"

Silence. Then another woman stood. "I tore Nami's robes and tried to hide it until I could fix it."

Another woman shouted, "I knew it was you!"

Madam held up her hand for silence. She approached the standing woman. Instead of striking her, she took the woman's chin in between her fingers and pulled her face up.

"That was very wrong of you. I am disappointed in your carelessness toward your fellow sister." The woman hung her head and Madam moved on.

She prowled the rows of kneeling women. She stopped behind a woman wearing road clothes, and Pax recognized her as the woman that offered to help him escape. His eyes lingered on her fearful face.

Madam looked at him, but he was already looking elsewhere. His eyes went back to her just in time to see Madam walk away. Pax looked through the crowd to see if he recognized anyone else.

He did. In the third row was the woman who brought him, Korivare, and Gerald to Jiang to treat him. His eyes bounced to Madam, making sure she wasn't looking at him and then back to the woman.

"You are being deceived, my sisters. Even now, the enemy betrays you."

Pax started looking around randomly, worried Madam had spotted him looking. He looked at each of his friends, but their heads were down. When his eyes went back to Madam, a priestess Pax hadn't seen before was whispering in her ear. She nodded. The other priestess walked away. Pax followed her with his eyes. She and three others took the two women Pax was looking at and held their arms to their backs.

The two women were marched by the priestesses up to the front to stand before Madam. "You have betrayed your sisters. Explain yourselves."

"I was threatened." One of the women said. "They escaped their cells, and the monster threatened to crush me until I promised to take him to his wizard friend."

"What is your mortal life compared to the salvation Her Majesty offers?" Madam demanded.

"My apologies Madam. It won't happen again."

"No. It won't." She turned to the other woman. The sunlight let Pax get a better look at her than the flickering light of candles. She was young, barely more than a girl. She was as skinny as a rail.

In fact, many of the women, now that he saw them better, seemed poorly nourished at best. Madam, and the women holding the two girls looked healthy and well fed. Anyone wearing robes seemed to be at least taken care of. Not one of the women in road clothes looked like they had eaten well in months.

"I heard them singing. I live just above them and I heard them talking to each other every night. They told stories and laughed with each other. I knew then that they couldn't be the villains you claim them to be. I may not know them well, but I do not believe they deserve to die."

Madam struck her hard across the face. She fell to the ground, and Madam kicked her once. "You blaspheme against Her Majesty's will. Your words are ashes on your tongue. You know nothing. How dare you question me?" She nodded and the young woman was pulled roughly to her feet. "Both of you will be sacrificed along with those vile men."

The other girl looked aghast. "Madam. I... you... have mercy. Please."

"You betrayed your sisters. Disloyalty and blasphemy are stains on our community. The only way to wash us clean of them is with your blood."

CHAPTER THIRTY-FOUR

Gifts for the Queen

The two girls were bound and brought to two other pegs on the wall. Madam was handed a book. She opened it and began reading.

"On the fifth day of the battle, the Lady of Rays went to her followers and said 'You are my daughters. Your men are my subjects and I will keep you safe in the coming fight. I shall be with you and go ahead of you. Your devotion is my strength; your resolve is my sword.'

"There was a great cheer from the crowd, and the women began to prepare their husbands and sons for battle. They gave them breastplates made by their wives and mothers. They armed them with sword and shield, and anointed their heads with oil.

"As promised, the Lady of Rays went ahead of her great army. Her own son drove her chariot. Her daughters sat in prayer, and with their faith, the army was strengthened. The fight lasted another two days. By the end, Her army was victorious, and the Night King was driven back."

She closed the book. "It is our faith, beyond anything else, that keeps the Night King at bay. Our faith gives our Lady strength, and in turn, she keeps the forces of evil back. If our faith waivers, the forces of our enemies would fall on us like rabid dogs, and we would all be slain."

The women that were still kneeling bowed their heads. They began another prayer. This one was so soft that, even with all of them chanting in time, Pax couldn't make out the words. As they reached the end of their prayer, Pax could swear the sunlight shinning down on them was brighter. He wasn't quite sure though.

They finished their prayer and Madam dismissed all the girls in road clothes to "attend to their duties." The priestesses, however, stayed. Madam had them rise in unison, and they turned to their, now six, prisoners. Their faces were unreadable, but Pax caught many of them lingering on the two women chained to the wall. He couldn't begin to know what they were thinking.

The priestesses that stood beside Madam took the prisoners' chains off their pegs, and pulled everyone roughly to their feet. Madam approached Pax and whispered so only he could hear, "I'm going to kill you last for what you did to me. That way your final moments in this world are spent completely alone and without a single friend to speak of."

Pax was silent. Her words didn't scare him anymore. He saw her for the manipulative crone she was. If he was going to die, he'd do it without giving her the satisfaction of seeing his fear.

They were marched up a set of stairs set into the wall opposite the door they had entered through. The stairs led to the top of the plateau. The harsh desert sunlight hurt Pax's eyes after a month of dark candlelit chambers. He had to blink the unrelenting light out of his eyes before he saw what was before him.

Six stone slabs covered in chains sat in a u-shape around the stone hole that served as a skylight to the room below. Each prisoner was led to their own slab and bound by their hands, feet, and chest in heavy iron. Madam stepped to the middle of the skylight, holding a vicious looking dagger with a gold and gem encrusted hilt. She reached out her hands and threw her head toward the sky, breathing deeply.

"Dear sisters, the moment has come for us to rid this world of not one, but two terrible evils. The evil of the faithless will be given over to the Lady of Rays along with the evil of the Night King. I—"

A shadow passed over them, and Madam paused. Something was circling above them. She smirked and looked toward Pax. "It would seem Her Majesty has sent an envoy to witness your destruction."

The shape descended, and Pax saw the tail, the wings, and the horns. It was a dragon. Pax's heart beat faster. If this thing was truly sent by their goddess, would it be under their control? Would it decide to shoot lightning down on the group instead? Perhaps it was the mate of the dragon they had slain come to take its revenge.

The dragon continued its descent, but another shape flew off it. It was much smaller, and roughly human shaped. The priestesses began to scramble around. Madam's face fell as the dragon landed, and its tail swept through her ranks of followers.

A hail of arrows flew from somewhere Pax couldn't see. They broke through the chains holding Pax and his friends to their slabs. Pax's eyes went wide, and he examined one of the arrows. It was made of a silvery blue metal that was so sharp Pax saw blood running down his fingers before he knew he'd been cut. His skin closed up quickly though.

The dragon roared on the other side of the plateau, and spit out a gout of flame. Pax scrambled away from the creature, trying desperately to not get burned. He stopped at a piece of stone that reached up out of the plateau like a shard of glass pointed toward the blue sky.

On top of the tall spire there was a fair skinned elf in leather armor. She was shooting arrows down at the women who were trying to get control of the dragon. "Get the others. We are getting out of here."

It took a moment for Pax to realize she was talking to him because she hadn't looked down. He didn't realize she knew he was there, but he nodded. He thought about what he was doing and that she wasn't looking at him. Instead, he said, "ok," and moved away toward his friends.

He moved carefully, not wanting to catch the attention of the dragon. He made it over to Gerald, who was trying to grab his harp without getting smacked by the dragon's tail.

"The elf-girl said we're leaving."

"Do you think we can trust her?"

Pax looked at her, still shooting arrows at the priestesses. "She seems to be on our side. Do we have another choice?"

Gerald shrugged and grabbed his harp. He started walking over to her, making gestures at Jiang and Korivare to follow him. Pax, on the other hand, wanted to make sure Madam didn't get out of this alive.

He marched around to where the dragon was biting and clawing, leaving at least one priestess in a bloody heap with each strike. Madam was toward the back, making her way to the stairs leading into the plateau. Pax yelled at her, and she turned.

He charged at her and she darted down the stairs. She wasn't quick enough, however, and Pax grabbed hold of her collar. He hauled her back up on top of the plateau. There was a whistle from behind Pax, but he didn't turn around. All his focus was on this low-life crone who had been the cause of so much of his suffering.

He held her by the robes over the edge of the plateau. He barely noticed the sounds of battle coming to a halt behind him. Madam clung desperately to his hands as she stared down at the ground at least a hundred feet below. Her eyes were full of fear, and Pax felt his

Rage stir and awaken inside his stomach. "Are you scared of dying? What is the end of a mortal life compared to the salvation your Lady promised you?"

She looked at him, panic-stricken, and he sneered back at her. "Pleases don't let go. I'll fall and..."

"Don't you trust your goddess to catch you? Or do you not really believe all that faith nonsense you preach about? Are you using those women like you used me? Is everyone just a toy to you?"

She didn't answer. She just clung helplessly to Pax's arms. Pax felt a hand on his shoulder. He turned to see the elf who had come to save him. "Put her down. Safely. You've made your point."

The look she gave him stilled his Rage, and he suddenly felt very ashamed for holding an aging woman over her own doom. He set her down on the solid stone of the plateau, but he wasn't too gentle. He wasn't that ashamed.

"You," Madam said. "You're one of His aren't you. To think, a woman like you, a slave to men." She spat the last word out like it was made of sand and ash

"I am no one's slave," the elf replied. "I serve my family. I am free and happy. You are the slave."

Madam continued her long-winded tirade, but the elf just gave her a witheringly stern look, turned and motioned Pax to follow her.

CHAPTER THIRTY-FIVE
New Allies

Pax pulled up short when the elf began climbing onto the dragon. "C'mon up. I promise you Raziren won't bite. At least, not so long as you don't look too much like food."

Her giggle afterward was the only thing that clued Pax into the fact that she was joking. He looked at the dragon's massive head and long serpentine neck. His scales and tight muscles spoke to a power that made Pax supremely uneasy.

The dragon looked at Pax. His mouth curved into something that could've either been a smile or a sneer. "Dah ti'n sarite Raziren," it said.

Pax didn't understand the creature's speech, but since the elf woman called the dragon Raziren, Pax guessed he had just introduced itself. He watched Korivare, Gerald, Jiang and the two women climb onto Raziren's back. Pax remembered the fire-breath and it paralyzed him.

The woman in road clothes looked at him with a deep emotion, but Pax couldn't figure out what it was. She appeared to be pleading with him to get on the dragon. His anxiety at the idea stirred his Rage. He reached out slowly to touch the dragon's scales. They were warm, but not hot.

The dragon's scales were smooth, hard and the color of bronze. Pax distanced his mind and his Rage from his actions as he climbed on the dragon's back. He couldn't see any other way to get his body anywhere near something that could breathe fire.

When Pax was seated firmly, Raziren beat his massive wings and lifted into the air. Pax felt the rush of air as they climbed higher and higher. The wind was loud in his ear, and he saw Gerald's mouth move, but he couldn't hear what was said. His lips seemed to say "(something something) incredible."

They landed somewhere in the desert wilderness. The elf helped the two young women down from the dragon, and as she did so, Pax noticed a saddle bag strapped to the dragon on the opposite side the he was clinging on to. Pax looked at his white-knuckled hands and tried to concentrate on releasing the tension he'd been holding.

He turned his attention back to the three women as the elf gave the other two packs from the saddle bag. The saddle bag was almost the same color as his scales, and Pax was so focused on not falling, he had assumed it was part of Raziren's leg. When the elf finished talking to the young women, she also gave them some money from her purse, and they walked away.

"Where are they going?" Gerald asked.

"I gave them directions to a city that's only about a day's walk from here. They have food and water, so they should make it."

"And what about us? Are you taking us back to Farhan? Also, how'd you get this... I mean, how'd you get Raziren over the Great Divide. I thought it was impassable."

"I didn't get him over it. He got me through it. Dragons weren't part of the treaties that separated the world, so they were given special privileges when it comes to crossing barriers like the Great Divide. Every dragon has a way through the mountains."

"No kidding. That must be how Jeremy got across the mountains. It was one of the only things I couldn't think of how to ask him. I'd only ever seen homespun like his once before, and that's a whole story itself."

Korivare smacked the back of Gerald's head. "My apologies ma'am. While the bard might talk loudly enough for four people, he does not speak for us. What was your name?"

She gave an almost embarrassed smile that was a steep contrast to the stern look she gave Madam. "My name is Telemnar Glanodel. I was sent here to find the four of you and take you to Mount Koyasha in the Great Divide." She moved to the saddle bag and started to rummage through it. "I expect you'll be needing these for the journey."

She presented Pax's bow and arrows, Korivare's halberd, and Jiang's slightly curved arming sword. Gerald made a confused face and looked in the bag. "How'd those stay in here? The halberd alone is longer than any side of this bag."

"Dragons have all sorts of useful magic at their disposal. I expect that's where you got that cloak." She pointed at Pax's cloak. It had turned a bright bronze color to match the scales of the dragon.

He smiled sheepishly. "We ran into a dragon that was less friendly than Raziren. I think its mate may still be after us, but we haven't seen it."

Telemnar nodded. "Not all dragons are kind. I'm sure you did what you had to do. Do you know why those cultists were going to kill you?"

"Because their goddess asked them to, apparently," Pax said. "We've been trying to figure out why the gods are out to get us. The only thing I can think of is that the gods think Gerald is as annoying as we do."

Gerald opened his mouth to respond, then closed it, thinking hard.

"Did you say, Mount Koyasha?" Korivare asked before Gerald could say anything.

"I did. The monks there are eager to have you home. There are many things that need explaining, and they wouldn't tell me anything until I found the four of you."

Pax looked at Korivare. His face was a mix of emotions. "I guess I'm going home," Korivare said.

Pax put a hand on Korivare's shoulder in what he hoped was a consoling gesture. Korivare rested his hand on top of Pax's. Pax genuinely couldn't tell if the man was excited, terrified, or some mix of several things.

Korivare nodded. He took his halberd and placed it into the saddle bag. They all put their things back in the dragon's saddle bag with it, and everyone climbed on to his back. Raziren's wings stretched out for a long moment. It took a moment for Pax to realize the dragon was warming them in the desert sun.

When he did flap them down, it created a spinning cloud of sand. Pax was reminded of the fight with the other dragon. He stilled his anxiety by reminding himself that, if Raziren wanted to kill them, he had a prime opportunity on the plateau. Instead, they simply climbed into the sky.

When they were in the air, Pax felt a rhythmic rumbling move through the dragon's body. He pressed his ear against Raziren's back and heard him speaking low in his long neck. He couldn't make out the words exactly, but they sounded very similar to the ones he spoke to Pax. He wondered if this was some kind of language that the dragon knew.

As the rumbling continued, the air began to shimmer. Pax looked down at the ground, and, after getting over the initial vertigo of being thousands of miles in the air. He realized that the land below wasn't just speeding by. It was shifting.

The sands of the desert gave way to rocky terrain more quickly than Pax thought possible. Wasn't the dessert supposed to be bigger than that? The mountains on the horizon were also getting bigger much faster than Pax would assume possible.

He put his ear to Raziren's back again. He listened to the rhythm. It was the same one that Jiang used for his spells. This dragon was using magic to move them toward the mountains at supernatural speeds. Pax sat in wonder at what else magic, draconic or otherwise, could accomplish.

Jiang had used magic to protect them from lightning and even summoned lightning of his own. The priestesses had used theirs to puppet Pax around. This dragon clearly knew some very useful spells. Then there was Deep Magic. The stuff of legend. Was there no end to what magic could accomplish?

CHAPTER THIRTY-SIX

The Foot of Koyasha

Raziren deposited the group of five in a valley at the foot of a mountain that was so large it loomed over the rest of the Great Divide like a disapproving father. The low clouds covered its peak, and Pax couldn't begin to guess how someone could live that high up.

Telemnar went into the saddle bag and handed out everyone's gear. Pax got a bow too heavy for anyone else to draw; two quivers of arrows, one with red fletching and one fletched with hawk feathers; and a backpack filled with food, a waterskin, a bundle of rope, and a bedroll. She handed one of these to each of them with their other possessions. Something occurred to Pax at that moment.

"You got these from our caravan, right?" Telemnar nodded. "Did Farhan say anything about us? Does he miss us?"

"The Caravan Master? He was very worried about you, but he explained this wasn't the first time you had disappeared. He told me to tell you all that he still considers you all members of his family, and that he doesn't hold these disappearances against you."

Pax caught the look Telemnar got before she could hide it. "We aren't going back. Are we?"

"I don't know. I still don't have the biggest piece of the story. The monks at the summit of this mountain promised me that if I delivered you four to them, they'd explain everything. I do know that the world is changing, and we are either to blame, or the ones who are going to stop it. I don't know which one or if it's both. I just don't know."

Pax thought about never seeing Farhan ever again. He thought about never getting to say good-bye to one of the first people that accepted him and treated him like a person. Would he ever know how much he meant to Pax?

He thought of Iris and Fertul. Would they be able to understand why some of their pack wasn't with them anymore? Pax looked up toward the mountain's hidden peak. He was already so far from where he'd started and he still had so much further to go.

Raziren made his good-byes to everyone, and Telemnar gave him a hug and a bow for taking her to Maskohma. Then he disappeared into the side of the mountain. As far as Pax could tell, he somehow shifted through solid stone.

Jiang and Korivare gathered stones to make a fire pit, Gerald found a spot for his bedroll, and Pax started oiling his bow. He hadn't been able to do that very much since their adventure started, but the wood was still smooth and uncracked. He let out a small sigh of relief at that.

When camp was set up, Telemnar put her fingers up against the sun. It was low in the sky and she was able to put three fingers between it and the horizon. "We have a few hours before it starts to get dark. I'm going to go see what sort of dinner I can catch."

"Why?" Gerald asked. "Don't we have food in our packs?"

"If you think any amount of food that can fit in that thing," she said as she pointed to the bag "will feed you for the time it takes us to climb this mountain, you're thicker than tree sap in a winter storm."

The packs weren't small. In fact, the packs were taller than Gerald, and Pax wondered if he would be able to carry his. "If we are going to survive," Telemnar continued, "we are going to have to save what's in our packs for when we can't find food. That'll be more common as we climb, and I don't want to be hungry for the last week of hiking. That'll be the hardest, and starving won't help matters."

She shouldered her bow. "I'll lay out a couple of traps. Hopefully at least a few of them will be sprung before we have to leave in the morning, and I won't have to do as much for our breakfast. Are any of you worth a damn at hunting?"

Pax spoke up. "A wind spirit taught us all how to catch cobras and scorpions in the desert. Is there anything like that out here? Something that digs itself a hole we can scare it out of?"

"There may be a few things, but this soil is shallow and there's nothing but rock underneath, so I'd suggest looking for cracked rocks instead of holes."

Pax nodded. He gestured to his bow. "In that case, I might be able to help you catch something a bit bigger."

"Are you any good with that?"

He made a gesture with his hand like balancing a scale. "I miss sometimes, but the bow itself is really heavy. So, if I do hit, it'll punch right through my target."

"Heavy?" Gerald said. "I've held that thing. It's no heavier than a normal bow."

Telemnar shook her head. "Heavy doesn't mean heavy when you're talking about bows. Let me see." Pax strung the bow and handed it to her. She tried to pull it back, failed, and hung the bowstring on her finger. "You're right. It's draw weight is like nothing I've ever seen. What's it made of?"

Pax shrugged. "The archer at House Morkae gave it to me. He said only someone with my strength could wield it properly."

"That may be true, but a bow like this is better suited for punching through a breastplate than hunting. For now, why don't I teach you how to set traps, and we'll see about finding a branch to make you a hunting bow."

Pax nodded enthusiastically and followed Telemnar out of the campsite. She taught him about snares and the force it takes to break a small animal's neck.

"A lot of snares are made out of saplings and other bendy materials," she explained. "Not a lot of them have the force behind them to give your prey whiplash. If you can set the snare up so it hits them against something hard and sharp like a rock, it can do the killing for you. The blood will attract predators, so it's usually a bad idea unless your particularly squeamish. Have you killed anything cute before?"

Pax nodded.

"Good. I don't need you getting sentimental when we collect our morning meal."

They set several snares before they ran into a huge beast with antlers like a deer and a hump on its back. The thing was larger than a bear, so when Telemnar crouched and pulled out her bow, Pax looked at her surprised. She winked at him, then shot. The arrow caught in the creature's eye, and it collapsed before Pax even realized it was dead.

"Where did you learn to do that?" he asked. He didn't bother hiding his amazement. She smiled proudly as she stood. They walked over to the creature, and Telemnar pulled out a long, slender hunting knife. She dressed the animal with more efficiency than anyone Pax had ever seen.

"I've been doing this a long time. I spent a season in the wilderness living off just my wits and my bow." She caressed her weapon lovingly. "Feraliana has served me well ever since I made her."

"Feraliana?"

"It's elvish. It means 'wild child'. The clerics who raised me used to call me that when I was younger. When I made my own bow, it was like I had my own child to look after, so it seemed appropriate. It sounds better in elvish though."

"Wild child has a certain ring to it, but not for a bow. Feraliana is better."

She smiled again. "Can you help me carry this? I don't want to drag it. Leaving a blood trail is just asking for trouble."

Pax bent and threw the animal over his shoulder. It was heavier than anything he'd lifted in a while, so he grunted, but once it rested on his shoulder, it was easy to carry.

It was Telemnar's turn to be impressed. He carried it back to the camp where Gerald presented them with a scrap of cloth filled with berries. They were a blue so dark they were almost black, and the juices that were seeping out was purple.

"I saw some rabbits eating them off the ground. That was good enough for me to assume they would be ok to eat."

Telemnar nodded and he set them down near the fire. "It's too bad we don't have a jar. These things are practically gushing with juice. We could make preserves."

Pax set down the beast they'd brought back, and everyone got their first good look at its size. In Pax's arms, it looked like a normal deer, though an oddly shaped one. On the ground the three other men got to see the size of it. They looked at Pax and Telemnar, the question forming on their faces: "how did the two of you take down that thing?" "what is this strange creature?" and "how are you not dead?"

Pax put a friendly arm around Telemnar's shoulders and gave his friends a smug look. Telemnar matched it and crossed her arms. The three men looked at each other and silently agreed that was as much of an explanation as they were going to get.

The fire pit was expanded to accommodate their extra-large kill. Even still, Telemnar had to use her knife to cut large hunks of it off and cook them individually. The group ate until their fingers were stained with juice and their mouths were dripping with grease.

Pax ate until he felt his body rejecting the food he put in his mouth. He was full to bursting, and they still had most of the creature's ribs and one leg left.

It was fully dark by the time they were finished, and Gerald was telling a story he called "the Copper Blade King."

"So, the King decided that stealing the horse would be too risky. There was no way the orcs wouldn't notice and chase him to the coast to get it back. Instead, he went into a nearby patch of woods and found a pool of water.

"He sat there for two days and three nights until the moon was full and reflecting off the water's surface. That's when he heard a buzzing followed by lots of tiny giggling.

"He knew that he'd found a portal to the Fae Realm. He ignored the buzzing. He knew pixies would be of no use to him. Then he heard the clomping of hooves, but he knew that a satyr couldn't help him either.

"Finally, he heard soft singing. 'Erutan verfalios. Silatria tempa mor atrio.'"

"If that's supposed to be Faen," Telemnar laughed, "you're doing a poor job of it." Telemnar was off to the side, digging a pit for the leftovers. She had said if they left them to smoke overnight, they'd keep better on their hike. Pax offered to help, but she said being tired from this sort of work helped her sleep.

"You know Faen then?"

"I know enough to know that what you just said sounded like 'wind-blown leaves fall. The horse's shoes are made of butter.'"

"I'm guessing you know how it's supposed to go."

"Erati vortempa latora. Selat te milto aria," she sung. "It means 'no wise man can see what my heart has lost. My song of sorrow is for you my love.'"

Gerald strummed his harp idly. "That does sound a lot better. Can you sing it again?"

She did, and Gerald matched the melody perfectly with his harp.

"Do you know the rest?"

There were no more stories that night. Gerald was distracted by learning a new song, and everyone else was mesmerized by the song itself. When Gerald declared he had the majority of it, Pax was almost asleep sitting up. They all bedded down for the night, Telemnar finishing the pit and setting the meat to smoke before she lay on her bedroll.

CHAPTER THIRTY-SEVEN

Surviving Among Stones

The next morning Pax awoke to a flurry of activity from Telemnar. The sun was barely peaking over the horizon, and she was already half way through dividing the smoked meat from last night's kill. Pax approached and asked if he could help. Telemnar shook her head. "I've been good at this for a while. It'll go faster if I do it myself."

Pax nodded and looked around the camp. All their bags were packed and ready. A fire was smoldering quietly inside their ring of stones. There was nothing left to be done accept check the traps and prepare breakfast. He started to head out of the camp when Telemnar sprang to her feet and took three long strides toward him. "Are you going to check the traps?"

"Yeah." Pax could hear a forced quality in her conversational tone.

"I'll come with you. I can teach you how to dress a smaller creature. Some people say the smaller ones are easier, but I've been known to have difficulty."

Pax looked at her and raised an eyebrow. "I know how to dress a kill. I grew up hunting my meals."

"Oh. I'm sure you're great at it, but I'd rather be there if you need my help."

So, the two went around to each of their traps, taking apart the ones that were empty and collecting the animals from the ones that weren't. Every time Pax dressed one of the squirrels or rabbits, he saw Telemnar's hands clench into fist, or she would hold one with the other. By the time they got to the last trap, sprung by a rabbit that was looking at them and trying to jerk free, he handed her the knife.

She made quick work of the tiny thing, and Pax had to admit she was much more efficient than he was. Still, being treated like he didn't know something felt a little too much like how people normally treated him. He didn't make an issue of it. It was clear something about the situation was bothering her, but he didn't know her that well. If she wanted to talk, she would.

They got back to camp, and Gerald was practicing the song he'd learned last night. Telemnar went over to correct a piece of the melody, and Pax brought the three squirrels, two rabbits and some kind of small, yellow bird that had surprised him given all their traps were ground-level, over to Jiang who was tending the morning fire.

The two of them talked idly while preparing their morning meal. Jiang had found some wild mint he brewed into a tea using his waterskin. They passed the tea between them as the meat cooked for their morning meal. They were through about half of the brew when the meat was ready and everyone dug in for their breakfast.

The breakfast was gamey and tough. It reminded Pax of his childhood running through the forest with falling leaves spinning around him. He and Telemnar seemed to be the only ones who enjoyed the texture, but only Gerald voiced his objection.

"Don't get me wrong," he said. "It's a damn sight better than the thorn bushes we had to eat with Meses. I just wish we could've tenderized it a bit beforehand."

"Get used to that not being the case," Telemnar said. "There's a reason Raziren didn't drop us off at the front door of the monastery."

She looked at Korivare. The two seemed to share a moment of understanding, but Pax didn't know what she was talking about. Korivare merely nodded. His expression was determined and solemn. Pax was not sure what made him so stoic, but he hoped Korivare wasn't dreading seeing the monks of his monastery. Pax knew so little about why Korivare left.

When they had finished eating, they picked up their packs and followed Telemnar up a steep mountain path. It wasn't long before they were high enough to see the entire valley that they had camped in.

The wind was blowing strong enough to hear it constantly, and Pax had to raise his voice a bit to get his friends to hear him whenever he spoke. Telemnar marched up the path without pause. She had adopted Korivare's determined look, and Pax had to jog several times to keep her from getting too far ahead. When the sun had just passed its zenith, Gerald demanded they break for lunch, and Telemnar looked at him confused.

"The rest of us have been running to keep up with those stilts you call legs. I'm tired and I need a break. Jiang didn't get to refill his waterskin after we drank the last of the tea. Finally, I don't think the monks will be angry if we take our time getting to them."

He gestured to the peak. It was still hidden by low clouds, and it didn't look any closer than when he'd seen it from the valley below. "I don't know what they want from us, but we're no good to them if we die of exhaustion."

Telemnar rolled her eyes. "You're being dramatic. You aren't going to die of exhaustion from a single day's hike." She looked around at the other three.

Pax was breathing heavy, but mostly fine. Jiang was stoic, but Pax noticed he was signing "tired" and breathing hard as well. Korivare was looking as red-faced as Gerald. "I suppose you are right though. We can take a short lunch break."

They found a spot near the trail to sit and rest. Pax broke off a couple of branches and asked Telemnar to show him how to make a hunting bow. She agreed and they got to work. They braided a few pieces of stripped bark into rough twine. Pax used some of it to lash two pieces of green wood together, and the last he used as a bowstring.

"It's rough," Telemnar said. "A good hunting bow takes more than an hour to make. This one might break at any point, but it's easy to fix and will be effective at short range. After we get done with the monks, I can show you a spot where you can get really good wood for a bow."

"I'd like that." Pax smiled. They finished eating from their provisions: hard sausage, trail bread, and apples they baked with sun-warmed stones and a heat-transfer spell Jiang knew. Then they were back on their hike up the mountain.

The wind grew stronger as they climbed. Soon, Pax couldn't shout above it, and resorted to copying Jiang's hand sings to convey emotions. He couldn't think of any way to convey other ideas, but he got his point across when he needed to.

The sun was still above the horizon when Telemnar guided them to a cave. It was little more than a crack in the mountain side, but it was big enough for the five of them, and it kept them out of the relentless wind.

Pax and Telemnar tried to hunt for dinner, but with this much wind and barely anything but stones around them, they couldn't find anything worth bothering. Pax took some branches off a thorny tree and showed Telemnar Meses' trick for shaving off the thorns to make the branches edible.

"Wood isn't particularly nutritious," she interjected. "I suppose it'll keep our bellies full though." She looked at the tree where Pax had broken off the branches. She sighed. "If I had paid better attention to the lessons the clerics tried to teach me, I might know a spell that could help draw the sap out of that tree." She shouldered her bow. "I was too busy though: climbing trees, target practice, and playing in the underbrush."

"Sounds like you had a nice childhood."

"I guess. Still, I wish I would've prepared more for my future."

Pax gave a low chuckle. "Target practice and playing in the underbrush didn't make you a better hunter?"

Telemnar smiled. "I guess it did. Didn't it?"

They gathered a few branches, and headed back to the cave. "It's gonna be a hungry night, gentlemen." Pax declared when they entered. He presented the group with the stripped branches. Gerald grumbled a bit, but ate his share. They each took another apple out of their packs to bake. After the woody texture of the branches, the apple was sweet and soft.

"This wind reminds me of a story," Gerald said.

"A rock can remind you of a story," Korivare commented.

"If it has a particularly interesting shape, I dare say it might. Still, this story isn't about a rock. It's about a sailor, who got lost at sea."

CHAPTER THIRTY-EIGHT

The Sailor's Tale

One day a fisherman was out on the water, pulling his net along with his boat, when it caught on something, and he was pulled off the boat. He tried to pull the net with him but realized it was a lost cause and abandoned it. He swam toward his boat, but a wave crashed against it, sending it toppling.

The fisherman clung to the capsized boat as a storm started to churn the water around him. Sea foam splashed against his face. Waves tossed him and his little boat up and down until he was so disoriented, he couldn't tell right from left.

He felt something touch his leg, and he jerked it away in fear. It touched his leg again, wrapping around his ankle. He expected a slimy tentacle, but it was some kind of rough cord. Pulling it up with his leg, he saw it was his net.

"The sea must be feeling merciful today," the fisherman said to no one in particular.

He grabbed the net and heaved with all his might. He climbed on to the bottom of the boat and pulled as hard as his strong muscles could bear. Eventually, what the net was caught on broke the surface.

Among all the flailing fish, there was a clay jar with a cork stopper in it. The side had strange writing on it. Although, in fairness, the fisherman couldn't read. Still, he knew the look of words, and these writings didn't look like anything he'd seen before.

He uncorked the jar, and a massive wind came spewing out of the jar. It pushed the jar into the fisherman's chest, and he flew up into the clouds. The wind carried him a long way, occasionally skipping his body on the waves the way you'd skip a stone across a slow-moving river.

Eventually, the jar lost all the wind it had been carrying, and the man was left floating in the churning ocean with no land in sight. He called out to the sea god saying, "every day I sacrifice the best of my catch to you, so you may feast on it in your pearl-colored palace. Are you so calloused that you would let such a faithful servant die?"

I still don't know if the sea god heard his cry, or if the man was simply lucky, but his prayer was answered. A massive wave loomed over his head, and it crashed down on top of him. When he broke the surface of the water again, he was able to set his feet on sand. He walked out of the sea onto a beach. He saw no people, nor the footprints in the wet sand that told him people had been there. It was just him and the mighty sea behind him.

For three days, he lived off what he could gather from the surrounding jungles. For three nights, be built a bonfire twice as tall as a man and hoped the light would signal to passing ships that he was trapped. On the fourth day, a man wearing nothing but beads woven into his hair approached the fisherman.

"Ho, traveler. What brings you to this place I call my home?"

"Sir," the fisherman said, trying not to stare at the man's nakedness, "I did not think anyone else was on this island. I have been here for three days and three nights and haven't seen anything more than my own footprints."

"Of course not. This place is for the Kal-kapula, the soul of the island. My people live on the other side of the jungle."

"Why only live on one side of the island?"

The stranger looked at him incredulous. "I already said. The west half of the island is for the Kal-kapula. Do you not know of the sacred agreement between men and the islands?"

The fisherman shook his head.

"Each island is divided. The east half is for man to make his home and to live his life. The west half is for the island. She tends to her children here: the animals and plants. We gather fruit and hunt on our side, but leave this side for them." The stranger gave the fisherman a solemn look. "You didn't take fruit from the trees on this half, did you?"

"Like I told you, sir. I have been here for three days and nights. I had to eat something or else I'd starve."

The stranger shook his head. "This is not good. The peace between men and islands must be maintained. I will take you to our Talakani, our holy man. He will decide what we must do to maintain peace."

The fisherman didn't like what he was hearing. Was this stranger going to kill him for violating this treaty? He had heard stories of savage cannibals that killed and ate men for the slightest insult. Still, there was nowhere for him to run. It was a small island and the stranger would certainly know it better than he would. So, he followed the stranger through the jungle to the other side of the island.

There he saw a small collection of strange houses. Their roofs were made of dried leaves and set on stilts. Instead of walls, the houses had some sort of woven fabric that resembled the canvas of his sail or the sackcloth he had to wear growing up. The fisherman's heart was filled with pity as he realized how poor these people must've been to be unable to afford proper walls for their houses.

He looked around and his heart was broken further. He had thought the stranger odd for not wearing any clothes, but now he could see that no one in his small village seemed to be able to afford even sackcloth. He tried to keep his eyes from lingering on the naked bodies around him, but he couldn't hide the pity from his face. This drew strange looks from the other people in the village.

The fisherman was led to a large building that seemed to be woven out of bark the way you'd weave a basket. Inside, an old man with gold armbands and beads woven into hair like the stranger's was sitting cross legged on the floor.

The fisherman realized that these, and the beads in the first man's hair, were the only adornments he had seen on any of the people. His eyes were closed, and he was muttering under his breath. When the stranger knelt before him, he opened his eyes and looked immediately at the fisherman.

"Who is this man that you have brought before me, my son?" the old man asked.

"He was brought by the ocean onto the western shore of the island. He has spent three days eating the Kal-kapula's fruit. I have come to seek your guidance for how we can maintain peace."

The old man nodded not looking away from the fisherman. "Three days you say? And he was brought here by the ocean?"

"Technically," the fisherman said, "I was brought here by a jar of wind."

"A jar of wind you say? You released one of the Erakani? A wind-spirit?"

"I supposed so. The wind was so powerful it blew me into the middle of the ocean. I prayed to the sea god to save me, and he dropped me on your island. If I had known that—"

The old man raised a hand for silence. "If the Lord of Oceans brought you to the western side of the island, there is no need to reconcile with the Kal-kapula. All of them know the will of the Ocean. If you were saved by him, you are under his protection."

The fisherman sighed in relief. He wasn't going to be killed and eaten, but he still had no way of getting home. When he told the old man this, he nodded. "Our Wayfinders will not be back for another month. You may stay in the village until they return. One of them will bring you back home."

The fisherman agreed. However, by the time the Wayfinders returned to the island, the fisherman had fallen in love with a woman named Lelani. He decided he would stay, and the old man, the Talakani married the two of them. They had many children, and when the fisherman died, he was placed on a boat and sent floating west in hopes that he would reach his long-forgotten home.

CHAPTER THIRTY-NINE

Up in Thin Air

When Gerald finished his story, Pax wanted to ask a dozen questions. What's a Wayfinder? How did the fisherman know the islander's language? Were they really that poor? All of the questions vied for space in his mind, but when Gerald set down his harp, Pax knew he was tired and wanted to sleep.

There would be time enough later for Pax to ask questions. He let his friend sleep, but the questions kept him awake and staring out into the night and the howling wind outside their cave. He didn't sleep for a long time, but when he did, he dreamed of the island.

The next day, Pax and Telemnar made another fruitless attempt at finding food, and the group ate out of their packs. As they climbed, the wind picked up still more. Pax's cloak was pulled tight like a flag, and the clasp pressed against his neck. Something made a noise behind him, and he turned only to have his hood thrown over him by the wind.

The cold of the wind started to leech into him as they climbed, and Pax wondered if they could survive the cold long enough to make it to the top of the mountain.

Korivare seemed to be doing his best to keep up with Telemnar. It was hard to tell, but Pax was under the impression that Telemnar was more familiar with the terrain than Korivare. That didn't seem to make much sense. Korivare had spent his life in the monastery they were going to. Why didn't he know more about this mountain?

Telemnar lead them to a pair of boulders that acted as a wind break. When they were behind the stones and out of the fierce winds, Telemnar told them to dig into their packs for warmer clothes. They each did so and found what she was talking about.

In the largest pocket of their packs, under the rope bundle and bed roll, there was a set of clothes that were lined with thick white fur. They were heavier than Pax expected, and when he put them on the fur was soft against his skin.

He was surprised that his fit him. He supposed on some level, the monks and Telemnar had chosen him out of convenience or due to some kind of random circumstance. Knowing that they took special care to make cold-weather clothes that fit his massive frame meant that him being here was no accident.

They sat a while longer to warm up a bit and used the break to eat. Their food was running low. Pax had one apple left, a piece of trail-bread no bigger than his palm, and one strip of smoked meat from the creature they hunted in the valley. It was enough for one more meal, and he still couldn't see the peak of the mountain through the clouds. There was no way to judge how far they had left to go.

After everyone changed and ate, they set out again. The wind still buffeted against Pax and threw off his footing at times. There was one moment where he had to step to the side to keep his feet under him, but his foot slipped off the side of the mountain path. The only thing that saved him was Jiang's quick reaction time. He had grabbed an outcropping of rock and Pax's hand at the same time, keeping Pax from falling while he pulled himself back up onto the path.

That experience alone made Pax realize just how dangerous this journey was. The path got narrower and the winds grew stronger as they made their way up the mountain path. The sun went down, but it was a long time before they found anything that offered them enough shelter from the wind that they could rest for the night. When they did, it was only a large stone laying on its side that was long enough to fit everyone under if they lay against it as they slept.

The howling wind made stories impossible, and Telemnar and Pax silently agreed there would be nothing up here worth eating. It was nothing but bare rock and the frosty beginnings of the snowy part of the mountain. Tomorrow would likely see them trudging through snow as well as fighting the screaming wind. Everyone ate from their packs, and tried not to think about the fact that they were now out of food as they went to sleep.

Pax woke to Telemnar's head resting on his forearm. She had fallen from her upright position, and Pax didn't know if he was supposed to prop her back up. If she woke up, would she assume he moved her? The weight of her resting against him felt intimate in a way he couldn't remember ever experiencing. She shivered a bit, and, with no better option, he put his arm around her, and nestled the both of them under his cloak.

When he was woken up next, it was from Telemnar stirring and stretching herself awake. She didn't say anything about waking up cuddled against him, and he didn't want to bring it up for fear of making her angry. The rest woke one by one, and, without any food to eat, they merely began their trek again.

They hiked for two more days through biting wind and driving snow before Pax looked at his hand. He was using it to block some of the wind so his eyes wouldn't tear up, when he saw the ring on his finger. Last time he tried to call Meses it didn't work. Would he answer them now? Gerald ran into Pax's back. Gerald muttered something that Pax couldn't hear over the wind, but the look the little gnome gave him communicated his anger well enough.

They had all grown testy with each other after three days without food. Sleep had become difficult as well. Finding shelter from the wind was getting harder, and everyone was getting fed up with sleeping against stones.

Pax gestured to his ring, and Gerald's eyes went wide with realization. He nodded vigorously, urging Pax to try. "Meses." The words were lost in the screaming wind, and Pax didn't know if the ring heard him. Then a thunderclap heralded the arrival of the wind spirit.

He was a massive figure, towering over the small mountain path as he floated off the edge of the drop-off. He didn't wear his normal fancy robe. Instead, he wore a doublet with gray fur peeking out. His legs were covered by a fur skirt that reached past his knees.

He threw out his hands and laughed a great booming laugh. "You truly have brought me to a wonderful place, my dear friend." The words weren't drowned out by the howling wind. Instead, they seemed to be carried by it. "How can I help you? If it is within my power, it will be yours."

"Why are you so big?" Pax asked.

Meses smiled. "Wherever I go, I am shaped by the winds. Where you met me, they were strong, but here, they are dominant. Stone has its place here, but the wind is ceaseless and powerful."

"That's actually one of our problems. We are trying to reach the peak of this mountain, but this wind is keeping us from making the progress we'd like, and it makes it difficult to set camp at night. Our other problem is that we ran out of food a couple days ago, and..." Pax trailed off as his stomach growled again.

"Ah. A guide. Is that all you need of me? Not to worry. Under my care, you will reach your destination, and you will do so like a Lord of the Winds." He clapped his hands once. It was like the clap of thunder.

The wind spun around, blowing and tumbling on itself. The blowing wind resolved into something like a table. It was clearly made of the air itself, but when Pax leaned on it, it was solid and supported his weight.

Then, the table was suddenly filled with delicious food: a boar bigger than the one in the Dream World; platters of grapes, apples, and figs; pies, cakes, and tarts. Pax had never seen a bounty like this. Gerald didn't hesitate. He dove into one of the pies with the ferocity of a feral dog.

Korivare was more reserved, but plainly excited. He plucked a handful of grapes and stuffed them into his mouth. Jiang cut off a piece of the boar and put it on top of a cake before eating the whole thing in three bites. Telemnar tore off an entire leg and ate it without hesitation. Her slender cheeks puffed out, and she closed her eyes as she savored the taste.

Pax started with three tarts that were each filled with a sour, acidic fruit he'd never had before. It made his lips pucker, but when he finished them, he smiled. Next, he tried one of the pies. He had expected a fruit pie, but what he got was a savory mix of meat chunks and a starchy filling that made him think of warm stew. The crust was flaky, the filling was creamy, and the meat was so greasy and tender that it had to have come from an animal that never knew a moment of hardship in its life.

The rest of the meal was a blur of one exquisite flavor after another. All the while, Meses looked on smiling warmly. When Pax attempted to stop, Meses clapped him on the back, handed him a cup of warm, mulled cider and said, "eat until you are sick my friend. This is the least I can do for you after you helped me get home."

Pax drank the whole cup in one warm swallow. The heat radiated through his body, and he felt muscles that had tensed against the cold relax for the first time in days. Everyone listened to Meses and ate until the idea of putting anything in their mouth made their stomachs turn. They sat back and Meses clapped his thunder-clap again. The table disappeared, and Pax braced himself for the return of the howling wind. The wind didn't come.

Pax looked toward Meses, who stood further up the trail. The wind jostled his skirt, but parted around him. Pax reached out a hand, and it met the howling wind and was thrown back. When he pulled it back however, it was met with nothing but still air.

CHAPTER FORTY

The Peak of the Mountain

They rested against the mountainside, Meses keeping the winds parted around them. Gerald sang for them for the first time in days. When he got to the drinking song, even Meses and Telemnar came in on the second refrain:

> Over rivers and under mountains
> We march through marshes
> We walk through woods
> To home and hearth
> Throwback our hoods
> Til adventure calls again.

When Gerald finished his verses, Pax tried one he'd been working on for a bit, and everyone clapped appreciatively. Gerald promised to make Pax a musician. Everyone laughed as Pax stumbled through a polite refusal.

"Well," Telemnar declared, standing up, "I think its time we tackle the rest of this mountain. We might get passed the clouds today and —" she stopped as she turned around. The clouds were gone, and they could see the peak of the mountain, or rather, they could see the tower that seemed to have replaced the tapered peak Pax had imagined the mountain having. The snow that reached to Pax's shins stopped a half mile from the base of the tower, and he could see the plants growing around it.

"I didn't do that," Meses said.

"It can't be no more than a day and a half of a hike," Telemnar said in amazement. "I had no idea how far we had come. I thought we still had at least a few days after we passed the clouds."

"This is Mount Koyasha, yes?" Meses asked.

Telemnar and Korivare nodded.

"I have heard of this place. The mountain is a test of sorts. It tests your will, your drive, and your cleverness. You have climbed it before yes?"

Telemnar nodded again.

"Was it different?"

"When I did it alone, there were more places to shelter and a lot more things to hunt. I didn't need to eat anything in my pack until I was past the clouds."

Meses nodded. "The mountain knows your limits. It knows what each of you is capable of and it tests you. Last time, it made you survive because you are a hunter. This time, you had different tools.

"You had each other to keep you strong, so the mountain knew you did not need food, or to sleep on soft ground. Each of you was tested by this mountain in some way as you traveled. And," Meses gestured to the tower above them, "it seems the mountain is satisfied with how you have fared."

"Are you saying that mountains are alive?" Pax asked.

"Many things are, in one way or another. Everything responds when its Name is called. But this mountain is more alive than most. It is a piece of the old days, still standing. That is why the Koyashian monks have made their home here. It is the biggest piece of the Deep Magic that is still left to them."

"But the Great Divide was made after the God Wars," Gerald said.

"The Divide, yes," Korivare said, "but this mountain is older than the ones around it. Some say the peak of it is where the Creator stood when he used his light to craft the world."

Pax stared up at the mountain in amazement. The very origin of all creation. The tower at the summit looked like it was carved out of the peak of the mountain, and Pax wondered if, at the top, there was a spot where a god once stood. He had been hiking toward the beginning of the whole world, being tested the whole way, and this mountain, the origin of creation, had declared him worthy. What did that mean?

Meses stood. "I believe my work is done. Your way is now clear. I will be leaving. Remember Pax, you can call me again for one last favor. After that, the ring will be nothing but a trinket. Take good care in choosing when you want to see me next. It will likely be the last time."

Pax nodded and the man disappeared in a whisper of a breeze. Pax braced and held up his arm for the return of the howling winds, but it didn't come back. Apparently, that was also part of the test.

When they settled in that night, Pax mentioned how he would've liked to still have some of the food Meses had given him. At which point, Gerald pulled a bunch of grapes, four apples, and a half dozen tarts wrapped in a linen cloth out of his pack.

"Those tarts were tricky. I had to figure out a place to hide them where they wouldn't get crushed. They might be a little flattened."

"You stole these from Meses?"

"Not technically seeing as how the food was for us. He did tell us to take our fill. I just understood that to mean 'fill your packs' as well as 'fill your bellies'."

Pax shook his head. The wind spirit had been amicable enough up until this point, but would he be offended at what Gerald did? Pax remembered something Farhan said. The good side of a wind spirit is a place you want to be. Pax hoped that referred to the bounties of food, and not some malicious power the wind spirit would wreak on you if you weren't on their good side.

Still, he was hungry, and Meses had made the table of food for them. If he did get upset with them over this, Pax would do his best to explain. Maybe they could do another favor for him to get back on his good side.

He ate. The tarts were a bit crushed, but they were still flaky and sour. The pieces fell apart and the juices from the filling made his hands sticky, so he licked his fingers clean. His friends did the same, and they all shared a laugh at their barbaric behavior.

Then everyone stood and they continued their hike at a more leisurely pace than they had made the last several days. Now that they knew they were close to their goal, it didn't seem as urgent. They weren't on the verge of starving or freezing in the thin mountain air.

In fact, when Pax drew a breath, he noticed it was easier to breathe. He wanted to pin this to the wind settling and letting his lungs pull in air that wasn't attacking his face, but even in the shelter of the stones or caves the air was difficult to pull in.

Up here it was greener too, under all the snow. Not as green as the valley they started in, nor as green as the forest he'd grown up in, but the bramble bushes that pushed through the ice around the path had buds on them. The stones were covered in lichen, and there were small saplings pushing their roots into the cold rocky ground. He could see the beginnings of something like a garden, and he wondered what season it was on this mountain.

In the deserts of Maskohma, he had learned there were two seasons: a dry season that could last as long as a few years, and a wet season that came when the wind stirred up a rare storm that drove itself from the mountains to the sea with little to get in its way. Where the clouds got so much water to rain down on the hot, arid wasteland no one knew.

Still, there was a reason the walls around the city-states were built of stone so well carved you couldn't fit a grain of sand between the blocks. Only part of that reason was for the city's protection from raiders and bandits and the occasional monster attack. The other was so that, when the storms came, and the rivers, oases, and sands flooded, the water would part against the walls and be sent on its way to the sea.

His forest home had a more regular cycle of four seasons: spring was for the beginnings of new life, animals had children, seeds sprouted, and trees grew new buds; summer was a season of growing, so warm and often carrying storms to wet the thirsty ground; fall was a time of change and slow deaths, the leaves fell, mothers sent their grown babes to fend for themselves, and plants drew back their blooming petals and leaves; finally, winter was a quiet time of bitter cold and little food. Then the cycle would repeat, birth, life, death, stillness.

Here on the mountain, cold winds seemed to dance among newly formed buds. Snow was present on this peak, but still the plants drank in sunlight and water. It was as if they were daring the bitter cold to take the life that they carved out away from them. The plants here had stubborn roots and thorny vines. They forced their survival on the world with a will as hard as the stones they grew out of. What kind of monks, or people of any kind, could make a home in a place like this?

A day and a half after the clouds parted, he got his answer. They were greeted at the gates by a man in dark gray robes and an iron ring hanging from a piece of twine around his neck. "Welcome to the Koyashian monastery honored guests. We are humbled by your presence. I invite you to enter and sit with me. I'm sure you have many questions."

Gerald sauntered through the open door. Jiang followed reverently with his eyes going to each corner of the room and then to each exit. Telemnar went next, nodding at the monk as she passed. Pax watched as Korivare gave the man a deep bow and then an embrace. Pax entered last of the five being closely followed by the monk.

The room was bare stone and featureless save for three doors including the one they walked through. Pax had sudden flashes of his time locked in the plateau by the cult of priestesses, but the stone there was a brownish-red. This was bare gray stone that matched the mountain so perfectly, Pax was now certain it had been carved from the mountain's peak.

The monk sat without preamble or introduction. The five friends followed suit. There was a moment of pause. Then Gerald said, "well? Are you going to tell us why we've been hunted from the coast to the mountains by dragons, bugs, and hateful priestesses?"

The monk looked at Korivare. "You remember the story we taught you, don't you? The story of how the world came to be?"

Korivare looked surprised. "Yes, of course. It's the first story you told me and the one you repeated most often." The monk nodded and made a gesture. Korivare cleared his throat and began to speak:

CHAPTER FORTY-ONE

The Beginning

In the beginning, there was nothing but chaos and darkness that held no form nor identity. Before long, however, a light came forth from this dark and nameless void. The Light became the Creator whose Name is lost. This is the god the Koyashian monks worship to this very day. This separation of Light and the Void allowed them both to gain identity.

Then the Creator used his shining light to create two children. The first was a daughter, whom he made the Sun that shines brightly in our daytime sky. The second child was a son that the Creator made the Moon that would watch over the shadowy night.

The Creator taught his children how to weave their own light into all the things that they would make in the world. The three of them began to craft the world as we know it today. Forming the great land masses and the oceans of the world, these three gods grew trees, flowers, and all other plants. Then they brought forth the beasts of the earth and birds of the sky to live on the land. As well, they made fish to live in the seas and oceans. In doing so, they became the first of the Seven we have come to know as the Makers.

While they were creating, the Void was not idle. It gave birth again to Starlight. He is the grandfather of all dragons, and from his light was born the Mother Dragon and the Father Dragon. These two embraced one another and gave birth to nine children.

All seven; the Void, the Creator, the Sun, the Moon, Starlight, Mother, and Father, came to be known as the Makers because they wrought the world out of their light. But the world they crafted was formless and without shape.

However, conflict among the three dragon gods arose soon after. Disagreements on how dragons should be made caused the Mother and Father Dragons to part ways. The Father took with him four of his children and they became the four heavenly dragons. The Mother took the other five children, and they became the first dragons of the earth. From them are born the five races of earthly dragons that still exist today.

The others continued to populate the world. Beasts roamed the newly created continents and ate from the fruits of trees and plants. In the sea, fish swam and storms churned. The sky had birds, insects, and bats. The Sun ruled the day and the Moon claimed the night, sharing it with Starlight and his children who he viewed as friends and who made the first constellations. Still the world was shapeless and without purpose.

The world felt incomplete to the seven Makers. They had made so many wondrous things, and yet, the world was still not yet done. The Light tried to make new gods, first a wife for his son, then a husband for his daughter. The four began having children.

The Moon and the Lady of Beasts sired the Master of the Arcane, the Master of Dreams, and the Lady of Storms. The Sun and her husband the Warrior King sired the Heavenly Wind, the Lady of Pain, and the Son of Battle. These children began to gather their own worshipers, and the pantheons we know today began to take shape.

Still, none of these new gods knew how to make the world complete. The Moon and the Lady of Beasts worked together to make the new and wondrous creatures to fill the land, but this did not complete creation. The Sun and her Husband shaped new lands and gave them new life, but this did not complete creation. Finally, the Void and the Light had an idea. They spoke with the other Makers, and they all agreed.

The Sun brought her flame which she'd fashioned into a mind. The Creator brought clay to form a body. The Moon brought air and shaped a name. The Void brought water and fashioned it into a spirit. Starlight gifted a piece of the aether that was his home, and with it he made presence. When they had finished, their creation stood before them. They called him the Adam, because he was the first thing with a purpose.

After this, many of the Makers set out to make their own version of the Adam. The Moon crafted the elves, and gave them the longest lifespan of any living creature. The Sun made the six fingered khaldabri, who are nimble and strong. The Mother Dragon and the Father Dragon embraced again to create dragons in this new way. Among all of these races, however, the Adam, who would be the father of humankind, was favored most by the Light.

In the end, seven were chosen, one by each of the seven Makers. These seven began shaping the world that had been created. In time, they had given everything that was created a Name, and, thus, they became known as the Namers. Soon these seven chosen people taught others how to find the Names they had given everything, and their disciples were also called Namers. When the seven Namers died, the seven Makers chose new people to hold their office. The office became known as the True Namers.

With each generation, new True Namers were chosen. They each became a guardian of the world and upheld its shape. Many of them became legends, and their names are still known to us: Siradyl, the swift; Kaleb, the bold; the Hero of Night's Hall. Each of these people were True Namers, and thus, wielded a power that is greater than any other. They are the guardians and practitioners of the Deep Magic, and they are the greatest among us.

This is the truth of how the world came to be. The Koyashians know it, and they share this truth with anyone who asks for it. These things are not hidden to those who seek it, but many people have forgotten these truths. Many more do not know where or how to find this truth, though they might seek it.

CHAPTER FORTY-TWO

True Namers

Pax waited until he was sure that Korivare was finished, but Gerald spoke up first. "What's that got to do with us? It's just a story about the seven Makers and the seven Namers. All of it is in the past."

"It is in the past," the monk agreed, "but it hardly has nothing to do with you. The office of True Namer died out after the Creator went into Exile. There were still Namers after that, and some claimed to be True Namers.

"However, once one of the Makers was not available to appoint his Namer, none could be appointed. The others abandoned the system of Making and Naming, and chose to guide their worlds as they saw fit. Conflict arose, and without anyone to act as arbiter, the Sun and Moon went to war."

"That's what started the God Wars," Telemnar said.

The monk nodded. "The True Namers were meant to preserve the balance. They acted as arbiters that allowed people to come to peaceful resolutions. Without them, the world descended into chaos, and only through division, could something like order be attained again."

"What does this have to do with us?" Gerald asked again.

The monk looked at him. "The Creator's influence is in resurgence. He is still in Exile, but he has sent visions to a prophet who has told us of a coming conflict. The only way to stop it is with the balancing forces of the True Namers."

"But you said they aren't around," Pax said. He was getting frustrated with this monk talking around Gerald's question.

"As I said, the Creator's influence is reemerging. With it, the office of the True Namers is returning as well. Each of the seven Makers has felt the resurgence and chosen their Namer."

Telemnar's eyes were far away. She looked like she was remembering something. "They have chosen already?"

The monk nodded. "The five of you have been chosen to be True Namers. Jiang was chosen by the Void, Korivare was chosen by Starlight, Gerald has found favor with the Father of Dragons, and Telemnar..."

"I have been chosen by the Moon himself. I am his Namer." She said it reverently. Her eyes were still far away, but Pax could see tears welling up in them.

"What about me?" Pax asked.

"You are the Namer of the Light himself master..." the monk trailed off.

"Pax," Korivare finished.

The monk looked at him quizzically. Pax explained, "Korivare said it was a word you used. It means peace."

The monk shook his head. "He misremembered the word. The word is not pax. It is pronounced as pakas. It doesn't mean peace either it means... hero."

Pax paused. His name meant hero. Better still, if Korivare was one of the True Namers, "does that mean Pakas is my Name?" he asked.

"Your Name will be something more complicated than that. Korivare probably, on an instinctive level, found a piece of your name and spoke it out to you as best as he could. If he chose to call you a hero, then he would likely have seen something in you that elicited that word."

Pax was a hero. Not just any hero, he was one of the legendary True Namers, guardians of the world. He felt a fluttering in his chest. Then he thought of all the blood on his hands. He thought of the woman in the tent, the paladin he almost killed, Farhan's father, and even the dragon. Was a hero truly someone who was surrounded by so much death and destruction?

"How can we be True Namers?" Gerald demanded. "I don't have any special powers. I have tried to get people to do what I want all my life and it only works half the time. I get beaten bloody as much as I get people to follow me."

"Being chosen does not give you the power all at once. It is the first step on your journey to mastering the subtle art of Naming. You will have an easier time of it than most. As we have already discussed, some of you have shown your talents. Have any of the rest of you noticed something odd about you?"

"The skulk," Jiang said, looking at Pax.

At first Pax didn't know what he meant. Then he remembered. "I told Fertul to stop and he just froze. He didn't seem to want to, but he did. Like he couldn't help but obey."

"You named a skulk Fertul?" the monk asked.

"It seemed like a good name at the time."

"Of course," Korivare said, "because you saw the protective instinct in him, and you used a word that fit that. Just like what I did with your name."

Pax sat back, stunned.

"Well, I couldn't get that thing to wag his tail for me," Gerald said testily.

"What about that strange language on the wall? You could read that even though none of us had ever seen it before."

"I told you that was an enchantment on the tomb. The people who built it wanted us to understand who was buried there."

"Tomb?" the monk asked.

Gerald told him the story, and he shook his head.

"Lethehotep didn't have magicians that could set up an enchantment that lasted that long. What you experienced was your prowess with all the languages that are derived from the language of the True Namers.

"That is to say, all languages. Every language spoken by the sentient races stems from the language first spoken by the original seven Namers. It was the language they used to shape the world, and it is the language that all Namers speak when they learn Names. As True Namers, you are naturally predisposed to learn this language. The more you master your powers, the easier the languages of the world will open their meaning to you."

"So, we can learn any language just by looking at it?" Pax asked.

The monk nodded his head back and forth. "Mostly. The further the language is from Truespeak, the more your mind will simply summarize things. You will find picking up these languages easier than others would, however."

The monk stood. "I have kept too much of your time to myself. Come, the others are eager to meet you, and we must begin your training if you are going to help us stop the coming conflict."

CHAPTER FORTY-THREE

Rooming with Monks

The monk led them through one of the two doors on the other side of the room. The door led into a much larger room, still of bare stone. It had a table that was too short to fit a chair under, and several more men and a small handful of women wearing the same gray robes were sitting on the floor. The hall had a large window that overlooked the eastern half of the mountains, but, since this didn't let in much light, the hall was lit by glowing orbs and candles.

The table itself was set with bread that was placed on a round, hot stone to keep it warm; a scattering of fruits, half of which Pax didn't recognize; and several sliced and smoked meats. It was a simple feast compared to the one Meses gave them, but it had a hearth-like charm. This was the sort of meal you'd eat with a family on a holiday, if your family celebrated holidays.

The monks welcomed them in with a gesture, and the five friends sat among them and ate. They hadn't eaten all day since Gerald could only hide away enough food for one meal, so Pax wasn't shy about taking half a loaf of bread, stuffing it with sliced meat, and eating it all together. A part of Pax thought they should mind what the monks were doing and follow their lead.

What the five adventurers were doing trampled on any semblance of politeness. The people around them didn't seem to take any offense, though. When they began eating like the savage ruffians they were, the whole hall cheered, and followed suit. Pax saw a bit of stiffness in their movements and could tell they were trying to mimic their supposed Namer heroes, but that this behavior wasn't normal for them.

While they ate, some of the monks mustered up the courage to make conversation with their guests. Gerald told a group of them the story of how they had gotten lost in the Dream World, embellishing the size of the boar, the fight with the tentacles, and claiming he had tricked the God of Dreams into revealing himself.

Jiang gave short, simple answers to the questions he was asked, and the monks took this as a polite request to be left alone. If they had known him better, they would've seen how engaged he was with their conversation, and how he'd signed "disappointed" when they stopped talking to him.

Telemnar told a story about how she'd survived in something called the Hunting Grounds for months with nothing but her bow and her training. She ended the story with her speaking to a god as well, and Pax wondered if she was embellishing, or if it was true.

Korivare seemed to be reuniting with a particular group of the monks Pax guessed were either friends or, based on the aged lines on their faces, the ones that had the greatest hand in raising him. They embraced several times, and Pax could see the beginnings of tears in the knight's eyes.

Pax was quietly absorbing all of this when a monk with a silver circle hanging around his neck approached him. "You are the Namer of Light. Is that correct?"

"That's what I was told. Still not sure you guys have the right troll though."

Pax smiled and the monk laughed a moment later.

"I am glad," the monk said, "to see you have humor in this. It is rare for one such as yourself to be chosen, but the Creator must see something special in you.

"According to legend, His Namers were often chosen from strange or unexpected circumstances. However, they were always the ones to rise best to being what the world needed. When the True Namers met, which was not often as they usually worked independently in the world, it was usually the Namer of the Void and the Namer of the Light that led them."

"I suppose it's a good thing that I already work so well with the Void's Namer."

Pax nodded to Jiang, who returned the nod.

"Yes. It was very lucky that so many of you found each other without our prompting. Though, perhaps it was not luck at all."

"You believe in destiny then, I take it."

The monk shrugged. "There are some here that do. I believe the Creator sets things in motion in a particular way. Before his Exile, I suspect he was more active in shaping the destiny of the world. However, since his Exile, his influence on the world has waned. It's hard for me to believe that he could foresee this far into the future."

"What does that mean? What is Exile? Did he die?"

"Some say he did. However, gods cannot die the same way mortals do. Many of them gain power from their worshipers, and if that power wanes, they can change form, or a new god can take their place. That only happens to the lower gods though, the children of the Makers.

"The Makers themselves are a constant. They are part of the very fabric of reality. The Creator allowed his influence on this world to retract, and his essence retreated from this world. But still, he awaits at the edges of reality. He listens for those who know his Name to Call him back."

"The story Korivare told us said that his Name was lost. How can we call it if no one knows it?"

"That is why we are glad you are here. You are the new True Namers. If anyone can rediscover his Name, it is you. You can call the Creator back so that balance can be restored."

"This all sounds like a lot of very difficult and confusing things. I don't know if I'll be able to help you, but I will try."

The monk bowed and touched his forehead to Pax's upper arm. The gesture was reverent, and Pax was a little uncomfortable by how much respect he was being shown. He continued eating, trying to ignore the whispers and looks he was getting from the monks. He was used to unwanted attention, and at least this time it wasn't fear they were showing him. Still, he wished he could just be treated like normal somewhere in the world.

The end of the meal was marked by a man standing at the head of the table. His circle was gold, and Pax guessed that made him some brand of leader. He held up his hand, and the monks immediately went silent. The five friends followed quickly.

The man spoke, "today, we are honored to have, as our guests, five of the True Namers. Ever since the Creator left the world behind, we have long awaited their return. At last, we can finally declare the Nameless Era has come to an end."

Everyone raised their stone cups in toast and drank the last of their water. Pax followed suit. Then the monks stood and walked out of the hall, leaving the five friends with the man in the gold-circle necklace.

He said, "I will show you each to your room. I hope they are to your liking. Tomorrow, we will begin your tutelage in the art of Naming."

He walked through a nearby door and the five fledgling guardians of the world followed him. He showed them each to a simple stone room with a desk, a mat on the floor, and a window overlooking the mountainside. Gerald grumbled about how, at this rate, he'd never get to sleep in a bed again. Korivare cuffed him upside the head. He apologized to the monk, but the monk merely nodded.

"We, of course, would give you more luxurious rooms if they were available. The monastery was built, however, with practicality in mind."

"These rooms are perfect Brother," Korivare said. "The bard merely lacks manners. We found him in the wilderness and had pity for him."

Gerald sneered at Korivare as he entered his room. "Just for that, I'm going to use this desk and all the paper I can find to write a ballad extolling your brilliant lusting after Farhan's camels."

The monk looked at Korivare, but he just shook his head. Pax entered the second to last room, giving the last to Korivare. His window looked out over the top of a sheet of white puffy clouds.

He had never seen the tops of clouds before, and he was dazzled by the way the light of the setting sun sparkled off them. He saw bright colors, many of which he'd never seen before. He stared at them until his eyes got heavy and he lay down on the mat to sleep.

CHAPTER FORTY-FOUR

Learning to Read

The next day the gold-circled monk, who introduced himself as Brother David, took the five friends to a library that was filled with more books than Pax had seen in his entire life, although that wasn't difficult. Pax could remember each specific time he'd seen a book in his life. He'd even seen the personal library of House Morkae, but that was contained in a single, albeit very large, room. The library they were brought to made up three full floors of the monastery's enormous tower.

Brother David explained, "The art of Naming is based on understanding the fundamental essence of a thing. Becoming a generalized Namer over a mere Adept requires you to have a deep understanding of the world as a whole.

"When the Libra Univertas stood millennia ago, Namers would congregate there to share everything they knew about that world. They would discuss philosophy, nature, magic, and all manner of scholarly pursuits. Debates would be held that would allow people to challenge any pre-established beliefs and traditions they had a mind to question. No topic was left undiscussed in those halls.

"Here we have done our best to collect as much of that knowledge as we can. We have also collected what has been discovered since that time. He have endeavored to make this place a storehouse for as much knowledge that exists in the world as possible."

Pax was getting more and more discouraged as he went on. Discounting the strangeness with the wall, he'd never been able to read before. If the first step of their journey required reading any number of these books, he was already failing.

195

He pulled Brother David aside, and Pax explained that he couldn't read. Brother David walked over to a shelf, removed a book from it, and handed it to Pax.

"This," he said reverently, "is the only surviving example of Truespeak in all the world. It is a precious and priceless thing."

Pax took it. He held it and waited for further instruction. Brother David gestured for him to open it. Pax did so, and the moment he began to read the text, he could understand it. Not in the general way he read the wall. That was mostly summaries and meaning without being able to translate any single word.

With this book, each word he landed on revealed its meaning in its entire. It was a book of beautiful poetry that seemed centered around the natural wilderness. The writer described stones, trees, and streams with the same excitement that a young man spoke of his new wife.

"This. It's all so beautiful. Thank you." He closed the book carefully and set it back on the shelf.

Brother David nodded. "There is more wisdom that we can help you uncover in these texts."

"Pax," Gerald asked gently, "do you not know how to read?"

Pax shook his head. He felt his skin get hot as he blushed. He didn't know why, but he was embarrassed to admit it. It made him feel stupid like the mindless troll so many thought he was.

Gerald stepped up and put a hand on Pax's forearm. "I can help you learn. There are a lot of books here from all over. They're in a ton of different languages too. I can help you learn how to read all of them."

Pax nodded vigorously. Pax told Brother David that he and Gerald would be staying in the library so he could learn to read. Brother David agreed to allow them to split off from the rest of the group as the continued the tour. Pax thanked him, then left to join Gerald in among the shelves of books.

Gerald was taking down books and examining them. He flipped through a few pages, considered, and ultimately put most of the books back where they were originally. He found one that made him turn his nose up as if it smelled of death or rotting meat.

"No reason we have to subject you to that kind of poetry," he said. "I detest an overly complicated rhyme scheme. Rhymes are meant to add emphasis. If the words that rhyme aren't near each other, no one will notice."

He chose another and raised an eyebrow. He put it on a nearby table. He did this with several books, some he put back and some he placed on the table.

When he finished, he gestured for Pax to sit. The table was another that was too low for chairs, so they sat on the stone floor. Gerald opened one of the books. "This book is in Lukorian, so I'm going to be teaching you to read and a new language. How does that sound?"

Pax shrugged. Gerald opened the book and sounded out the words, pointing to the symbols that made the sounds. He explained how the letters get put together to make words.

The words themselves were unfamiliar to Pax, so Gerald had to explain those as well. He helped Pax sound out each word as they went through the book. After each sentence, Pax understood both the summary of it, his Namer instincts helped with that, and the words that made them up.

By the time they were done with the first page, Pax felt like he was getting the hang of it. Gerald turned the page, and it was filled with hundreds of more unfamiliar words. Gerald was patient, and the second page took just as long, if not longer than, the first.

"Can you tell me what the book may be about?" Gerald asked.

"It's a," Pax couldn't think of the word, "a book about a person."

Gerald nodded. "A biography. Specifically, an autobiography, since it was written by the person who it's about."

Pax nodded. Gerald turned back to the first page and had Pax read it on his own. He made it through the first page and half the second one before he stumbled over a word.

Gerald clapped him on the back and smiled. "That's really good. I dare say it may only take the rest of the day before you can read as well as the rest of us."

Pax smiled. They continued through the book. The man in the book was a king of somewhere called Strophe. He talked about several battles he'd led, and a rebellion he had suppressed. To Pax, it didn't sound like the peaceful and prosperous rule that the man insisted it was. Pax asked Gerald about this.

Gerald shrugged. "Strophe is a relatively new kingdom, and it's beginnings were as bloody as any other nation. This was one of the founding rulers of Strophe, and a handful of rebellions and border skirmishes were as peaceful as he could've hoped for.

"They're probably more established and better respected now, though I think they're still a small kingdom. The fact that the University Arcanum is within their borders helps them be recognized."

They were about half way done with the book when a deep chime from a large bell sounded through the room. Brother David came in shortly after to explain that the bell was what they used to call everyone to meals. Gerald happily set down the book, and Pax followed them both to the hall where they had their introductory meal.

CHAPTER FORTY-FIVE

Dining Sequestered

This meal was even more simple: bread, an assortment of jams, and a large cauldron of stew that had been placed inside a hole in the middle of the table. When Pax asked about it, one of the monks explained that a piece of the table was removable, so they didn't have to risk breaking the table with their cast iron cauldrons.

The stew was thick and creamy. The bread was once again kept warm by round stones, so the butter and jam warmed and soaked into it. Pax watched some of the monks use hunks of bread to sponge up the remnants of their stew while others placed a slice of bread face down on the hot stone so it'd come away slightly toasted.

None of them simply ate. They all found small ways to get the most out of their simple meals, and it seemed like they were having fun with it. To Pax, it seemed almost like a game. Who could do the most with just bread and stew? Who knew the best combination of jams to put between two slices of bread?

Gerald was goaded into joining, and he took a whole loaf of bread, carved out the middle, and used it as a bowl for his stew. The monks looked at him aghast, and Pax thought they were angry until one of them grabbed another loaf and did the same. The long, narrow shape made an awkward bowl, but Pax heard some of the monks talking about shaping the loaf differently for dinner and doing away with the stone bowls entirely.

Pax asked Korivare and Jiang how their tour went. Jiang gave a simple "well," as Pax should've expected. Korivare mentioned that a great deal had changed since he left, and he had mixed feelings about it.

"Maybe it feels different because everyone is treating us with so much reverence," Pax said. "Some of the monks have even started copying our eating habits." He nodded to the monks watching and imitating Gerald.

Korivare shook his head. "It's not just that. There's a tension here that didn't exist when I was growing up. Whatever this conflict is that they want us to solve, it has a lot of them, including Brother David, very scared."

"Gerald was helping me read a biography on a king that had to fight a bunch of wars to keep his kingdom. Maybe they just need diplomats to help everyone figure out their borders."

Korivare shook his head. "True Namers don't bother with stuff like border disputes. That's not what is meant by preserving the shape of the world. We are meant to guard against things that go against the natural progression of the world. Squabbling nations are as natural as predators and prey. We are meant to prevent things like the God Wars: World-ending threats."

"Is that why those gods wanted us dead? They are trying to end the world?"

Korivare looked pensive. "I don't know. The Sun Queen is one of the seven Makers, so the idea that she would want the Namers dead is disturbing. It suggests she's abandoned the old ways, or she's gotten used to things being done without us."

"If she doesn't want the Namers back, does that mean there are only six chosen?"

"I don't know. There's only five of us so far. We are still missing the Mother's Namer and the Sun's Namer. The fact that it could be anyone disturbs me."

"Well," Pax gestured with a piece of bread, "whatever happens, there's five of us and, at most, two of them. I'm sure we can take them."

Korivare raised an eyebrow. "Even if the Sun's Namer is someone like Madam?"

Pax's face went dark. He looked at the knight, but he held firm.

Pax sighed. "You're right. There's no way for us to know who they are or what sort of powers they may have. For all we know, they could be done with their training while we are only beginning ours."

Korivare looked down at his bread. His eyes were far away. Pax could tell his friend was genuinely worried, and that, more than anything, made Pax anxious.

"The only thing we can do is learn about our powers and do our best to master them as quickly as possible," he finally said.

Pax nodded in agreement.

"The Powers. Learning. It's not easy."

Pax nodded again. He hadn't realized Jiang was listening, but he was glad they all seemed to agree.

"If Naming is really based on knowledge," Pax said, "then I'm especially at a loss. I feel like half the time I don't understand what's going on."

Korivare touched Pax's forearm. "You're smarter than you give yourself credit for. I see it in the questions you ask. You understand more than you realize. The fact that the world is doubly complicated doesn't make you stupid."

Pax looked down at the knight. This was more than friendly comfort. Pax saw in his eyes that he was serious. Pax had to look away to stop himself from crying into the stew.

They finished their meal, and Pax asked Gerald if it was alright that they take the afternoon to see the rest of the monastery. Gerald agreed, saying that the library's light would be getting worse as the day wore on, and he'd rather wait until tomorrow to continue.

They asked a monk that had also just finished eating if she could show them around. She wanted to, but explained that she had duties to attend to. Pax offered to assist, and she stammered out an acceptance.

"Ugh. Chores?" Gerald whined. "Fine, but I don't wash dishes."

The monk nodded solemnly not understanding that Gerald was making a joke. She led them down to a sublayer with several wooden wash basins filled with warm water and piles of gray robes. The outside of the basins was covered in strange sigils that were carved into the wood.

Gerald examined them, but he declared he couldn't make sense of them. The monk didn't understand them either, but explained the basins were designed to keep water warm as they cleaned the clothes.

Pax took several robes over to a basin and began washing them. The monk did the same at a different basin. They gathered the clean robes into a pile and Gerald hung them on a line to dry.

It all took less than an hour and the monk was deeply appreciative. She explained that that chore generally took her a good chunk of the afternoon, and that she had a great deal of extra time to devote to their "service." That word made Pax uneasy.

CHAPTER FORTY-SIX

The Tour of the Tower

She brought them first to the gardens that supplied some of the monk's food. She explained that many people on both sides of the Great Divide recognize the Koyashians as the servants of the Creator. Though many people suspect that he is no longer active in the world, they still wish to show their reverence by making gifts to the god that gave life to their gods.

"It has a sort of roundabout logic to it. Like 'sure I give money to *my* god's temple, but I also honor my god's god by giving gifts to his monastery,'" Gerald said.

The monk nodded and continued their tour. They were brought to the chamber that acted as their center of worship. As best as Pax could tell, it was at the center of the tower's base, and so all the light in it was shed by candles or the glowing balls. Gerald called them magelight.

At the center of the room was a brazier that was large enough to house a huge bonfire. Pax imagined the leaping flames licking the top of the high stone ceiling. Around the brazier, there were wooden benches: the only seats Pax had seen in the entire monastery.

The walls were painted in a beautiful mural that depicted a shining light in the shape of a person standing on a mountain. Their rays reached around the circular room and, as they got further away, they resolved into tress, water, sky, and animals of various kinds. Pax recognized about half of them.

"According to legend, the Creator took one day to make His Children. Then three days were spent crafting the world from their light, and the last two were spent resting and celebrating.

"That's why we spend Virtal in our rooms, only coming out for meals. Most of us also stay silent for the whole day. It's supposed to be a day for prayer and meditation. Then we break our silent sequestration on Yolewa with a service in this room.

"Yolewa is in two days," Gerald thought out loud.

The monk nodded. "Brother David has devoted our entire service on Yolewa to the resurgence of the True Namers and the Light's return to the world. There will be songs and prayers. We'll build a huge bonfire and tell stories of the Light's influence on our lives. It's my favorite day of the week. I can't wait to see what this one will be like with the five of you here with us."

"Are we expected to speak?" Pax asked.

The monk shrugged. "Brother David is the only one that speaks every week. Everyone else speaks when they wish. I'm sure many of those here would listen if you had something to say."

The idea scared Pax. Gerald was the eloquent one, and Pax had no doubt he had a story for the occasion or had started working on one at that very moment. Korivare grew up here, and no doubt had experience talking to these people. Pax didn't know of anything he'd want to say.

They were shown around the monks' quarters. Each was identical to the rooms they were given accept only some had windows. Others were merely lit by candles or more magelight. Many of the desks had several papers strewn about on them, in various states of full with writing. Others had books on the desk and pages on the floor.

"Many of the monks here spend their free time copying books from the library. Those get sold all over the continent to further support the monastery," the monk giving the tour explained.

The final stop on their tour was the kitchens. There were monks baking bread for dinner, and Gerald helped them mold the dough into a round shape that looked like a large, symmetrical, river stone. When these came out of the oven, he cut out the middle and made about twenty bowls. It wasn't enough that everyone would get one, but the monks agreed to put them out with the other loaves of bread and allow people to take them. First come, first served.

After the tour, they went back to the dining hall for dinner. Gerald's bowls were a big hit, being taken by the first people to sit down. That left the rest with stone bowls, and everyone was gracious about it on the surface. However, Pax sensed an underlying tension, and wondered if the anxiety of looming conflict had something to do with it.

Pax looked out the large window. He still couldn't see through the clouds, but he imagined looking down on a valley similar to the one they had started their hike in. He imagined looking down on the desert where Farhan was leading his caravan.

The world was so much bigger than the forest he grew up in. Now he was being asked to play such a big part in it, and he barely knew anything about it. There was so much to learn, so much to know. The idea of the fate of the world resting on his decisions made him feel overwhelmed and anxious. Despite the name Korivare had given him, he didn't feel like a hero.

Pax looked down the table to where Gerald was telling a story to two monks. They sat listening intently. Gerald knew so many stories and things about the world around him.

Pax thought back to all the times Gerald had the answer to something Pax simply didn't understand. He thought of how Gerald closely rivaled Jeremy, who came from a long line of master storytellers, with his knowledge. It was easy to see how someone like Gerald could be asked to protect and influence the shape of the world.

He turned his head and watched Korivare. He was deep in an ethics debate with Brother David. He knew so much about what was right and what was wrong. He had magic that could save people from dying, skill in combat, and the wisdom on how to use both. He was everything Pax thought a hero should be. Guarding the world from evil was something he was born to do.

Pax looked across from him at Jiang and Telemnar. Both of them were as skilled warriors as Korivare. Jiang was quiet, but he was smart. He was the first person to think of Pax as a person. That kind of compassion would mean a lot to people.

Telemnar was the newest of Pax's group, but Pax didn't have any reservations about thinking of her as a friend. She was a patient teacher and always willing to show Pax how she did things. He noticed that she preferred to do things herself, but shouldn't she? She was the most skilled hunter and survivalist he'd ever known. Both of them would make fine protectors of the world.

Then there was Pax: the troll. The monster who had stumbled into the story at the wrong time, and everyone was too polite or kind to tell him so. What could he offer to a group so well rounded and ready to take on this great conflict? All he had was anxiety, fear, and the sleeping Rage in his belly. He fingered the clasp on his cloak. Maybe he was better off leaving them to take on this threat without him.

Someone touched his forearm and Pax jumped.

"Excuse me, I'm sorry to startle you. Are you the Namer of Light?" The speaker was a small woman wearing a copper circle around her neck. The robe came down a bit too far like it was too big for her. Did she not have one that fit properly?

Pax nodded.

"Brother David said you needed help reading?"

Another nod.

She handed him a thick leather-bound tome. "This book is how I learned when I first got here. I came from a small town and reading wasn't really a priority for us. There's lots of really good stories in there." She gave him an embarrassed smile. "Some of them are a bit…" she trailed off. Then she looked up and continued, "I hope it helps."

Pax looked at the title on the cover: "One Hundred and One Tales of Heroism."

"Thank you," Pax said. "This will probably be more interesting than the biography of a king I've never heard of." Pax smiled and the woman laughed. Pax opened the book, and picked out a couple of familiar words, but most of it was still unclear to him. He set it on the table and pointed, "how do you say this word?"

She helped him along the first story. It was about a prince who tricked a dragon and won a sword. He used it to slay a giant and rescue a princess. Pax remembered at least three stories Gerald told that sounded very similar. He wondered if these princes were the same person, or if there was a part of the world with a giant problem. He chuckled.

"What?" the woman asked.

"I just thought of something funny, but it would take too much explaining. Can we continue?"

"Oh." She looked up. Pax followed her eyes around the dining hall. He had been so engrossed in the story that he hadn't noticed everyone finish their meal and leave. "I'd better get to my room."

"Wait. There's a magelight in my room. If you want, you could come continue teaching me there." Pax tried to keep the desperation out of his voice. He needed to be able to read this book.

The woman blushed a deep red. "I don't know. What would the other monks say?"

"Gerald has been teaching me in the library, and no one seemed to mind then. What's the difference?"

She looked at him blankly. "You mean... you actually want..." she stammered.

Realization hit Pax like a boar tusk. "Oh. No. I mean yes. I just want... I wasn't trying to... I don't..." He fell silent. His face felt hot.

The woman looked at him for a moment. "My name is Rhea. I guess you should know that if I'm going to spend the night in your room."

Pax's face got hotter.

She nudged him on the arm. "I'm just teasing. I guess we're both a little nervous about this whole thing huh?"

Pax nodded.

"If you want my help, I'll gladly give it. Any service I can lend one of our great heroes is an honor." She made a deep bow that seemed very reverent.

"It's nice to meet you Sister Rhea."

Rhea waved dismissively. "You don't have to call me 'sister'. Brother David is really the only one that insists on that sort of thing. Everyone else just calls me Rhea."

Pax nodded and led Rhea to his room where the magelight was already giving off its warm yellow glow. The desk wasn't big enough for both of them, so they sat with the book open between them on the floor. She helped him sound out words and learn their meaning late into the night. The stars were out and the waxing crescent moon was high when they finished the third story and Pax's eyelids were getting heavy.

Rhea stood. "If I stay, I'll fall asleep on your floor. Then, everyone in the monastery will have questions for us in the morning."

"I'm guessing you aren't allowed to have relationships."

Rhea shrugged. "It's not forbidden. Though," she gestured out the window, "there aren't a great deal of options. Still, I'd rather not have people making assumptions about what we were doing."

Pax nodded and she walked out of the room, giving him a friendly wave as she closed the door. He lay back on his mat. His head was spinning with the stories he'd just read. He thought about the similarities between the different heroes.

He thought of the heroes in Gerald's stories. They were all very different from each other, but one thing was common across the board. Each of them was certain they were doing the right thing. That, more than anything else, was what made Pax different. Pax was still thinking about this when he fell asleep.

CHAPTER FORTY-SEVEN

Late Night Dreaming

That night, Pax had two very vivid dreams. In the first, he was moving through a forest that reminded of him of his childhood home. He tried to move toward the cave he and his parents lived in.

As he did, the whole scene shifted. He was reminded of his adventure in the Dream World, and Pax suddenly realized he was dreaming.

Korivare had said that the dreams people experienced were the adventures their mind went on in the Dream World as their body slept. Did that mean he was actually back in the Dream World, or did the fact that it was only his mind make it not count? He watched the scene shift as he pondered this question.

The cave he was running to changed. It became a cave of dark stone surrounded by sickly looking plants. Pax looked around at trees that had no leaves. They had deep gouges cut into them by something with massive claws.

Pax crouched on the ground and touched a plant with yellowing and wilting leaves. He tried his best to think of where he might be and what all these dying plants might mean, but for all his familiarity with forests and the wilderness, he couldn't recognize any of the plants around him. There were no animals, which was its own kind of unsettling.

A massive shadow blocked the light of the sun from around Pax. It appeared too fast to be a cloud, and he spun around. His eyes locked with shinning green eyes that shot him with a cold feeling of dread. Before he could take in anything else about the creature, he was hit with a cloud of noxious fumes that burned his throat and he began coughing and wheezing.

He tried to suck in a breath, but his breathing became labored. It felt like he was trying to breath through a wet cloth as he forced air into his lungs. He felt his chest burning and his breathing became even more labored. He started to panic as he gasped for air.

At the edges of Pax's vision, a darkness was creeping in. He tried to remind himself that it was only a dream. He thought of the room he fell asleep in at the monastery. He was safe, but it didn't matter. As far as he was aware, he was suffocating, and he couldn't do anything but panic.

With his heart beating in his ears, Pax tried to look up at the beast that had cast a shadow over him. When he looked up, however, his eyes filled with tears and started burning. He could only make out a vague, incredibly large shape. It might have been green, but that also might have been the green of the forest around them. Then the darkness overtook his vision, and he fell into shadow.

#

Pax found himself in the chamber with the large brazier in the foundations of the monastery. The brazier was lit, and fire cast light and shadow in equal measure on the walls with the creation murals on them. Pax was standing near the last row of wooden benches until a deep resonating voice commanded him to approach.

Pax looked around for the source of the voice, but he couldn't see anyone else in the room. He reminded himself that he was still dreaming, and he approached the burning brazier.

When he was in front of the first set of benches, but not close enough that he could touch the brazier, the voice spoke again. "Son of Light, you stand before me as my chosen Namer. You, who lay under the protection of my most devoted followers, now stand in the chamber they have prepared for me."

"What? The Koyashians follow you? Would that make you..." Pax asked before he failed to remember how to refer to this god. He'd heard so many titles for so many gods that he couldn't remember what this one was supposed to be called.

"I am the Creator of the World. I am he who Exiled himself, and I am the one who chose you as my Namer."

"Why did you leave the world? What is going to happen that the True Namers had to be chosen again? Are you coming back?"

"I know you have many questions. I am sorry that I cannot answer them all for you. I have come to you now because of the question you fear to ask. I would have you ask it now."

Pax swallowed. He knew what question he wanted to ask, but he feared what the answer would be. Was this all a mistake? Was he really meant to be a True Namer of a world he barely understood?

Pax took a breath. He wasn't sure if his heart was racing out of fear, or if it was lingering adrenaline from his dream of suffocating. He said, "why did you choose me to be your Namer?"

The question seemed to linger in the quiet chamber for many moments before the fire in the brazier spoke again. "You were chosen as my Namer because of your strength of spirit and enduring will.

"Even in Exile, I am aware of the adversity you have faced in your life. Yet, when you reach out to the people of the world, you expect nothing but the best of them. No matter how many times the world fails you, you never forget to hope that its people can be better."

Pax didn't know what he expected the answer to be, but this was not it. He was chosen because of his spirit and will? What did that mean? "Who, of all seven Makers, chose first?"

"What you are asking is if I wished to choose any of the other Namers above you. This is not how the Makers choose their Namers. Each of you is chosen by one of us with council and advice from the other six. None of you were meant to be any other Namer than the Namer you are."

"But surely there are people in this world that are better for the job you are asking me to do. Why are you choosing me to do it?"

"You are my choice. You will be the champion of my will in this world. This is my choice."

Pax could feel himself coming awake again, but he had many more questions to ask. As the dream started to fade, only one left his lips, "am I meant to summon you back to the world?"

The was no answer.

CHAPTER FORTY-EIGHT

On Top of the World

Brother David sat silently. Pax had described his dream encounter with The Creator to the man. They were sitting in Brother David's room. Brother David looked out the window for the time it takes to draw a full, slow breath.

"The dream you describe is something not many receive. Fewer still since the Creator went into Exile. As my brothers and sisters in the monastery have no doubt made clear, the Creator's influence on this world is seeing its first resurgence since before the God Wars. This, I think, is yet another sign of that resurgence."

"What does it mean?"

Brother David looked at Pax and gave him a frank look. "I'd think the words spoken are rather clear. The Creator sensed your doubt. He wants to make it absolutely clear that he stands behind you. You are His Namer, and He believes that you will do great things."

That sparked something in Pax. A god chose him, and it wasn't by accident. He hadn't stumbled into his part in this story. Did that mean he had something to contribute? What did the Creator see in him?

"What about what He called me? What does Son of Light mean?"

"The Koyashians call each other 'brother' and 'sister' because we recognize the Creator as our parent. We are one family in worshiping Him. The fact that he has claimed you as His son means you are also part of that family."

Pax sat motionless. "I have... you are... family?" He thought about something Jiang said to him when they first spoke to each other. "Family does not make you a slave." Was he right? Should he be a part of this family instead of House Morkae?

"You are more than just our family, Pax. As His chosen Namer, you will, when you are ready, be the person this monastery looks to for guidance. You will, in effect, be treated as our eldest sibling."

Not just in the family, then. He would be taking a leading role in the future of this monastery. "Would I be expected to stay here?"

Brother David shook his head. "Namers generally do not stay so far away from the world. It would be unwise to have a guardian of the world cloistered away at the top of a mountain. You need to be accessible to the people.

"However, your actions, words, and your life will be seen as an example to us. Future generations of Koyashians will model themselves on how you comport yourself. This is both a great honor, and a huge responsibility."

"I don't know if I'm ready for all that."

Brother David looked at him. "Of course not. That is why we must train you. The five of you were brought here to learn the truth about your powers and how to command them. We offer you what guidance we can.

"However, your powers come from wisdom and knowledge. These are things best gained in the world. Once we have given you everything we know, you will go out into the world, and you will learn. Only when you understand the inner turnings of the world can you know how best to protect it."

He stood. "Speaking of which, it is time for us to go meet with the others. Today begins your first lesson in Naming."

Pax followed Brother David to the sanctuary where the brazier was kept. There, Korivare, Jiang, Gerald, and Telemnar were waiting for them. The five friends sat on one of the benches, and Brother David stood in front of the brazier. He took on an air of formality that Pax hadn't seen on him yet.

"Naming was the first magic," he began. "It is the magic that draws on the fundamental aspects of reality. It is the core of Deep Magic. All other kinds of magic; the arcane, faith magic, and primal magic, are pale shadows of Deep Magic. They are fishing boats sailing over a deep ocean. When you master your powers, you will command a force that will put you on a level equal to the Makers themselves.

"I say this not to scare or inspire you. It is a warning. This world and its people are in balance. Wars are fought, conflicts arise between nations, disease and famine snuff out lives like you would snuff a candle.

"These are minor tragedies compared to a world that is thrown out of balance. The God Wars and the chaos that followed were this world's closest brush with the kind of disaster that would come if any of you do not take your duty seriously. With your powers, you could unravel the fabric of existence and send all creation tumbling into the Nameless Void."

Pax raised a hand. Brother David nodded to him. "If existence does go into the Void, wouldn't it just remake everything the way the Void did the first time? It is one of the seven Makers isn't it? The origin of creation?"

Brother David nodded. "It is possible that the Void would recreate *a* world. But it is impossible to know for sure, and impossible still to know if the world it creates would be the same one as ours. Are you willing to be the one to take that chance?"

Seeing Pax's stricken expression, he gave a comforting smile. "If you take your duties as a True Namer seriously, you will not be the one to destroy the world. This is a warning against complacency. The seven True Namers must be a proactive part of the world if it is to keep its balance."

Pax raised a hand again. "If the True Namers are so essential to reality, and there haven't been any for so long, why hasn't the world crumbled?"

"Another good question. You show your wisdom Namer of Light. The simple answer is, we almost did. As I said, the God Wars were a close brush with worldwide destruction. Since then, the world has been maintained by the remaining Makers.

"When the unsteady peace that ended the God Wars was forged, and the land divided, the world's balance was hung on that peace. Now that peace is being abandoned, and the need for True Namers is greater than ever before."

Pax caught an edge of anxiety in the man's voice. Whatever it was that he thought was coming, Pax felt it shake the man to his core. Pax understood that kind of fear, and it made him uneasy as well. There was so much about this he didn't understand or know. Did they have time to learn it all?

"How do we start?" Korivare asked. His face was a mask of determination. Doing a duty came as easily as breathing to him.

"As I have said. The old Namers spent a great deal of time learning about the world through study. Many others traveled the world to learn about it in a more practical way. All of them spent years learning before they began to know even their first Names.

"We do not have that kind of time. Luckily, you are no regular Namers. You are the seven True Namers and this power already resides in you. There is no need to instill you with deep knowing. Your office grants you that. Our job is merely to connect you with that knowing."

Brother David beckoned them to follow, and he brought them out onto a high stone balcony that reached out toward the northern clouds. It had no railing or guard to keep people from falling through the sky and striking the stony ground below.

"This is a place of ritual. The sanctuary is where we worship, but here, on an edge that stretches above the world, is where we seek meaning and truth. The five of you will spend a great deal of time out here among the clouds, wind and stone. When you begin to hear creation whispering to you, you will know you have touched the power that lies inside you."

Brother David left them there. All Pax could hear was the howling wind. It was much more vicious than the wind at the base of the tower, and it reminded Pax of his hike up the mountain. Pax watched as Jiang sat in a crossed-legged, straight back position. He closed his eyes and folded his hands in his lap. Korivare knelt and did something similar. Gerald merely lay back on the bare stone and closed his eyes as if he were napping.

Pax looked at Telemnar for some guidance, but she looked very uncomfortable. She was pressing her back against the outside wall of the tower. Pax chose a spot at the edge of the balcony and looked out over the clouds surrounding them. The blowing wind was cold on his face, but his fur-lined clothes kept most of him warm. He felt a twinge of vertigo as he imagined the drop from up here to the stone mountainside.

He remembered the moment he was dropped by the dragon. Before he hit the ground, there was a feeling of weightlessness. He wondered if that was what it was like to fly. He remembered being on top of the broad back of Raziren and looking down at the vast expanse of land beneath him.

Was the feeling different between dragons and birds? Dragons were much heavier, but they also had much bigger wings. These thoughts led him down a path of wonder toward the vast world around him. He wondered what it was like to be a bird, a fish, a tree, and a cloud.

He let his mind wander, and it began gathering questions. How does a bird fly? Can a tree feel pain? Do clouds hold rain like a waterskin, or are they somehow made of it? These questions and more kept him staring out at the clouds and imagining the vast world underneath them until Brother David came back to fetch them.

It was time for lunch, which meant they had spent about three hours out on the balcony listening to the wind and looking at the clouds. Gerald had spent the time napping, Korivare and Jiang had spent the time doing something called meditating, and Telemnar had watched Pax for a bit, prayed, and sat against the outer wall of the tower trying not to think about the way-far-down drop.

When they went to lunch, more of Gerald's loaf-bowls had been made for stew. There were also cheeses, jams, regularly shaped loaves of bread, and even mutton. The last surprised Pax because he couldn't recall another meal where they had meat that wasn't made into stew.

Three of the friends continued to interact with the monks around them in their own ways. Korivare continued discussing theology with the same monks he'd been conversing with before. Jiang made a greater effort to speak to the monks the way they spoke to him. Gerald ate unabated by the monks asking him questions.

Only Pax and Telemnar seemed to eat sparingly. Pax was still preoccupied with his dream from the night before, both the one with the Creator and the one where he suffocated. When he finished eating a polite amount of food, he turned to Telemnar.

He gave her a questioning look. She noticed and shrugged her shoulders nervously. He wanted to ask what was bothering her, but she seemed so closed off from everyone. He didn't know if trying to ask her would be prying too much.

As Pax hesitated, the moment was lost when Brother David stood and asked the five True-Namers-in-training to accompany him to the library. The five friends stood and he lead them out of the dining hall and up the stairs to the library filled with books.

CHAPTER FORTY-NINE

Stories from Everywhere

Brother David explained that the group was to spend the afternoons in the library learning everything they could about the outside world from the books they had available. "I will also," he said, "be sending several of the monks to you as well. Not everything can be learned from books, and it will be good for you to draw wisdom from the experiences of the monks that have found their way here."

Brother David left them to their research as he went to fetch the first set of monks for them to meet. Gerald was helping Pax read through a book on the anatomy of birds when Brother David returned with two other monks.

"Gentlemen," he said. He turned to Telemnar, "m'lady. This is Deruk and Joshua. They came to this monastery years ago, and they have agreed to tell you what brought them here."

One of them, Deruk, was short and stout with a barrel chest and broad shoulders. The other man, Joshua, was tall and lanky with fingers that drummed at his sides. Pax recognized the habit. It was similar to his tendency to shake when his anxieties got the better of him. He wondered if this man was nervous about being in the same room as the True Namers, or as a troll.

Brother David finished introductions, and left them with the newcomers. Both of them stood awkwardly by the door until Gerald offered them a seat next to him and Pax. Deruk nodded and sat, but Joshua leaned against a nearby shelf.

"I guess I'll start then," Deruk said. He had a slight accent that Gerald picked up on immediately.

"You're from the north clans, right? Your accent is very slight, but you seem to have kept it."

Deruk looked surprised, but not offended. "Aye, I'm not used to people catching my accent so quickly. Most days it seems like I've lost it."

"I have very clever ears. Please continue."

"Well, I don't know how much you know about the dwarves, but a lot of us are crafters. Livin' under the mountains gives you plenty of access to lots of metals, which is also how some of the clansmiths became bankers, I suppose. I don't know much about that though. My father was a workaday blacksmith. Nuthin' fancy, but he was proud of it and wanted his only son to follow in his footsteps.

"I didn't care for it though. The forge was hot, and it made me sweat more than I liked. I could never get a good grip on the hammer and, more than once, it went flying across the workshop. You can prolly imagine the reaction when I told my da I didn't think I was up to being a blacksmith. He kicked me out, and, without anywhere else to go, I ended up here. Been a part of this family ever since.

"I can't hold a hammer worth a damn, but I found out while I was here that I have good penmanship, and holding a quill doesn't take as much grip strength. I've been making myself useful copying down as many of these books as I can, and I've learned a lot along the way. Not a lot of it is useful, but I like knowing things."

"I'm happy to hear the monastery could give you a home Brother Deruk," Korivare said. Deruk looked at him with his eyebrows raised.

"You've been spendin' too much time with Brother David lad. Call me Deruk, please. I appreciate these people giving me a new home and all, but callin' me Brother all the time feels unnatural. Like you're trying to remind me of who I am."

"My apologies."

Deruk shook his head. "Is he always this formal?"

"Nah," Gerald said. "Usually, he's much worse. I'm surprised he's even sitting and not standing in parade rest."

Deruk gave them both a look that said he was unsure if the small bard was joking. Then he cracked a grin when he saw Gerald squeak while trying to contain his laughter. Korivare gave him an exasperated sigh.

"What about you?" Korivare asked the man leaning against the bookshelves. "Joshua, was it? Do you have something you'd like to share?"

The man looked at the group then down at his feet. "My parents are farmers. I came here because I wanted to learn to read and they didn't have money to pay for schooling or a tutor. Every copper penny we had went back into the farm or on our table."

It seemed pretty straightforward to Pax. "What made you want to learn to read?" he asked.

"I don't know. I just did." Joshua kept his eyes low and continued drumming his fingers against his thigh.

"Is that because your anxious?" Pax asked, gesturing toward Joshua's fingers. "I tend to shake a lot when I get nervous, but that seems a little subtler."

Joshua looked at him with an expression of surprise. "What makes you anxious?"

"Talking to people. Mostly strangers, but large crowds do it as well. I spent most of my life alone, so being around people always makes me feel like I'm going to say or do something that will upset them."

Joshua's fingers stopped drumming and he looked at Pax for a long moment. Pax started to feel uncomfortable, but Joshua spoke up, "I feel that way a lot too. I'm usually afraid someone will yell at me for doing something wrong."

Pax nodded. "My mother used to do that a lot. I guess she got annoyed at me sometimes, and she didn't really care to hide it."

"But…" Joshua scrunched his faced and Pax could tell he was trying to think of a polite way to phrase his question. "I thought you were a… Aren't the True Namers supposed to be powerful mages or something?"

"That's what they keep telling me, but even if I am, it doesn't seem to stop the anxiety." Pax looked into Joshua's eyes. The boy was staring again, but it didn't make him uncomfortable this time.

It was like they were having a moment. Neither of them was a monk, Namer, farm boy, or a troll. They were just two people who were trying to live with their anxieties. It felt nice to Pax to know other people felt the way he did.

CHAPTER FIFTY

Naming

Days passed like that. The mornings were spent listening to the wind and watching the clouds from the balcony. When Gerald was done napping, or when Telemnar's anxiety about being so high up made her wake him, they gathered everyone in the center of the balcony and sang, told stories, and shared their impressions of everyone from the monks they met in the library to Brother David to Farhan and the caravan.

In the afternoon, they would meet in the library to read about all manner of places and things. There were biographies and travel logs, books of legends and folk tales, and several legal codices from various place around the world.

Pax found the last to be dry and boring, but found the fact that the city-states of the Northern Deserts in Maskohma were unusual in the wider world surprising. Most places organized themselves into Kingdoms, Nations, or, in the case of Calcut, Theocratic Church-states, whatever that meant.

Gerald explained that the vast desert wilderness that separated places where people could build cities meant that a single, central power in the region was almost impossible to maintain. The Kings of the Desert managed to do it, but that was, apparently, a feat that was too difficult for anyone to accomplish since the fall of the Araka Empire.

The only break in the day-to-day routine was the two days the monks spent, first in quiet contemplation, then in worship every week. The five friends were invited to the worship services, and Korivare and Gerald even spoke at some. The rest merely participated in the ritual. Pax didn't know what was expected of him, but he noticed Telemnar and Jiang were very reserved during the services.

He asked them both privately about it. Telemnar explained that she preferred the worship of the Moon God, and didn't want to offend him. Jiang tried to explain his interpretation of the gods and their will and activity in the world, but it sounded very confusing to Pax.

"I'm sorry. I still don't get it. The gods made the world, but don't participate in it?"

"Yes."

"But they do have aspects, these spiritual splinters you mentioned, that *do* act in the world."

"Yes."

"And that is not the gods acting in the world."

"No. Spirits are their own. The Gods' wills are not the wills of the spirits. The spirits are a piece of power from the gods, but they have their own will."

"Does this will go against the will of the god that they splintered from?"

He made a sign that Pax had learned meant "both yes and no." "Complicated. A spirit's will is close to the god's will. Not the same."

Pax nodded. He was still confused, but he thought he had the bones of it.

The first week passed. Then the second week. By the third week, Gerald said that he was tired of stories, and Pax tried his hand at making one up. It was about a rabbit that got scared out of her den, and found a world much bigger than her small grassy field.

Pax stumbled a bit in places, but Gerald encouraged him, saying he was enjoying the little rabbit's adventures. The rest of that week passed with the group debating whether the rabbit's new helmet was a leather cap or a steel helm.

In the middle of the fourth week, it finally happened. Pax heard something. More accurately, he felt something. It came from deep inside him. It was deeper than his Rage, deeper than his anxiety, and even deeper than where the name Korivare had given him settled in his gut.

He felt the whispering rhythm of all creation slowly humming away. He could feel the beginnings of a sweet melody. The melody had a number of discordant notes in it, and Pax wondered if those were the small sufferings Brother David was talking about. In that moment, Pax felt aware of it enough to smooth those over and make things right in the world around him.

"I have it." His voice was quiet and much calmer than he'd expected. Gerald opened his eyes and looked at Pax.

"I have it," Pax repeated. "I can feel... something." It was soft and delicate, and Pax feared if he moved too quickly or spoke too loudly it would disappear.

"Well," Gerald said, "I don't feel any different. Maybe I've had access to this power all my life."

"Or maybe," Korivare countered, "Pax has actually been trying while you've spent your mornings out here napping."

"You just assume my napping had nothing to do with what we were doing? I'm sure I'm not the only one that has noticed his dreams being different since we got back from the Dream World. I've had lucid dreams before, but not every night."

"What's a lucid dream?" Pax asked before Korivare could respond.

"It's a dream where you know you're asleep and you have more control over the dream. I have been having them most nights since we got back from the Dream World, and I started using them to explore certain things."

"Things like what?"

"Well, originally I was using them to practice songs. When these monks explained the True Namer thing, I decided I may be able to use it to explore other things as well."

"So, you've been, what, trying to Name things in your dreams?" Korivare asked.

"Pretty much. Sometimes I feel something, and it works. I haven't been able to translate it into the waking world yet, but I'm close. Where are you at Jiang? The meditation helping?"

"Yes. Also no. Complicated. I hear the world, but it is weak."

"Well, I've been too scared of falling off the edge of this balcony to do anything productive," Telemnar said from the outer wall of the monastery. "Is there anywhere else we can go to listen to the world? Maybe a tree that's a little closer to the ground?" She took in a shaky breath.

Pax looked at the nervous elf for a long moment. She looked different. It wasn't in any of the details, but there was a change in how Pax saw her. He looked her up and down and heard a small whisper of something as he did. Telemnar looked at him as he strained his ears to hear it.

He heard the melody of the world again. It felt different, but he landed on a piece of the tune that didn't feel right. He matched the rest of the melody as best as he could, and tried to move the discordant notes into their proper places.

Telemnar's body grew still, and her breathing became steady. Some color came back to her pale face, and she stopped looking like she was going to be sick. "What did you do?" she asked.

"I... I don't know. When I looked at you, I heard something, and I... just..." Pax trailed off.

Korivare gave him an amazed look. "You heard her Name," he said. "You used it to calm her down."

"I'm sorry. I didn't mean to. You just looked like you were going to throw up or pass out. I just wanted to help."

Telemnar raised a hand, and Pax fell silent. "If you did hear my Name, and that's what you chose to do with it, I am grateful. I feel like I can stay on this balcony for the rest of today without worry."

Pax smiled. They all gathered around and started talking about how each of them felt when they drew near to the power Brother David was talking about. Gerald described it in terms of music, and Pax understood where he was coming from. Korivare said it sounded like a prayer.

"It's more just a feeling for me," Pax explained. "The music description makes sense to me. It's sort of like a song but just in how it makes me feel. There really isn't a music like what you play. It's just... I don't know the word for it."

"It sounds like it's different for each of you," Telemnar said. "I remember when I went on my survival trip, I met someone who gave me his Name and told me to say it. When I did, he looked more solid. It was like I had reaffirmed his existence. I wonder if I'll experience it like that when I get to."

They continued their discussion until Brother David came to fetch them, and they told him the good news. Not only did Pax hear the whispers of creation, but he used his powers to calm Telemnar's fear of heights.

Brother David smiled openly and gave the troll a congratulatory clap on the back. They mentioned Telemnar's suggestion of finding other places to rouse their powers. He admitted that he perhaps was a bit too single-minded to consider other possible paths to their powers. He agreed to let the rest of them find other places in the monastery to reflect.

"This was the sort of place old Namers were brought to, as best as we can tell from what few records we have of their training. It was meant to be a place where wind and stone, danger and safety, sight and blindness met." He gestured toward the clouds. "If these were cleared away, this would be a view to rival any in the known world."

"I could sense it," Pax said. "The first time you brought me here, I felt like I could see the whole world if the clouds weren't in the way."

Brother David nodded. "That is the way it feels to know a Name."

"You say that like you have experience," Gerald noted. "Have you been holding out on us all this time?"

Brother David paused, considering his words carefully. "The regiment I have been putting you through... this is what I did to try and search for the secret to Naming. When I first came here, it had nothing to do with my devotion to the Light. Though that devotion has grown, my true reason for staying here has always been to become the first Namer in centuries."

"And?"

"I have learned a great deal about the world, the people in this monastery, and myself. As for Names, however," he touched the gold circle that hung from his neck, "the only one I know is that of this symbol hanging around my neck. I learned her Name soon after I had risen high enough in the ranks here to have earned her."

"You know the name of gold?" Korivare asked.

Brother David shook his head. "Not gold. My necklace. It has the name of gold in it somewhere, though I don't know what part, and I hardly think I could figure it out.

"I know the name of this holy symbol, this badge of honor. For that, and many other reasons, she is the most precious thing I have ever held." He took the circle in his hands, and looked at it as if it were his only child. Pax could feel the love radiating off him like a bonfire.

He had never noticed before, but Brother David was very fatherly. He was a practiced mentor and a strong leader. When he looked at the piece of gold in his hands, Pax could see all the protective instincts, will to provide, and strength to carry on that Pax wanted out of his father. Pax decided in that moment that, whatever family Brother David had built at this monastery, Pax wanted to be a part of it.

CHAPTER FIFTY-ONE

Speaking in Service

After that day, Brother David gave Pax's four friends the run of the monastery for their mornings. Telemnar and Jiang spent their time in the gardens. Korivare helped many of the monks with their chores. Gerald slept in, but, after his explanation of why he was spending so much time asleep, Korivare only woke him early about a third of the time.

Pax was asked by Brother David to give that week's sermon to the monastery, and he spent a lot of time in the library reading the Light's Path. It was a collection of hymns and poems dedicated to the Creator. Brother David explained that a great deal of the Koyashian faith was founded on the principles outlined in the book.

When Pax told his friends what he was doing at lunch that day. Gerald gave him a disgusted sneer. "Religion is the driest reason for storytelling. Make it a poem, and it gets so much worse. I'd rather have Korivare run me through with his halberd than spend an entire week reading that."

"I'd rather run you through with my halberd than listen to you bad mouth my religion," Korivare said darkly.

The bard looked at his friend. He had opened his mouth to retort, but seeing the knight's face, he decided it was better to leave it alone.

"I just don't want to make a fool of myself when I speak at the service. I thought getting to know their religion a bit better might help."

"What have you learned?" Korivare asked.

Pax shrugged. "There's a lot in the poems about the beauty of justice, compassion, and shinning lights in dark places. I think it's supposed to mean something, but I've only been reading for a month now, and it seems like there's a lot going over my head."

Korivare nodded. "The poetry can be a bit esoteric. There's a book by a cleric from a long time ago that puts a lot of the concepts into parables. It's called the Book of Shinning Beacons. I think they have a copy or two in the library. I'll show it to you after lunch."

They finished eating and Korivare showed Pax the book he was talking about. True to his word, the book had several short stories that pointed toward a moral. Sometimes the moral was explicit at the end, but sometimes the story just ended. Korivare explained that these stories were meant to be a point of discussion among the Koyashians.

One such story was about a judge who presided over a trail. The trial was concerning the murder of a young man who had been beaten and hung from a tree. There were some witnesses and a small amount of evidence that pointed to one of three men: the victim's brother, a local blacksmith, or the lord that held the lands.

There was no way to know which of the three was guilty and which two were innocent. The judge thought on it for several days while the three men sat in prison. By the end, the judge had all three executed.

"What do you think?" Korivare asked after they had read this story.

"He killed two people who were innocent."

Korivare nodded. "The decision he made guaranteed that two people were punished for a crime they didn't commit. However, it also guaranteed that the person who did commit the crime paid for it."

"That doesn't excuse it. He took two innocent lives because he couldn't figure out which one of them was guilty. If that was going to be his solution, he should've just burned the whole town to its foundations. It's the same thing."

"I have met some who would argue that the young man's life was taken by the town. That the society is partially responsible when someone does something as heinous as murder."

"Ridiculous. One person killed that man. They should be the only one to pay for it. If you can't figure out who it is, I'd rather let a murderer go free than kill even one innocent life."

Korivare smiled. "You feel very strongly about this don't you?"

"Don't you?"

"I have strong opinions on many of the moral dilemmas contained in this book. I read it constantly as a child and asked the monks an endless stream of questions about it. That, I think, is what lead me to a place of such strong faith.

"I began to believe that, fundamentally, the Creator made this world to work in a particular way. That if everything in the world was brought to the same conclusion about truth, ethics, morality, all of it, the world would be a perfect place."

"Do you still believe that?"

"I do. But I'm less willing to point a sword at someone over the issue than I used to be. If threats are how you convince someone, then you haven't really convinced them. You just scared them into compliance."

"Maybe that's what all of this is. What we feel when we touch our powers is the way the world is supposed to work."

"I hear too much about famine and war in the prayer when I hear it for me to believe that. However, perhaps there is something underlying it that may point in the right direction. After all, our powers and office give us insight into how the world is meant to work. Maybe we can use that wisdom to shape a better world."

"I don't know about that. I'm pretty sure we're supposed to be preserving the way the world is, not changing it."

Korivare nodded. He was quiet for a moment, then he brought them back to the next story. It was clear he wanted to move on, but Pax was still thinking about what he said when he went to bed that night.

Pax spent the rest of the week preparing for his sermon. On the fifth day, the monks stayed in their rooms as usual, only coming out to eat silently. This was the fifth one of these days Pax had been a part of since he'd gotten to the monastery, and they always seemed unsettlingly still.

The five friends were allowed to go where they pleased, but breaking the silent stillness of the monastery seemed irreverent. They always talked in whispers and moved through the halls as quietly as possible. Telemnar was the best at this, with Gerald being a close second.

Compared to them, Pax made more noise than a band of drummers and trumpeters declaring the arrival of a king. At least, that's how Gerald described him. Pax thought of himself more as a lumbering bear.

The next day, Pax awoke with a knot in his gut that felt like a stone. He worried over every word he had planned. Gerald had helped him write them down so he wouldn't forget, but the bard's tight, tidy handwriting was more difficult to read than most of the books he'd been studying from.

He worried that the sweat from his hand would make the ink run. He worried he'd stutter or stumble over a word and lose his place. He worried that the sermon wouldn't resonate with anyone the way Brother David's often did. He worried he'd talk too loudly and hurt someone's ears or too softly so no one could hear him. Worry. Worry. Worry.

The service began as it always did. The brazier was lit and Brother David led everyone in a series of hymns chosen specifically to fit the theme of that week's lesson. He brought Gerald up to tell a story about one of the Creator's True Namers stopping a dragon from burning down a town.

The man used the dragon's name to keep it from flying or breathing fire, and forced it to speak to the mayor of the town. In the end, they settled their disagreement and came to a truce. The True Namer used a Binding, whatever that was, to make sure that everyone stuck to their agreement.

A second round of hymns, and it was Pax's turn to stand next to the brazier and speak. He swallowed hard against the dryness in his throat. He walked forward, whispering "relax" to himself the whole way there.

"Hi," he began. "My... name is... Pax." He took a breath. He calmed a bit and continued, looking down at the paper in his sweaty hands. "Many of you have seen me around the monastery. Still more of you have no doubt heard why my friends and I are here.

"If what Brother David believes of us is true, we are the first True Namers in a long time. Many of you are nervous about the coming conflict and few of us know much about it. I wanted to tell all of you that, whatever this conflict is, my friends and I are here to protect you from it.

"Just this week I have begun to feel the deep shape of the world that my powers and office make known to me. I used my powers to calm my friend, Telemnar, who was afraid of falling off the balcony here in the monastery. I used her Name to set her at ease."

A small murmur washed through the crowd. Pax took the time to read ahead and get his thoughts in order. He looked up, and everyone's attention fell back on him. "My friends and I will master our powers. We will preserve the balance of this world as best as we can. You don't have to be afraid anymore."

Everyone clapped loudly. Pax looked at the faces in the crowd, lit by the brazier behind him. At many times since he had met his new friends, he'd done things a hero does. He'd slain a dragon, rescued slaves, spoken to two different gods, and escaped a group of cultists in the desert. This, however, was the first time he truly believed that he could be the hero of this story.

CHAPTER FIFTY-TWO

Final Favor

"That was really well done," Telemnar said. "I would've been shaking from my knees to my elbows if it had been me up there."

"I was shaking. I hid it well with the shadow the brazier was casting on me," Pax said.

She shrugged. Korivare came up and gave Pax a sideways hug. "You really showed us your best up there. Give it a couple more tries and you'll be better at public speaking than the bard."

Pax smiled as Gerald made a gesture of partial agreement. "He's right about you doing well. I probably could've done better, but I see no reason to give a bunch of stuffy religious folk my best. What would I give to my better audiences?"

Korivare punched him lightly on the arm. Jiang was stoic, but he signed "vast approval" with his left hand. Pax felt himself glow with pride at all the compliments his friends were giving him. It made all the worrying and fussing over the wording of his speech worth it.

After that day, progress in their powers began to compound. Telemnar finally began to feel something, and she described it as a chorus of animal calls: bird songs, wolf howls, the yipping of a fox, and the screaming of a rutting stag. The last one didn't sound pleasant to Pax, but she seemed to think it was beautiful.

The rest of them began to slip in and out of the feeling more easily. Gerald learned the Name of the wind that whipped around the balcony, and sang it until the wind was stilled. Korivare used the

Name of fire to light the brazier before one of the services. Jiang said that he began to understand the Name of his sword and was whispering it every night while he oiled and sharpened it. He said it started to feel more balanced and flexible. This all came to a head when Brother David announced one day that they would be leaving the monastery.

"Finally," Gerald said when they were given the news. "If I have to sleep on cold stone for much longer, I'm going to develop a hunch."

Korivare cuffed him.

"Are you sure we're ready?" Pax asked.

"There's no way to know for sure, but each of you has already advanced beyond the point where anyone in this monastery can mentor you in any meaningful way. Now it's time for the five of you to find your own path."

"Where do we go from here then?" Telemnar asked.

"Out into the world. Learn about the places you are sworn to protect. Discover things and speak to people. Only then can you gain the wisdom to stop whatever is coming."

Pax didn't care for this plan much. Where could he possibly go? The only place outside of this monastery that offered to accept him was House Morkae. However, seeing as their caravan is now destroyed, Pax didn't expect a warm welcome from them.

Brother David left them in the Library to read and make plans on where to go. Pax asked each of his friends what their plan was.

"This is wonderful," Gerald said when Brother David had left. "If I could find a troupe of Wanderers when we get out of here, I bet I could convince them to let me travel with them. Think of all the stories and songs I could learn."

"We are supposed to be learning how to use our powers," Korivare pointed out.

"Brother David said we were to learn about the shape of the world. The shape of the world in contained in stories and no one knows more stories than the Wanderers."

"Well, I am going to be visiting the churches and temples of the world. I'm sure the devoted followers of the gods can provide whatever insight I need to protect this world. After all, the gods are responsible for its creation and maintenance."

"Until we get our powers. Then it'll be our job," Gerald said. He winked at Pax, and Pax smiled back at him.

Pax looked at Telemnar and Jiang. "What about the two of you?"

"Home," Jiang said.

Pax heard an edge of anxiety in his voice. Pax signed "questioning". Jiang signed "scared."

"Lord Minamoto will not be happy. I was meant to protect his silk in the desert. It was lost with the caravan."

"Do you want me to come with you and help explain?" Pax asked.

Jiang shook his head vigorously. He signed "deep refusal". "I must face it myself. Outsiders are not allowed in Lord Minamoto's court."

Pax tried to hide his disappointment. He didn't have anywhere else to go, and all his friends seemed to be very excited about going their separate ways. He didn't want them to leave him behind, but he didn't want to hold them back either. He looked at Telemnar.

"There's a forest in Lukor that is populated by wood elves," Telemnar said. "According to legend all of their villages and cities are invisible, but I doubt that. I want to see if I can find one and get to know the people there."

Another place it sounded like Pax would be more of a hindrance than any sort of help. He wished there was a place in the world for people like him. If he could find a place for the people the world had turned their back on, maybe he could start learning from people just like his other friends.

The places his friends were going to all sounded like amazing and fun adventures, but Pax didn't think he'd fit in with any of them. He was wringing his hands thinking of what to do when his fingers glided over his ring. There was one stone that still wasn't dark. One more favor from Meses.

"Guys," Pax said without thinking. Everyone stopped talking and looked at him. "Before we go our separate ways, could you help me think of what to ask Meses?"

Korivare looked at the ring on Pax's hand. "What were you thinking of asking him?"

Pax didn't want to say his first request would've been for them all to stay together. He stood quiet for a moment. He thought of the way he'd been treated by so many people: The ringmaster, the priestesses, and that guard who had arrested him. Then he remembered the look of the old beggar he'd saved. A new idea came to his mind.

"I want to ask him for a place for everyone who has been forgotten or cast aside by society. I want to give a home to every orphan and beggar who needs help."

Korivare nodded, but Gerald looked unconvinced. "It sounds like a big ask. Where would you put these people? We would need land for them to till, housing, food, an army of tailors for clothes..." The bard would've continued, but Korivare gestured to Pax. He wasn't listening. His eyes were far away.

"It sounds like the request of a true hero. There is no harm in asking," Korivare said.

Pax whispered "Meses," and the final stone grew dark. The elderly wind spirit appeared before them, his robes back on his body, and a bronze circlet on his head.

"Thought of your..." Meses trailed off. "You look different." He looked around at the other four. "All of you look different from when I last saw you. What have you been up to?"

"We found out why we were getting attacked. Turns out we are the new generation of True Namers," Pax said.

Meses raised his eyebrows. "Are you now?" He looked the troll up and down. "I suppose you are. Your countenance is different. It does remind me of the old days." He smiled, then laughed. "Well, I guess I'm lucky then. Who knows what a powerful True Namer would've asked of me if I needed your help to get home now?"

"I wouldn't have kept you here just to get more out of you." Pax sounded hurt.

"No? Then you're a fool. A True Namer at his full power could send me home as easily as breathing, and he would've known how desperate I was to get there. Any man who doesn't take full advantage of that situation is doing himself a disservice."

"If that's where you belong, then it would be my duty as a guardian of the world to get you there no matter what you'd give me in return."

Meses thought about that for a moment. "I suppose. Still, you shouldn't sell your powers for simple things. Yours is a rare ability, and shouldn't be squandered."

Pax didn't like the idea of "selling" his powers, but they had gotten far enough off track. "I'm ready for my final favor. I need your help to make a home for the people who have none. A place where they can live peacefully."

Meses didn't say anything. He merely ran his fingers through his short beard. He looked down, but his eyes were distant and calculating.

"That is a large request," he said finally. "Is it necessary that all the forgotten people of the world be there? Would you settle, say, for building a place where some of those people live and letting the others come to it in time?"

"Is that all you can offer me?"

Meses tried to look offended, but when Pax looked into his eyes, he could see the limitations of the wind spirit's power.

"If you help me build a place for them," Pax said, "I will do the rest."

Meses nodded. He clapped his hands, and suddenly a whirlwind swept through the library. It swirled around the six people and everything became blurry. When the wind stopped, they were standing in a field. Pax could hear a stream bubbling somewhere in the distance, and he could see a clump of trees in the distance that could be the beginnings of a forest.

"Welcome!" Meses declared, throwing up his hands and spinning around. "To the sight of your new town. But," he put up a single finger, "what's a town without citizens?"

He clapped his hands again, and suddenly a hundred ragged and half-starved people were looking around the place confused. Pax looked at Meses with wide eyes. "What did you do?"

"I brought you your own citizens. You said you wanted this to be a place for the forgotten. Might as well start with these people."

He turned to the crowd, lifting his hand. The ground under him and Pax forced its way up until they were standing above the milling throng of confused beggars.

"People of Lukor," he began in a new language. It was the one Pax had been learning with Gerald. "You have led lives of hardship and suffering. That is, until today. My friend," he gestured to Pax, "has decided to give you homes here in this lovely land. Alas, we need your help to build them. We, and our four heroic friends, will give you the trades and skills you need to make this barren plain into a thriving metropolis."

The crowd looked at him and Pax. They all began to whisper among themselves. Pax could see hopeful sparkles in the eyes of several people, but most looked stricken and fearful. What did they think of this strange man and troll telling them they'd have new homes here?

Pax put a hand on Meses' shoulder. "We can't kidnap people to build this town. We have to let people come here of their own free will."

Meses waved the comment aside. "Free will is an overrated concept among mortals. It does nothing but lead to tears. Better to let people with a larger view of things tell you what is expected of you, and simply do it."

Pax wanted to argue, but Meses moved quickly through the crowd, speaking in several different languages. Pax looked out at the people Meses had brought to him. Most were human, but there were several fair-skinned elves, tan halflings, and hairy dwarves.

Everyone was wearing sackcloth, canvas, and other scraps of fabric that gave the barest impression of clothes. Pax did believe he could help them, but he didn't want to start by stealing them away from where they lived. He wanted these people to come to him in their own time.

Meses waved Pax over. Pax walked over to where he was standing in front of a tiny girl wearing a canvas dress wrapped with hemp rope. "Elise, this is Pax."

Elise stepped away with a fearful expression. Pax crouched and held out his hand. He smiled, but kept it small enough to not show teeth. She looked into his eyes, and he felt words boil up out of him. "Elise, can you help me help them?"

Elise looked at him. Her fear turned to stunned surprise. Pax didn't know why, but she flung herself into his arms. He gave her a gentle hug and patted down her messy brown hair. She started to cry, and Pax could barely keep his own tears back.

"This doesn't change the fact that you stole these people," Pax told Meses when he stood up.

"How do you expect people who can't afford to eat to find a way to travel to you?" Meses asked.

Pax didn't have an answer.

"The winds carry many things to me. One of these things is the whispered hopes of many people. Every one of these hundred people have, at some point, dreamed of going somewhere better.

"Their whispered prayers were brought to me by the winds. By bringing them here to you, I am not only granting your wish to have someone to help. I am also granting the wishes of these people by giving them to someone who can help them."

Pax looked at the faces around him. They saw how he treated Elise, and many of them looked relieved. Some still looked suspicious of him. It dawned on him that they weren't scared of him, they were just afraid.

They had spent most of their lives afraid of hunger, afraid of disease, afraid of the cold winters or harsh storms. They were afraid like he used to be, like he still was sometimes. Fear had become as natural to them as their own skin, and they wore it like their dirty rags. They didn't have anything else to wear.

Pax nodded. He would change that.

CHAPTER FIFTY-THREE

A New People

Meses helped translate Pax's message to those that didn't speak either Arakkan or Lukorian. His message was simple: "we will help you develop a skill or trade, and ask you to build a piece of the town. Once the town is done, everyone would be free to stay or leave.

"Those who stayed would be given one of the houses they had helped to build and the land under it. Those who left would be given enough money to get them to the closest major city."

Pax mentioned to Meses that all his money had been taken by the priestesses, but Meses said he'd take care of financial needs as well as any resources they find useful.

Telemnar took a group of people into the nearby forest. She taught them how to hunt, trap, and gather food for the townspeople. She explained to them that, since the farms wouldn't start producing crops until fall, they were responsible for the town's food supply in the meantime.

Jiang said he'd learned how to work a forge when he crafted his sword. They let him teach a handful of people the basics of blacksmithing. Meses provided high quality steel, and some of the dwarves he'd brought on turned out to have some skill in metallurgy.

By the end of the season, seven of the ten people had gotten good enough to make a full set of their own tools. The final three remained as apprentices under Ferren, a human man who had taken especially well to blacksmithing.

One of the first projects Jiang used to teach the blacksmiths was to forge twenty spear heads. It took a week longer than Pax had hoped, but Korivare was able to get them fitted onto handles, and he began training twenty people to be town guards. They practiced simple formations and drills for the rest of spring.

At one point Pax noted a familiar face among them. He approached Korivare to ask about it. "Do you know who that man is in the front line?" Pax asked pointing him out.

"Osaim? He's taking well to the drills I have given them. I suspect he might have experience in battle or some kind of training. Why?"

"Look closer. We have met him before." Korivare looked at him for a long moment, but shook his head.

Pax approached the group of practicing guards. Korivare called for attention before Pax could get in the way, and Pax approached the man he had pointed out. He had a copper complexion and a lean face. He stood straight and proud. He was the very image of a soldier.

"Do you know who I am?" Pax asked.

"Sir, you are the lord of this town sir."

"Do you know anything else about me?"

The man glanced at him for a brief moment, then went back to staring ahead. "Sir, you—" he stopped as he clenched his jaw.

"You're the beggar that I brought to those priestesses."

The man stumbled forward and Pax caught him in an embrace.

"You have no idea what that meant to me," Osaim said. "After I left the army, I tried to…"

His words were muffled as he buried his face in Pax's chest. "Then you showed up. I was so scared because I thought you were some thug, about to beat me senseless, but I didn't have the strength to run. You gave me the coin and brought the priestesses to me.

"I should've died that day, but I didn't. You saved me, and now I'm here. I want to protect you and these people. I want to be useful again."

"And you will be." Pax turned to Korivare. "Once these people are trained up to your satisfaction, Osaim here will take over. He will be our Captain of the Guard. I have no doubt his military experience will prove useful to us."

Osaim gathered himself together and stood at attention again. Pax left them to their training, smiling.

Gerald took five people and taught them his best negotiating tactics. He said they'd make fine merchants. Pax pretended not to notice him also teaching them how to have fingers light enough to pickpockets. According to Gerald, this was a skill they already possessed, and he'd merely been correcting their mistakes because "doing something like that so poorly offends me."

Pax didn't have much skill in anything, but his strength was endlessly useful in building houses and shops. Meses took about a dozen people to a lumberyard they had built in the first handful of days. There, he taught them basic carpentry techniques.

Rather, he had a servant from his court teach them. Meses admitted he didn't have many hands-on skills himself. Still, the people he brought from his court and the resources such as steel, seed, and clay for pots and roofing tiles were endlessly useful.

The rest of the townsfolk were given the task of building houses, shops, and barns. Meses explained that they had to work fast or they'd miss the already waning days of the planting season. When mid-spring hit and Pax understood that not all the buildings would be done in time, he broke the team in half and sent one to simply start planting.

When summer did hit, and it got too hot to work in the field all day, there was still a lot to be done around the town. Korivare dismissed the guards from training duty earlier and earlier, so they could help with the building and farming. Tools and plows broke and the blacksmiths were brought to fix them.

The merchants left soon after Gerald declared them fit for duty. They had taken everything the town could spare and headed west to trade for supplies and livestock from other towns and villages. Pax hoped they'd be back by the fall harvest.

Meses gave less and less of his own riches to the townspeople over time. When Pax asked him about it, he explained that he had planted the seed.

"Now it's time for your town to blossom into a flower, or wither on the vine," Meses said. "I can't keep giving you everything you need. The people here have the skills they need to survive. That is enough."

Pax wanted to say more, but there was a more pressing issue he needed to discuss with Meses. "Where are we? You brought us to an open field near a stream and forest, but why does no one else live here?"

"The simple answer? Because you are largely nowhere. The land under your feet is fine enough for farming, but there is better. There aren't any major roads around here, and the closest river is ten miles west of here. But there is another reason no one else is here. This is technically disputed territory.

"You happen to be right in between the Kingdom of Strophe and the Antorn Confederacy. There are treaties outlining the borders, but, according to those treaties, the boarder is a river.

"The Antorn Confederacy says the river the treaty refers to is the one thirty miles northeast, putting this strip of land in their borders. If you ask the King of Strophe, however, the river is the one ten miles west, and you're standing on his land.

"Neither of them is willing to go back to war over it because, as I pointed out, there's nothing out here. Just don't swear fealty to either of them, and you should be fine."

Pax didn't find that reassuring. Was there any part of this town that Meses hadn't stolen? Pax supposed that was partly his fault. He did ask for this, in a way.

Still, it seemed like Meses was being less than truthful about something. The land here was plenty fertile and the stream was good for water. There was just no good reason for there to not be some kind of settlement out here.

Meses declared the town fully functional the next day. He threw a large feast to celebrate and declared Pax lord of all the land they had tilled and planted. Many of the townsfolk spent the whole day in a drunken revelry. Meses brought the five friends aside before they could get too drunk.

"It's time for me to leave. If I stay too much longer, I'll be trapped in this world until one of you becomes a full Namer and can send me home."

"Thank you," Pax said, tearing up a bit. "You helped us in so many different ways. Your friendship will always mean a lot to me."

Meses smiled. "Wind spirits don't have friends, but I am glad to have known you as well. I can't wait to see how this True Namer thing shakes out for you. Feel free to stop by when you get your powers. I'd love to host one of the guardians of all creation." He gave

Pax a wink. Everyone said their goodbyes, and Meses disappeared in a clap of thunder.

CHAPTER FIFTY-FOUR

A New Threat

A dragon. That was the reason no one lived here that Meses failed to mention. It was possible that he didn't know, but Pax doubted it. If he could hear the whispered prayers of lost people, then he could undoubtedly hear a snoring dragon.

About a week after Meses left, the woodsmen Telemnar trained had come back from scouting with a dire report. There were signs of a massive beast somewhere in the unexplored places in the forest. Pax sent Telemnar to investigate, and she had confirmed, saying it was likely a dragon of some kind.

"If you follow the signs of the beast, you get to a part of the forest where all the plants are stunted. It's as if the ground has been poisoned. There are hardly any animals to speak of, but there are plenty of rotting carcasses strewn about. I didn't go much further. I don't know if it's hostile, and I don't want to find out while I'm alone."

Pax cursed. The last dragon that attacked almost killed them, and they had to flee when its mate showed up. Could they face another one?

"You know the dragons on this side of the world better than I do," Pax said. Technically, she probably knew dragons on both sides of the mountains better than him, but there were townspeople listening. He didn't want to look clueless. "What is our best option?"

"We have plenty of guards, and my scouts are skilled enough to cover them." Telemnar shrugged. "I would've preferred this sort of thing happen when they have years of training, not months, but there are a lot of them."

Pax thought for a long moment. He didn't want to throw citizens lives away on something like this. On the other hand, if the dragon was hostile, it could be the entire town's doom.

"Sir," Osaim said, "My men are ready to defend their homes from anything. I don't relish the idea of dying to the fangs or poison of a dragon, but..." he trailed off.

The man had adopted Elise, the orphan girl Pax had first spoken to when they were all brought here. Fatherhood suited him. It made him stand taller and firmer, and he had become even more invested in keeping the town safe since.

Pax nodded in understanding. "You give credit to the position we gave you. If it means protecting our people, we will fight. Go and gather your bravest men. I'll need at least ten. The rest will stay here and watch over the town."

Osaim nodded and gave a salute before running off.

Pax turned to Telemnar. "Can I rely on you to find me our five best archers and have them meet us at the edge of the forest?"

Telemnar looked at him with over-acted shock. "You can rely on me for anything, my lord." She said the last with a playful grin. Pax hadn't taken to the title, and didn't insist on it. His friends, however, decided it was a funny nickname, and used it anytime they could.

Pax stepped up on the raised piece of earth Meses had created when he first brought everyone here. They had since begun to use it for announcements, and built the rest of the town so that this raised platform sat at the center of the town square.

"My people, your attention, please," Pax began as he forced his anxiety down. He let the Rage inside of him swallow it, and pushed the beast aside. "Our scouts have discovered a threat in the forest. I am joining a group of our finest warriors and archers to deal with it, but I need your cooperation in the meantime.

"The normal guard rotation must be changed so that those who are needed in the forest can be there. Until we return, I would ask everyone to stay in your homes or shops, and keep yourselves and your families safe."

Pax stepped down from the platform as the guards who were on duty jumped quickly and efficiently to the task of ushering everyone into the nearest building. It took less than five minutes for the street to be cleared, and when it was, Osaim and nine others were standing before Pax in leather jerkins and holding slightly lopsided spears. "Sir," Osaim said, "we're ready."

They walked to the edge of the forest. While they were still a half mile away, Pax saw eight figures standing at the forest's edge. As they got closer, he recognized four of Telemnar's woodsmen, Telemnar herself, Korivare, Gerald, and Jiang. Pax looked at Telemnar who gave him a frank look.

"You think I'm going to let you face down a dragon alone? I'm coming too. Besides, like I said, I'd rather have someone with years of training going into those woods than someone with months of training."

"I heard there was a dragon. Are we going to slay it?" Korivare said. Pax looked at him with stunned confusion. Korivare looked back at him. "You aren't facing down a beast like that without your best knight."

"Best? No. I am his best. I will go too." Of course, Jiang wanted to come. How could Pax not have thought of telling him?

"When I heard that these three were going," Gerald said from near Pax's knees, "I guessed that, if I try and stay here at this point, I'll look like a jerk." He hefted his harp. "I'm not much of a fighter, but my healing magic should be worth something."

Pax blinked away the tears that were welling up in his eyes. He nodded solemnly and turned to look at Osaim. "Captain, we are ready to face the dragon."

Osaim nodded. He gave the order and the town guards formed two lines of five men. The archers stood near the center of the line to ensure their safety in the event of an ambush. The five friends found their place within the line: Pax and Jiang stayed near the back, Korivare and Gerald remained with the archers, and Telemnar stayed at the front to help with tracking.

CHAPTER FIFTY-FIVE

Poisoned Grounds

Telemnar led them to the edge of the patch of forest she had mentioned. She was right, the grasses, trees, and even the vines were all stunted. The trees around them stood tall and proud, but the ones in this part of the forest were barely more than sickly looking saplings. One had been cut down by something, and Pax counted ten almost imperceptively small rings. Whatever this creature was doing to the surrounding ground, it was making any kind of growth very difficult.

Pax thought of the crops they had planted. They had seemed fine, and none of the townspeople remarked on them being oddly small, but most of them had never farmed before. He looked at the trees that stood tall and quietly hoped that they marked the boundary of whatever poison was in the soil.

Telemnar stood from where she was examining the ground. "This is as far as I went. The dragon's burrow will likely be somewhere in this patch of forest. If it isn't out hunting, we'll find it there. Let's just hope it is taking a midday nap and we can catch it by surprise."

She turned to her scouts. "You and you." She pointed at random. "Take the north half. You and you. You search to the south. I'm going to try and find the center. Meet back here for a report in an hour. If you find something interesting, come back sooner."

They nodded and moved swiftly and quietly through the underbrush. When Telemnar set out, however, she was perfectly silent. Her step didn't leave a trace of her passing. Pax wondered quietly how long it took her to learn how to do something like that.

"Our original plan of having the archers in the trees isn't going to work out if they're all like this," Osaim told Pax.

Pax nodded. "They don't have a lot of places to hide either. If we do find the dragon, it'll know your men have bows to cover them."

Osaim chuckled low in his throat. "They way I hear it, most dragons don't have to worry about a normal bow. Their scales are so hard nothing but a proper elvish longbow like the one your friend has is any kind of useful. Makes me wonder if our spears will do anything either."

"We will do whatever we must to keep the people of the town safe," Korivare declared. His eyes were locked on the path Telemnar had taken as she sought the center of the stunted patch of forest.

"Do all dragons have poison like this?" Pax asked. He couldn't remember the other dragon doing anything but breathing lightning and smacking them with its tail.

Korivare shrugged, but Gerald spoke up. "Many have some kind of venom. We were lucky to not get bitten by the one we faced. I suspect living in the desert made its venom very potent. This is different, however. A dragon's venom doesn't do this sort of thing to plants. The only thing I can think of is..." He trailed off.

Pax wanted to ask, but he could tell the bard was too frightened to speak about it. His reaction made Pax shiver. Anything that could take away the bard's normally jolly disposition was not something he wanted to face. Still, the town needed protecting.

The two scouts that had been sent to the south half returned before the hours was up. "There's a large cave five leagues south by southeast of here. We heard a low rumble inside that could either be snoring or growling. We have no idea which."

Pax turned to Osaim and Korivare. "We have fifteen minutes before everyone else is due back."

He took a breath, forcing more anxiety down the throat of his Rage. He forced the beast down as well. "I want us to have a plan before they get back. What's the terrain look like?"

The question was directed at the scout that gave the report.

"Mostly the same as here. All the plants are tiny and look like they're on death's door. We mostly kept off to the sides of the cave, so nothing inside could see us, but there's not really anywhere else to hide."

"How far is the top of the cave from the opening?"

"A few dozen feet."

"High enough for a good archer perch?"

"Sure, but you can only fit one person up there. Two if they get close, but they'd have to get really close."

"Are the two of you OK with being that close?"

They looked at each other and blushed. "I suppose not," one of them said. Pax grew intrigued, but didn't comment.

"Osaim, would your men run if they saw the dragon coming out of the cave?"

"If they did, I'd brand them a deserter and leave them in the forest for whatever beast wants them."

A few of them paled at this, but they stood firm.

"You will make a spear wall at the mouth of the cave. These two will perch above to give you cover. Give the dragon enough room to emerge, so they can shoot it. If it gets too close, go for its underbelly. I hear those scales are a bit softer."

Gerald interjected. "That's largely a myth. Go for where the wing connects to the body. It's soft to give the dragon mobility in flight. There are some exposed tendons and blood vessels there. You might hit one."

The soldiers nodded, and Pax thanked Gerald for the correction. "You and Korivare," he continued, "will standby as field medics. I don't want to lose anyone if we can help it. Jiang and I will form a back-line." He hefted his bow. "It's not elven made, but mine kicks like a donkey. Jiang has range with his magic. With any luck, we may just come out of this alive."

When Telemnar and the other scouts got back, they reviewed the plan with them. Telemnar suggested putting her and the other two scouts on the flanks to enclose the dragon. "It will still be able to fly away, assuming none of our spearmen cripple it. But then we get at least a couple of clear shots before it's gone."

"I have a question." One of the scouts said. She was one of the ones that explored the northern half. "How do we know this dragon is hostile. Aren't some dragons... good?"

"This dragon is definitely far from good," Gerald said.

Telemnar nodded. "I was thinking something similar. When I originally saw these plants, I thought they'd been poisoned. Now that I've seen more of this place, I can tell it's something else entirely.

"The rotting carcasses haven't been touched my scavengers or predators. The plants that grow big enough get trampled or poisoned. This dragon isn't just a big predator trying to feed itself. It... hates the life around it. I don't know why, but it seems to want everything within a certain distance dead. I can only assume that radius is going to get bigger the longer it stays here."

The scouts lead the team to the cave they found. It was a huge piece of rock that jutted out of the ground and cracked open in the middle. Pax heard the rumbling they mentioned. They were right, it could be a growl, but Pax was sure it was snoring. It was too regular to be an angry growl. He whispered this to Telemnar and she nodded.

She stepped in front of the line of spears. Pax went to grab her, but she made a sharp gesture, and he backed off. She made her silent way into the cave. Pax listened hard to the snoring, waiting for any sign that she had been detected. When he couldn't see her anymore, he swallowed and felt his heart start to race.

CHAPTER FIFTY-SIX
Battle for Home

Everything was still. Pax nocked an arrow and looked around at the others. Korivare and Gerald wore their worry plain, but Jiang was stoic. He did sign "anxious". Pax took a breath to slow his heart rate.

Before he could let it out an angry roar came from inside the cave. Pax took a step forward, but Jiang held out his arm to block the troll. A huge dragon with scales the color of moss, and frills down its neck and back burst out of the cave's mouth.

It reared up on its hind legs and spat a yellow gas into the air above them.

"Kor sath dirkal thersal," it shouted at the soldiers.

Pax didn't understand what it was saying. But the sounds of the dragon's voice made his blood turn to ice. He knew the voice that was speaking those words. He'd been dreaming of being under the shadow of this dragon since the first night in the monastery.

The cloud settled down on the band of spearmen. Pax realized too late what was about to happen. When he took in his next breath, he coughed it back out. The dragon had breathed out a cloud of corrosive, poisonous, gas.

The fog was thick and settled on the group. It burned Pax's throat, and he heard the coughing of the others as well. The gas didn't seem to be dissipating on it's own, and Pax wondered if it stuck to itself the way water sometimes does on a small leaf.

He heard the thrum of Gerald's harp, and Jiang began to choke out an arcane chant. Soon there was a stiff breeze that dispersed the fog. Still Pax had to hold his breath for a couple minutes before the air around him was clear.

He looked down at the spearmen. All of them were clutching their throats and choking on their own breath. Pax looked at Korivare, who nodded and got to work. He laid his hands on the closest spearman and the soft light of his healing magic surrounded the man's throat.

Gerald continued to play his harp. It's song floated out from his fingers and lingered in the air where the acrid gas had been pushed out from. Pax felt his regenerative abilities invigorated by the song. It didn't take long before the burning sensation had left his throat.

Pax hefted his bow. There were already arrows flying from several directions. The dragon lashed out at the closest archer, but the young elf woman simply jumped back and kept firing. The arrows were merely glancing off the hardened scales of the dragon's hide. The archers continued to fire, attempting to find a weak spot, but it was to no avail.

Pax decided that, if anyone was going to slay this dragon, it would be him. He loosed an arrow, aiming for the creature's wing. It was batted away as the dragon spread its wings to take off.

Pax looked down at his quivers. Dare he use an explosive arrow on this thing? What would it do to the people around it?

An arrow sprouted from the meat just under the dragon's shoulder. It roared in pain. The other archers looked confused. Their arrows had been bouncing off the creature's hide.

Telemnar stepped out of the cave clutching her leg. She leaned against the mouth of the cave and shot again. Her arrow hit the dragon where its wing connected to its body. A spurt of blood sprayed out, and covered the ground below the dragon. The small plants began to wilt more.

Pax shot another arrow, aiming for the dragon's broad side. It dug in just above the dragon's hind leg. The dragons tail swept toward Pax, but he caught it and stood his ground.

With all the strength he could muster, he lurched the dragon back, pulling it off its feet. An arrow sprouted from the creature's eye. One of the archers from atop the cave had found a weak point.

The dragon writhed in pain while letting out a colossal roar. It swung its tail, and Pax was pulled to the ground. Korivare stopped his healing and picked up his halberd. He sprinted toward the flailing dragon.

It caught sight of him with its good eye, but it didn't have time to react. Korivare hefted the blade of his halberd, and it fell on the dragon's neck, severing its head from its body.

Everyone that was not already on the ground collapsed into a heap of sweat and exhaustion. Pax got to his feet and went to assist Telemnar. With his help, she was able to limp over to the other rangers as they approached the slain dragon.

"That was quite the battle. How many are injured? Did we lose anyone?" Telemnar asked.

Pax took a quick survey of the battlefield. Each of the soldiers that had succumbed to the poisonous gas were still moving, and Korivare had returned to healing with Gerald's magical music supporting his efforts.

"I don't think anyone is dead, but any of our soldiers that get out of this without permanent damage to their throats will be lucky," Pax said.

He turned his attention to the cave from whence the dragon had come. Something about it unsettled him, and he couldn't help but feel the true threat was still inside.

"What is there?" Jiang asked. He was standing by Pax's side. He signed "nervous curiosity."

Pax nodded in agreement. "Something is still inside. I don't know what, but I have been having dreams about this dragon and this cave since we got to the monastery. I don't think it's a coincidence that we are here."

Jiang nodded his agreement, and they both walked into the cave to face whatever was inside.

CHAPTER FIFTY-SEVEN

Into the Belly of the Beast

The moment Pax stepped inside the cave, he felt a strangely familiar sensation. The cave felt somehow insubstantial, like it was not yet fully formed. Pax couldn't help but feel like there was something just beyond his senses that made this place feel all too familiar. Then the maniacal laugh started to reverberate through the walls, and his blood turned icy cold.

He knew that laugh. He knew the voice and the god from which it bellowed. Somehow, for some reason, the god of chaos was speaking to them inside this cave.

"Ode to the conquering heroes!" the voice hissed out from the cave walls. "Hooray for the great True Namers from days of old. They have slain the mighty dragon and have come to claim it's treasure."

"What do you want from us? Why are you here?" Pax demanded. He felt his fear and anxiety stirring the Rage inside of him. He tried to keep it pinned down in his gut, but it seemed to grow stronger as the voice continued to speak.

"What do I want? Isn't that quite the age old question? God of chaos and as unpredictable as anything can be. What could something so unknowable and completely unhinged possibly want in any given moment?" The voice gave another hissing laugh.

"Wrong," Jiang said. "Something is wrong."

"Ah, the silent stoic speaks. And in speaking, he states the obvious. Of course there is something wrong, you fool."

The walls of the cave turned to shadow, and Pax felt himself sinking into darkness. He remembered the dreams again: the dreams he had been having since his first day in the monastery. They had been of the dragon and his choking breath, but there was also always a swallowing of shadow as well. Was this what the God of Dreams wanted? To kill them once they had realized they were meant to be the saviors of the world? Why?

"I was hoping you would bring your thieving friends in here when I summoned you. Especially that little gnome. I wanted all of you to pay dearly for stealing from me all at once, but I'll have to kill you all separately."

"We haven't stolen anything. We were only in your realm for a day or two. We did what we needed to survive until we could get to you. When would we have time to steal from you? We left after speaking to you."

"Then I suppose its merely a coincidence that your friend's halberd is an exact match to the one he had in my world. You know nothing, you stupid monster."

Pax heard the word, and the Rage roared up in him at the sound of it. He fought and clawed and the swallowing shadows around him. He didn't know if doing so would harm the god that threatened his life and slandered his friends. Still, he thrashed about, sinking claws into shadows that seemed more substantial than a mere absence of light could account for.

"Be the beast you know you are. Attack me as your instincts demand. You have no power to defend yourself from a god, you tiny thing."

Pax paused suddenly. The voice was right. He was powerless to defend himself from this thing. He could no more harm Chaos Incarnate than he could throw a stone at the moon.

"The Moon," he whispered.

"My father cannot help you here. This is my domain, and my grievance. He will not protect you from me."

The Rage inside of Pax was made silent by something deeper in him. He felt it call to him, and he listened carefully. He closed his eyes and strained his hearing against the hissing laughter of the Chaos God, and tried to listen to the small voice of his deeper nature.

Pax the Troll had nothing to use to stand against a god, but Pax was more than just a troll. Pax was the True Namer of the Light of All Creation. He opened his eyes and looked out into the shadows before him.

He looked and saw the swirling, shifting names of the World of Dreams before him. It was the world of chaos, yes, but it was a world of potential as well. It was a world of limitless possibilities that were all unbound by the laws of the natural world. It was a world where a troll could learn to fly merely by wishing it for himself.

At the center of it, there was something else. There was a thing at the center of it all that seemed to have no Name. Pax could feel the limits of his power as a True Namer. This thing, the God of Chaos had no Name that Pax could turn against it. The world around him, however.

Pax spoke the swirling Name that ebbed and flowed around him. He listened to the quiet rhythm of creation and shaped a small piece of it around the Nameless God. He remembered the cage he was kept in by the ringmaster, and he built bars out of blackness. He remembered the cell he was kept in by a town guard in a far-away city, and he shaped walls out of shadows. He remembered being sealed in a plateau of red stone by a group of fanatical cultists, and he created a door out of darkness. Finally, he spoke a Name to seal the door shut with the Nameless God behind it.

"There," Pax said to himself as his powers began to recede back into him, "you will stay. You are bound to the world you created, and you may never leave it to threaten anyone ever again."

As Pax's powers began to fade and he returned to his normal self, the shadows too began to recede from the cavern around them. Pax moved to Jiang's side as the warrior emerged from the receding darkness. He had collapsed, at some point, on to all fours and he was clutching his throat like he had just been underwater.

"The god. Is he gone?"

Pax nodded. "I think I sealed him away with my powers as a True Namer. I hope that he stays that way. If he does get out, he'll be looking for us for more than just theft."

Jiang looked up, and Pax followed his gaze. When they had entered, the cave was small and empty, but that must've been an illusion or a trick by the god of chaos. Now, what they were seeing was a huge cave filled with treasure just like the one they had found from the first dragon they fought.

Pax and Jiang shared a look, and then a smile. They both stood up and walked out of the cave to retrieve their friends and inform them of what had just transpired.

CHAPTER FIFTY-EIGHT

To The Victors

Pax gave the quickest summary of what had just transpired in the cave to his friends and fellow dragon-slayers. They had several questions, and many of them couldn't believe what he was saying. Apparently, from their perspective, the two had gone into the cave, and merely a moment later walked out of the cave claiming they had sealed away an angry god. Pax's fellow True Namers, having experience with the power of a Name, more readily believed him, but they still had several questions.

Those had to wait, however, because Telemnar's leg was still bleeding heavily, and the soldiers were still lying on the ground with Korivare doing everything he could to heal their throats. Telemnar gestured for Pax to come near to her. When he did, she said, "there wasn't an angry god in there when I went inside to draw out the dragon, but I do remember seeing a staff with berries growing out of it. Did you see it too?"

Pax nodded.

"Get it. I think those berries might have healing magic."

He nodded again and sprinted into the cave. A moment later, he emerged with a staff of dark wood that, by its appearance, seemed to be little more than a stripped tree branch. He tried to hand it to Telemnar, but she shook her head.

"I don't know what to do with it. Are the berries on it?"

"Yes, there's four, but I don't know what to do with them either.

258

Are they supposed to be eaten?"

One of the rangers spoke up and said, "no, you don't eat them. I know how to use it."

Pax handed her the staff and she took it over to one of the soldiers that was still coughing. His cough sounded dry and harsh. She began chanting and touched the staff to his throat, and one of the berries shriveled and fell off the branch.

Instantly he stopped coughing and breathed normally. He took a few deep, experimental breaths. He smiled up at the young woman and choked out a "thank you" before tears made him go silent.

There were only three berries left. Pax asked her to start with Osaim, but he stopped her hand before it could touch him. He pointed at one of the other soldiers. When Pax tried to protest, he pointed more vigorously. Pax let the girl follow his orders. She healed three other soldiers and Korivare was able to heal another one before nearly collapsing from exhaustion. Pax made him stop.

Seven. Seven of the ten soldiers were able to keep their voices. Osaim was not among them. On their hike back to the town, Jiang showed him a few simple gestures to express his mood. He and the other two soldiers learned attentively. When they got back to town, they had five simple gestures to mean sad, angry, happy, confused, and indifferent.

Elise was confused when her father tried to sign happy to her. When she looked at Pax he explained, "your father was injured fighting a dragon. His throat is damaged, and he won't be able to speak for a while." He tried not to mention his greater fear. Osaim and the others may never get their voices back.

Elise gave Pax a reproachful look. "Why didn't you save him? He is my daddy. Don't you care?"

Osaim pulled Elise's arm and made her look at him. He signed angry, but the emotion was plain on his face. He gestured toward Pax, made a sharp motion of negation, then pointed at himself. Elise looked confused for a moment, but she understood when he repeated the gesture. He made his choice, and it wasn't Pax's fault he got hurt.

Except it was. Pax had asked Meses to bring them here. Pax had asked him to fight that dragon. It was Pax's plan that got his throat burned by that gas. This little girl would never hear her father say he loved her again, and it was Pax's fault.

The elvish woman that had used the staff took Osaim and the other two to her house to care for them further. When they were gone, the townsfolk that had gathered began asking about the dragon.

"What did you do with the hide?" one of them said from the back. Pax hadn't thought of it, but everyone else insisted that someone go retrieve it. They explained that a dragon's hide, if properly tanned, could be worth a fortune. Pax asked if anyone knew how to tan dragon hide, and the man who spoke up raised his hand.

"I used to tan hides before a guild put me out of business. Never tanned dragon before, but I can give it my best shot."

Pax nodded. "I'll bring a few scouts to help me retrieve the body. It's going to be heavy, but I think I can manage it if someone can lash together a sled for me to put it on."

"Use my cart." One of the townspeople said.

"The dragon is too large for a cart, and it's body would no doubt crack your wheels. I'm going to need two iron rods and the strongest fabric we can find."

Everyone darted around the town. Within an hour they had produced several scraps of canvas, no doubt someone's old clothes, and two hefty rods of iron as long as Pax was tall. They brought a long piece of hemp rope, and used it to tie the dragon's body to the sled. The scouts offered to help pull, but Pax was able to get the whole thing into town with only a bit of a struggle.

"Besides," he said when they had reached the edge of the forest, "this is a good workout for me. I've always been naturally strong, so the chance to push my limits is rare."

They nodded uneasily. He could tell he hadn't convinced them, but it was true. He had learned from Korivare and Jiang that difficult work can be good for pushing your limits and growing stronger. Now that he wasn't merely trying to survive, Pax was curious just how strong his body could become.

When they got to town, the man that had offered to tan the hide took a look at it. Pax hadn't yet caught the man's name, so he asked in the politest way he could think of.

"Oh, it's Thayden, your lordship."

"Good to meet you Thayden. What do you think you can make of this creature's hide?"

"We're dealing with quite the large beast here, your lordship. I'd say we're looking at at least six full sides of leather if we can get the whole thing off in one piece. That should be easy enough, but I wouldn't want to start cutting into it beyond that without knowing what we're going to be doing with it."

"Sides?" Pax asked.

"Most leather workers I've ever known measure things by side. A single side is about half the hide of a cow, but this creature is a whole heck of a lot bigger than a cow. Reckon we could get about as much leather as three cows out of it, so that'd be about six sides."

Pax nodded. He left the man to removing the hide, while he went about town trying to find the best thing to use the leather for.

While he worked on that problem, he went to visit the injured soldiers. "How did you know how to use that staff?" he asked the scout that was tending them.

"My mother was a healer in a small village just outside the wood elves' forest. I left the village because I wanted to make something of myself in the big city. Turns out they don't have much use for 'witch doctors' there."

"Well, I don't care what kind of doctor you are. If you can help these men, I will be very grateful."

She shrugged. "Their throats are still raw. I don't know much magic, so I can't regenerate what they lost. Whatever does comeback will be scar tissue.

"I do know some herblore though. If you don't mind a more mundane approach, I can at least ease them through the next few days while their throats heal."

"Whatever you can do to help them will be worth the time. I don't want them to be mute the rest of their lives."

The woman shook her head. "I can't regenerate what they lost. Like I said, I ain't got any magic, and I don't know if the berries on that staff will regrow in time to save their voices. The flesh in their throats will scar over, but that won't help them speak. It'll just stop hurting as much... eventually."

Pax's face fell and she gave him an apologetic grimace. "Whatever you can do for them," Pax said. "Please, it would mean a lot to me."

"Sure thing, sir." She handed Pax a water cup and told him to keep them hydrated. She walked out of the door of her cottage and walked into the forest. When she returned, she had an armload of herbs that she hung from her rafters. After she was done, she dismissed Pax, telling him her patients needed rest.

CHAPTER FIFTY-NINE

The Price and Prize of Victory

Over the next few days, the woman, who Pax learned was named Selena, brewed tea that she said would ease the pains of the three soldiers. They worked on their new hand language, and by the time Selena deemed them well enough to not need her care, Osaim could thank her, give basic orders to his men, and tell his daughter he loved her.

He still needed a lieutenant to shout the orders when his men couldn't see his hands, but he was able to continue serving as Pax's guard captain. He still had a home and a place in this town, and that's what Pax wanted to give all of them.

While the soldiers where being treated, Pax noticed the berries grew back on the staff he'd given Selena. She nodded and explained the staff had been imbued with magic that ensured that any life that was attached to it would always be renewed in time.

"Which means I may be able to develop a salve out of those berries. It'll take some experimenting, but I think I can manage it."

She paused for a moment, and Pax could feel a question on her lips. He gave her a look, telling her to speak. She took a breath and began, "as a troll, your blood carries a great deal of your restorative ability. It may help with my experimenting if I could..."

"Is there a safe way for you to collect it?"

She nodded vigorously. "I can disinfect the knife we use, and I know enough about anatomy to avoid anything vital."

"If it will help you heal people, you can have as much of my blood as you need."

She was as good as her word. She made a small cut toward the top of his forearm with a knife that had been polished with alcohol. When they were done, she had filled a small clay jar and Pax was feeling a bit light headed. She gave him a cup of water and a bit of smoked meat and told him to stay sitting for at least the rest of the hour.

The next two days were spent clearing out the cave the dragon had been using to hoard its possessions. In total, they had four wood statues depicting a mighty looking orc standing on a skull that looked human, a dancing elf, a signing gnome that Gerald insisted looked just like him, and a human with a crown on his head; six slabs of wood with a mix of carving and burning to depict several nature scenes; a second staff that looked nothing like the one in Selena's house; and two hundred gold coins that Gerald identified as Strophe crowns. Altogether, it was worth a king's ransom.

Thayden announced he would be able to make two full sets of armor, and, after Pax had him measured, Osaim had one set made for him. The other Thayden had made much too large for anyone else in town. When Pax asked about it, he explained that their lord shouldn't be anything less than the most well-armed-and-armored man in a hundred miles. Pax tried on the armor, and found it fit him perfectly.

Telemnar insisted the blood not be allowed to seep into the ground, and, after seeing what had become of the plants around them while they were fighting it, Pax agreed. Unfortunately, this was after Pax had dragged the body across the forest floor, and Telemnar said they'd merely have to deal with that problem as it arose.

However, they were able to put together enough clay to make a wide basin in which they bled-out the rest of the dragon. Gerald mentioned it might be worth something to an alchemist if they could find one, and they agreed to collect it in large clay jugs. They were tightly stoppered and kept in the cellar beneath Pax's house.

The meat of the dragon was brought to the smoke house they had built for deer and other large game. It was smoked, and Pax portioned it out so that each household got at least a stoan of meat. The ten soldiers and five scouts got five stoan, and there was still enough left over for a victory feast to celebrate the town being safe.

Finally, there were the bones and viscera. The bones were more like large bird bones than Pax had expected. They were filled with holes and incredibly light. Gerald explained that they had to be less dense or the dragon wouldn't be able to fly.

Pax was disappointed, as he'd hoped he could carve some kind of weapon out of the large ones, but they were far too brittle. Korivare said he'd heard that dragonash was a useful substance for some clerical rituals. That was good enough for Pax, so they burned what they couldn't use and put the ash into jars. The merchants would be coming back soon, and maybe they could find someone to sell it to.

Pax did everything he could to find a use for every piece of the dragon, and Telemnar said she was proud of his resourcefulness. She explained that, despite the dragon being hateful toward the surrounding wildlife, she was sad that such a rare and noble creature had to be put down. Seeing its remains put to good use made its death more bearable. Pax felt similarly, and regretted not doing something similar with the first dragon they'd killed. He hoped it'd end up useful to some kind of desert creature.

CHAPTER SIXTY

The Lonely Road

With the extra meat from the dragon and all the wealth its hoard offered, the town had everything they could need and even some luxuries by the time the harvest came in. Pax was able to pay for a road to be constructed from the nearby river to their town, the smiths had to build a second forge for all the tools that were being bought, one of the townsfolk decided to open an inn and asked for the dragon's head to be mounted above their fireplace. However, the head was rotted and decaying by the time they went back for it, so the innkeeper settled for having the skull cleaned and set in the corner of the inn.

By the time the harvest was coming in, word had spread about a new town that cropped up, that its lord had killed a dragon, and that the people were rich and the streets were paved with gold. This brought several curious travelers into the town, and the farmers were able to hire dozens of extra hands to help pull in the harvest.

Pax heard talk of a festival, and Gerald explained to him that almost every culture on this side of the mountains had some kind of harvest festival. Pax announced that, once the harvest was done being taken in, they'd have a full week of feasting, games, and performances from a certain bard.

Gerald was saved from having to do all the performances, though. A troupe of Wanderers were passing through the town two days before the festivities were scheduled, and the townsfolk convinced them to stay for the festival. It didn't take much, as the Wanderers mentioned in passing that the townsfolk were the most generous they had seen in a long time.

They set up a stage on the raised bit of earth at the town square, and from sunup to sundown there were plays, music, and stories. The innkeeper opened a cask of special mead he'd claimed cost him two silver nobles. Pax tried it. It was sweet and spiced with the barest hint of a kick. He gave the innkeeper one of the crowns he'd saved and told him not to charge anyone for their share of the cask. The man grinned, bowed, and said "as you wish, my lord."

The festival ended on the first truly cold day that marked the beginning of winter. The town felt still and quiet afterward. It was like an endless indrawn breath. When the snow came, people spent as much time as they could huddled up in their houses and keeping warm. Pax and his friends shared the manor house the town had built for him. He didn't want such a large living space, but they'd insisted that their lord ought to play the part.

It felt full and cozy with his friends there. However they spent more and more time planning their departure. Telemnar still wanted to find the mysterious wood elves that seemed to elude any outside travelers. The more she spoke about it, the more Pax came to realize she was treating like some kind of test of her worth as a tracker. Korivare still wanted to visit other monasteries and temples. Pax and Jiang's run-in with the god of chaos seemed to have made him more anxious about the state of the divine pantheons. Gerald had asked the Wanderer troupe that had performed at the festival to come back by the town when the weather turned, and he was planning on joining with them for the time being.

Jiang was the only one that was quiet about his plans, and Pax hoped that was because he'd decided to stay. Except, when he brought this up to the stoic warmage, Jiang simply shook his head and said, "I must go. Speak to my lord."

This town had quickly become a home to Pax. He thought his friends felt the same way, but they were still planning on leaving. More than once, when he was alone in his rooms, the thought of his friends leaving forced tears out of his eyes. He'd cry himself into exhaustion and fall asleep feeling more alone than ever.

Gerald and Korivare tried to make him feel better by promising to come back to visit when they could.

Jiang said, "Friends. Always together. Though far away, still together."

Pax wasn't sure what he meant, but he knew the man was trying to help. Telemnar was more distant. When the others tried to comfort Pax, she chimed in, but never of her own accord. Pax started to feel like she had never thought of them as friends, but he found out that was far from the case.

"Of course, you are my friend," she said one day when he mentioned it to her. "You all are better friends than any I've ever had. That's what makes this so difficult for me. I grew up in an isolated temple far from anywhere. After that, I went to the Hunting Grounds for my survival test. After that, I roamed the wilderness for a while until the Night Hunter gave me a vision that told me to find the Koyashians. I'd never been around people that I didn't know before I met you guys."

That sounded so familiar Pax barely kept from grinning. "You and I are a lot alike," he said. "Neither of us have had much in the way of friends. You were raised by clerics, right?"

She nodded.

"I was raised by parents who thought of me as little more than a nuisance. Then I got lost in a cave one day and was captured by a bunch of thugs who sold me to a circus. When that burned down, I ran away.

"I had to survive on my own until some scouts from House Morkae found me. When they took me in and found out I was strong, they told me to guard a caravan. That's where I met them." Pax gestured to the others sitting by the fire on the other side of the room.

"They were your first friends. The first people who liked you for you and not because you were useful to them."

"Jiang was the first one to ask me my name. When I told him I didn't have one, he seemed confused. That was the first time anyone had ever looked at me like a person. And now you're all leaving and I don't know what to do."

Telemnar put one of her hands on Pax's hands where they were folded on the table. "You have built a wonderful town that is a home to many people who haven't had such a luxury. I think what you are doing now is exactly what you should be doing."

"But I'm supposed to save the world. How can I do that from here?"

Telemnar looked out the window to the homes and shops lit by lamp light. "That's exactly what you are doing. You're saving the world, one group of hopeless beggars and orphans at a time."

Pax looked out the window as well. He could see through the window into the house Osaim and Elise shared. Elise was singing, and Osaim was giving a wide fatherly smile.

Spring came sooner than Pax wanted, and the roads thawed and dried. Caravans, with real dwarvish Caravan Masters, started to come in. They were nothing like the Shatka, but Pax recognized a lifetime of haggling in the way they spoke about their wares.

Pax's friends made a deal with one of these caravans to bring them as far as the nearest major city, Risdel. The Caravan Master was a dwarf named Berûn and he had a halfling wife name Rosie. They seemed like pleasant company for his friends to begin their next journey with. Still, Pax was sad to see them go.

Pax said his good-byes, telling Gerald to pick up a few new songs he could teach the troll on his way back through these parts. Korivare said he'd keep Pax in his daily prayers, Jiang told him to be strong, and Telemnar warned that there were boars in the forest.

"I remember what you told me about the last time you tried to fight a boar. Those lopsided spears your guards carry won't do much better."

Pax thanked her and gave her a big hug. She let out a strangled "oh," and he softened it a bit but didn't let go.

When the Caravan Master was yelling about wanting to get a move on, the friends began their journey away from Pax's safe, little town and into the wider world. Pax didn't stop the tears rolling down his face. When they were over the horizon and he could no longer see them, he already started to miss them.

The End of Book One